The Scandal At Bletchley

by
Jack Treby

Preface

Few people have heard of Bletchley Park these days.

The government did a pretty good job of covering everything up after the war. The machines were dismantled, the blueprints destroyed and an entire generation of spotty, bespectacled crossword enthusiasts were sent home to live with their mothers.

Nowadays, I hear, the place is virtually derelict.

Not that I knew anything of the code-breaking activities there during the Second World War. It was only later that I heard all the gory details. Very hush hush, but terminally dull. For my part, I spent the war years abroad, like any decent Englishman, doing work that was a damn sight more useful than anything the boffins at Station X ever managed.

No, my only memory of Bletchley Park was of a rather peculiar weekend there in October 1929.

It was a private residence back then, the country pile of Sir Herbert Leon and his second wife Fanny. The place was renowned at that time for its lavish parties. David Lloyd George – that great Welsh windbag – was a regular visitor. And even though the well-connected Sir Herbert had popped his clogs in 1926, dear old Fanny had kept up the tradition. She was a stern, Edwardian matriarch of the best kind and it was no surprise that Bletchley Park was thought an appropriate venue for a departmental knees-up.

The Security Service was looking to celebrate its twentieth anniversary and as Sir Vincent Kelly, the director of MI5, was a close personal friend of Fanny, it was hardly surprising that Bletchley Park should have been pencilled in.

The Colonel – as we all knew him – had been the head of MI5 since the early days, running the organisation from one small office in Victoria Street from October 1909.

I had been recruited a couple of years later.

Being part of the Security Service in those days was not the glamorous job you might suppose. John Buchan wrote a load of old nonsense about it and Ian Fleming is scarcely any better these days. I spent most of my time at MI5 trawling through 1911 census information, looking for German nationals and deciding whether or not they posed a threat to national security. It was deadly dull work, but it was useful all the same. The day war broke out we arrested damn near every Kraut spy in England (and one or two other people whose names I had surreptitiously added to the list). That was pretty much my only experience as a spy in the pre-war era, apart from one abortive field trip in 1912, which I don't have time to relate here.

Despite the brevity of my career, the Colonel was kind enough to invite me along to his twentieth anniversary bash, to be held at Bletchley Park over the weekend of 26th and 27th October. A select few former and current employees would be gathering to celebrate (as Sir Vincent put it) two decades of being only slightly less incompetent than MI6. I was happy to accept the invitation.

If I could have foreseen something of the disaster that would ensue, perhaps I would have been less happy to do so.

No records were kept of the events of that weekend. Even Ramsay MacDonald, the Prime Minister of the day, was not informed. The witnesses were sworn to secrecy and only a handful of people ever knew the whole story.

I am the only one left now. Sir Vincent Kelly died in 1942, after thirty years of loyal service and precious little thanks. No, if I don't put pen to paper, no one will. And they can't exactly hang me for it now. My doctor tells me I will soon be dead in any case (he's a cheerful bastard, that one). I must confess the idea of taking the secret to my grave does have a certain perverse appeal – especially as the undertakers are already waiting in the wings – but causing one last bit of mischief before I die holds an even greater attraction.

I only pray I have the time left to do it justice.

This then is the true story of Bletchley Park in 1929. I saw it all with my own eyes and was at least partly responsible for some of it. My name, by the way, is Hilary Manningham-Butler. I was born on 24th April 1889 – a girl, much to my father's horror, though I have lived most of my life as a man. History will probably judge me a villain, but at the very least I am an honest one. I died, according to an obituary in the Daily Mail, on Sunday 27th October 1929, two days before the Great Wall Street Crash.

But you should never believe anything you read in the newspapers.

Sir Hilary Manningham-Butler
28th July 1967

Chapter One

The gales that struck southern England on Thursday 24th October 1929 could hardly be described as apocalyptic. A ninety mile an hour whirlwind was reported to have thrown great lumps of lead across the Wellington Road, near Lord's Cricket Ground and the rain certainly battered the windows of No. 93 Curzon Street, where I was comfortably tucked up in bed that evening. It was scarcely a repeat of the Great Storm of 1871, however, and I managed to sleep comfortably through the worst of it. Indeed, the whole affair would have passed me by if my man Hargreaves had not told me of the devastation when he delivered my usual pick-me-up at eight thirty on Friday morning.

The headline on the front page of the Mail was typically sensational: *"Whirlwind's Havoc"*. Oddly, it was not the most prominent headline of the day. The banner that really caught my eye as I settled myself down at the breakfast table was *"Greatest Crash in Wall Street History"*. Needless to say, given the newspaper in question, the story was somewhat overblown. The Times, which I had closer to hand, had relegated the news to an altogether more restrained page fourteen. The markets may have taken a tumble – as they had been tumbling, to a greater or lesser extent, for most of the previous month – but Wall Street had rallied by the end of the day, and things did not seem as severe as the journalists at the Daily Mail would have us believe.

I have never been fond of that particular periodical. If it had been up to me, I would not have allowed it in the house. But my wife – who was sitting opposite me, engrossed as ever in the sordid details of the society columns – had always been partial to a bit of tittle-tattle and as she had control of the purse strings (at least where the household was concerned) I could scarcely object.

For my part, I much preferred the Times.

I poured out some tea from the pot and added a couple of spoonfuls of sugar from the bowl.

Elizabeth glanced up from her newspaper. 'Are you taking the car today?' she enquired.

'No, dear, I thought I'd walk to Buckinghamshire.'

There was an icy pause.

'There's no need to be facetious, Hilary.'

I buttered myself a slice of toast from the rack. I had already mentioned that I would be away for the weekend but this was the first time Elizabeth had shown any interest in the matter.

'I thought you might be going by train,' she added.

That was hardly likely. Bletchley Park was on the main line from Euston Station, but I would need to take a cab to get across London. Far better to use the car and avoid all that expense.

Why Buckinghamshire? I wondered irritably. It seemed an odd place to hold a reunion. Why not London, where the office was located? And come to that, why invite me? I had left the Security Service on good terms, but that was fifteen years ago. There was no reason for anyone there to remember me.

The invitation had arrived out of the blue on Tuesday morning. It was not part of the regular post. There had been no postmark on the envelope. Quite how it had materialised in my letters tray even our house maid Jenny was unable to say.

The note was written in a typically oblique fashion.

'The Colonel requests the pleasure of HMB for WW&S to celebrate 20 years of SSB.'

I crunched at my toast.

I was HMB, of course. SSB stood for Secret Service Bureau and my best guess at WW&S was Wine, Women and Song. There was a blank space underneath, but no date or location provided. Lemon juice had probably been used – or some unmentionable bodily fluid – to render the rest of the invitation invisible. Sir Vincent Kelly had a rather peculiar sense of humour. I had to warm the card over a hot stove before the words "*Bletchley Park*" appeared.

I was not the only one to receive an invitation. An American friend of mine, Harry Latimer, had also been targeted. He'd done a bit of work for MI5 during the war. He phoned me up on Wednesday afternoon, long distance, saying he was away in France for a few days on business but would be back in town on Friday morning and could I give him a lift? I hadn't told Elizabeth about that. I knew what she would think. But the time had come to tell her now.

I took a quick slurp of tea. 'I…er…I promised to pick up Harry Latimer on the way.' That was as good a reason as any for taking the car. 'Why? Were you planning on going out?'

Elizabeth shook her head. 'I shall be entertaining at home this weekend,' she replied, returning pointedly to her newspaper.

Another one of her fancy men, no doubt. For such a profoundly trivial woman, Elizabeth was surprisingly popular with the men. Perhaps it was her frivolity that made her popular. It was certainly not her looks. If Helen of Troy had the face that launched a thousand ships, Elizabeth had the one that scuttled them. She had been plain when I'd married her at seventeen. At thirty-three, she looked positively granular. Yet still the young men flocked around her. I couldn't tell you why.

I suppose I should have objected to some of these dalliances, but it was not as if our union had ever been anything more than a marriage of convenience.

Elizabeth had been the daughter of a wealthy industrialist and I had married her for her money. She in her turn had married me for my title. I was a baronet and any wife of mine was entitled to be called a lady. It was a comfortable arrangement based on a healthy ignorance of each other's private lives.

To this day, I cannot say if she ever realised I was a woman. She had certainly never seen me in a state of undress. It was not the done thing in those days. The marital bed was occupied only once, on the night of our wedding, and the combination of a darkened room, a bizarre French marital aid and an astonishingly ignorant bride served to satisfy the legalities of the situation.

Since then, we had lived separate lives. If my wife had any suspicions of me, she never voiced them. I had in any case been blessed with a fairly masculine aspect – stocky shoulders, square jaw and a rather deep voice – which always helped to maintain the illusion. Having spent the greater part of my life masquerading as a man, I pride myself I had become rather good at it. I didn't just act like a man, I *thought* like one too (and certainly had more balls than most real men of my acquaintance). It was only the flesh beneath the starched cloth that gave away the biological truth, and that was always kept firmly under wraps. Well, mostly under wraps. But I'll get to that later.

From a virginal bride, Elizabeth had gradually transformed into a rapacious socialite. She was always discreet, however, and together we maintained a façade of matrimonial harmony.

She kept her hands on the purse strings, though, and in fairness her frugality was probably the only thing that had kept us on an even keel over the years. And at least – with the markets plunging around us that weekend – the bulk of the wealth she had inherited from her father was in the land and not in stocks and shares.

There was a knock at the door and Hargreaves poked his head around the corner. He was a short, balding man, slim and well turned out but with a slightly shifty air born of badly concealed nerves. 'There's a telephone call for you, sir. Mr Latimer. It sounded quite urgent.'

I dabbed a napkin to my lips irritably. 'I'm in the middle of breakfast. Can't I call him back?'

'I don't think so, sir. He's phoning from a call box.'

'Oh very well.' I placed the napkin back down on the table, took a last bite of toast and rose to my feet. 'Excuse me, my dear.' Elizabeth was glaring at me once again. She had never approved of my association with Harry Latimer. I can't say I blame her. He was a man who spent his life on the borders of legality and it was difficult to associate with him without getting one's hands burnt occasionally.

'Did you fill up the car?' I asked as I passed Hargreaves in the doorway.

'Just seeing to it now, sir. You did say eleven o'clock.'

'So I did. Get to it, then.'

Hargreaves moved off and I crossed the hall to the telephone. I picked up the receiver and braced myself.

'Good morning, Harry.'

'Morning, old man. Sorry to drag you away from the breakfast table.' Harry Latimer spoke with a smooth transatlantic accent, the kind of voice that oozed charm but lacked any real warmth.

'I was expecting to pick you up at Claridges at eleven thirty.'

'Change of plan. Had a bit of trouble with the weather last night. I was meant to catch a train up to London, but there was a tree on the line and nothing was running. Hey, did you hear about Lords?'

'Yes, I was just reading about it in the Times. So where *are* you, if you're not in London?'

'I wish I could tell you, old man.'

An operator interrupted him, demanding more money in a polite Devonshire brogue. A few moments of silence followed as Harry fumbled for a coin. Bloody telephones, I thought, not for the first time. The world would be a better place without them.

'I was meant to be in Hastings,' he continued eventually, 'but I guess I ended up a few miles down the coast. Looks like I'll have to make my own way up to Aylesbury, so I reckon lunch is off. But there's a little business in London that needs taking care of first. That's why I called you.'

I tried to stop myself from sighing. 'Go on,' I said, bowing to the inevitable.

'I need you to do me a favour…'

The clock at Waterloo Station is possibly the least imaginative place one could think of to arrange an illicit rendezvous. Harry Latimer was known for his style, not for his imagination. The area directly beneath the multi-sided clock was already jam-packed with grubby schoolchildren. It was half past ten and by the looks of them, the children were fresh off the train from

Reading or some other god-awful backwater. I was in a foul mood. I had been looking forward to a quiet morning pootling around the house, followed by a leisurely drive out into the country and a nice pub lunch, instead of which I was now criss-crossing the centre of London like an overworked errand boy. If it had been anyone but Harry, I would have told them where to get off. But Harry Latimer could be damnably persuasive.

'I don't like to put a price on gratitude, old man,' he'd told me on the phone, 'but shall we say...forty pounds?'

'Make it fifty,' I said. 'And you can pay for lunch.'

A schoolmistress in a straw boater was busily checking off the children, making sure none of the little darlings had been misplaced between the train and the concourse. One little girl was throwing a tantrum. 'I don't wanna go to the blinkin' British Museum!' she bawled. The mistress slapped her across the back of the head.

I took out my pocket watch to check the time. A little boy pulled at my trouser leg and pointed up to the rather large clock looming above us. I took the point – my watch was somewhat superfluous – but I fetched the snotty little brat a solid wallop across the ear for his impertinence.

The school mistress gave me a nod of appreciation. I tipped my hat to her as she began herding the rabble in the direction of the street. It took some moments for the group to depart and for a second or two I thought the woman had made a mistake and left one of the grubby little mongrels behind.

I looked down at the child in irritation, concerned that I might have to drag him after the school mistress, but then did a double take as I realised it was not a child at all. It was a rather small man. He was bald and rounded, an odd looking fellow by any standards, a diminutive baked potato in a cheap suit, with a distinctly menacing air.

In his right hand he gripped a large brown holdall.

This was the fellow I had been instructed to meet. Reluctantly, I introduced myself. The man peered up at me suspiciously. 'You ain't Latimer,' he growled. Harry had obviously failed to pass on the change of plan.

'No, I'm not,' I barked. '*Mister* Latimer couldn't come.

9

That's why I'm here. To collect the holdall,' I added, just in case there was any doubt.

The baked potato looked dubious. 'How do I know Mr Latimer sent you?'

'You don't,' I snapped. 'But I don't see anybody else waiting around here for you.' Actually, there were quite a lot of people milling about, but we were the only ones underneath the clock. 'Harry said you might be difficult. He told me to tell you: "Mr Monroe owes you a favour".'

The little man considered this for a moment. 'All right,' he agreed, lifting up the holdall and handing it across. 'Here you go.' I could tell he was reluctant, however. He'd held onto the handle for a fraction too long.

'You're too kind,' I said, pulling the bag firmly away from him. The nerve of the fellow. What was Harry thinking of, associating with an ill-bred brute like that?

Hargreaves was waiting outside the station. He looked rather dapper, standing next to my gleaming blue Morris Oxford in his immaculately laundered chauffeur's uniform. He always scrubbed up well, did Hargreaves, though he was not a handsome man. He opened the passenger door for me and returned to the driver's seat.

Thomas Hargreaves had been my valet since before the war and, though it pains me to admit it, he was rather good at his job. The badly organised parade of half-wits who have followed him in recent years have reinforced in my mind what a useful fellow he was, though I would never have admitted it at the time. No, Hargreaves was a loyal and dependable servant whose devotion to my well-being would have been insufferable had it not been so damned useful. He knew his place and more importantly, he knew how to keep a secret. Which was just as well. He had known the truth about me from the day my father had employed him – how could he not, when it was he who dressed me every morning and ran my bath every Monday and Thursday night – but he had protected that secret over many years with the single-minded devotion of an overgrown wolf cub. I suppose I should have been grateful, but he was paid well enough for the job.

Harry's brown holdall was now resting firmly in my lap. It was a rather tatty looking thing, but the lock was well secured. I had no idea what was inside it, but it didn't take a mathematician to work out that the contents could not be – as the Jews would say – strictly kosher. Not that this bothered me unduly. Whatever Harry was up to – smuggling, blackmail, forgery – it was his business, not mine. So long as he paid me the fifty pounds, I would happily deliver the goods, whatever they might be. What are friends for, after all?

I clicked my fingers and Hargreaves produced a penknife from his trouser pocket. He handed it across and I set to work on the lock.

Friendship is one thing, curiosity quite another.

Hargreaves watched patiently as I forced the mechanism. The man was a better pick lock than I was – he could probably have sprung it in half the time – but I was not about to give him the satisfaction. Servants are there for the donkey work, not the fun. And breaking into somebody's holdall is dashed good fun, especially when you know the contents are unlikely to be anything legal. I unclipped the fastener and peered inside.

There was a large stash of money. About £20,000 in French Francs, though whether they were genuine or counterfeit notes I could not immediately tell. A small revolver nestled in a side pocket together with a round of ammunition. Knowing Harry, that was probably just for insurance. At the bottom of the bag, there was a thin cardboard folder containing some rather risqué photographs. These were almost certainly obscene, according to the letter of the law. Harry did have a penchant for the fairer sex but these photos were strictly business. Even so, I shielded the naked images from my valet.

I have never been attracted to women – too many wobbly bits for my taste – but having lived the life of a man for so many years I had developed a fairly robust understanding of the male mind. I knew what would happen if Hargreaves caught even a glimpse of such explicit images. I clipped the holdall shut before he got the chance. The last thing I needed was my valet getting hot under the collar.

I secured the lock and threw the bag onto the back seat.

'Blackmail, I think. Or perhaps a pay off.' Nothing out of the ordinary. I glanced across at Hargreaves, who was waiting patiently for my instructions. 'Well, get on with it!' I snapped. 'We have an appointment to keep!'

The Copper Kettle tearooms were situated at the far end of Buckingham Street, slap bang in the middle of Aylesbury. Harry Latimer was standing in the doorway and he waved a cheery greeting as we chugged to a halt outside. His large, wide brimmed hat obscured most of his face, but the brilliant white of his perfectly chiselled teeth shone out even in the dull October afternoon. I waved my hand in return as Hargreaves came around to open the car door.

Harry stepped forward, eyeing the holdall as I pulled myself up. 'Good to see you old man,' he grinned, shaking my hand. He was an amiable fellow, a veritable grizzly bear of a man. He was handsome too, in a boyish way; perhaps not quite Rudolph Valentino but a passable Ivor Novello. He had an easygoing charm and a roguish demeanour that made him irresistible to a certain type of woman. The girls all swooned and their irate husbands waited in line to smack him in the face. Thankfully, I had been inoculated against his charms early on, when he had tried – unsuccessfully – to seduce my wife. Elizabeth adored young men but she had an abiding hatred of all things American, and this certainly included Harry Latimer. Our friendship had blossomed from then on.

We left Hargreaves to park the car and made our way inside the Copper Kettle. Harry had to duck his head to get through the door. It was one of those irritatingly quaint outfits that make a virtue of being old-fashioned. All oak beams and tiny windows.

'Sorry to put all this on you,' Harry said. 'I hope it wasn't too much trouble.'

'It was an awful lot of trouble,' I grumbled good-naturedly. 'But I was happy to be of service.'

He grinned, gesturing to a table. 'For the right fee, of

course.'

We settled ourselves near a window overlooking the street. A waiter came across to take our order and the tea and scones duly arrived. It was not quite a pub lunch – the licensing laws precluded that at three o'clock in the afternoon – but Harry had come prepared, producing a small metal canister from his jacket and using it top up my teapot, before adding a dash of brandy to his own coffee.

I shuffled the holdall towards him under the table and he lifted up the case. 'I'm obliged to you, old man,' he said, examining the lock. 'Shame I couldn't get down there myself. That damn storm last night. I nearly drowned.' He looked down at the case. 'I'm guessing you picked the lock and had a quick rummage inside?'

'Of course not, Harry. I wouldn't dream of prying.'

'Yeah. That's what I figured.' He smiled indulgently. 'Just so long as you didn't take anything that didn't belong to you, old man.' A flash of steel flickered briefly behind those sparkling eyes. There were limits even to friendship.

I raised up my hands. 'We're friends, Harry. No double dealing.'

That seemed to satisfy him. 'Fair enough.' He pulled out his wallet. 'We said thirty, didn't we?'

'Fifty, I think.'

'Are you sure it wasn't forty?'

'You can pick up your own bloody briefcase next time.'

'Just checking old man, just checking. Can I write you a cheque?' He grinned, catching my sour expression. 'Cash it is then.' He opened the wallet and quickly counted out ten crisp five-pound notes. I held each one up to the light, just to be sure. 'They're genuine, old man. I wouldn't try to palm anything off on you.'

'What about the French Francs? Are they genuine?'

Harry gave a non-committal shrug.

'So what are you up to this time, "Mr Monroe"? A bit of blackmail? Or just another elaborate scam?'

'Oh, you know…something like that.'

'Just so long as you're not intending to shoot anybody.'

13

A .32 calibre revolver was not exactly friendly, no matter who was carrying it.

Harry looked hurt. 'Just a bit of insurance, old man. You can't be too careful these days.'

I pocketed the cash and took a sip of tea. The brandy Harry had added gave a pleasant aftertaste. 'So are you looking forward to our little reunion?'

Harry placed the holdall on the floor and leaned back in his chair. 'Oh, sure, sure. I haven't seen the Colonel in years.'

'No, neither have I. Though why he would choose to invite an old reprobate like you is beyond me. You're not exactly his favourite person in the world.'

Harry had worked in the New York office of MI5 during the Great War – trying to persuade the Yanks to join in the mindless slaughter – but since then he had been a free agent and about as disreputable as they came. He was not exactly a gangster – though he'd done a bit of bootlegging in his time – but most of his business was on the wrong side of the law. Confidence tricks and racketeering mostly. Not something I was ever terribly interested in, but I admired his nerve. He got away with it too, most of the time, though there were warrants out for his arrest in several states back home.

'Perhaps he wants to introduce me to his niece,' Harry suggested, hopefully. The rogue had always had an eye for the ladies.

'He never forgave you for the last one.' The Colonel had only just managed to keep that affair out of the newspapers. If the scandal had broken, poor Annabel Cartwright would have been ruined. 'Come to that,' I added, 'I can't think why he invited me either. I'm all for a bit of a knees-up, but I only worked for him for five minutes.'

Harry smiled. 'I guess he likes you, old man.' He added a bit more brandy to his coffee and pocketed the canteen. 'Can't imagine why,' he said.

Chapter Two

The mansion house at Bletchley Park was a crude and rather odd building, a vulgar mishmash of late-Victorian architecture, all archways, porticoes and shocking red brick, situated on the edge of an otherwise pleasant estate, itself sandwiched between a railway siding and the small Buckinghamshire town of Bletchley. It was an architect's nightmare, but I rather liked it.

The estate, though modest, was heavily wooded, with a small lake surrounded by trees, colourful flowerbeds, neatly trimmed lawns and a short driveway leading on to the traditional carriage turnaround at the front of the house. Three or four cars were already parked there as our little Morris Oxford chugged up past the lake and onto the roundabout.

Two large stone griffins guarded the main door of the mansion. At the sound of the car, a tall well-dressed gentleman emerged from the faux-Jacobean arch. He had aged quite a bit since I had last seen him, but I recognised at once the familiar form of Sir Vincent Kelly, my former boss at MI5. This was Britain's most trusted civil servant, the Colonel himself; probably the last man in England who could get away with wearing a monocle and not look like a complete idiot.

He came forward to greet us.

'Afternoon, Butler. Delighted you could make it. I wasn't sure whether you'd got our little note.'

We shook hands warmly.

'Oh, I got it all right. Though it took me a while to decode it. Honestly! Invisible ink. This isn't the nineteenth century, you know.'

'Just a bit of fun. Sets the tone, what?'

I nodded amiably. 'So, did you provide your own?' The idea of the Colonel disappearing into the little boys' room to manufacture his own ink was strangely appealing.

His thin lips formed a brief approximation of a smile. 'Not my department. Ha ha!' I had forgotten the Colonel's extraordinary laugh. It was more of a bark than a chortle; the kind of verbal affront that would have done a Labrador proud.

The man slapped me on the back good-naturedly. 'You haven't changed, Butler. Ha ha! It's good to see you.'

The smile vanished as Harry Latimer stepped out of the car behind me. The Colonel gave him a curt nod. 'Latimer.'

Handshakes were exchanged but with considerably less warmth.

'It's been too long, old man,' Harry schmoozed. 'How's that little niece of yours?'

The Colonel ignored the barb. 'Had a devil of a job tracking you down. What exactly are you up to these days?'

'Oh, this and that. A bit of import, export. A bit of trading.'

Sir Vincent raised an eyebrow. 'That's what most of my chaps say.' The Colonel was a rather severe looking man in his early fifties. At first glance, you would think him a cold-hearted military type, the kind of officer who would happily send thousands of young men over the top to face heavy machine gun fire. He had a long, thin face, a clipped moustache and the sort of neatly groomed black hair that invites suspicion in a man of his age. The reality was somewhat different. The Colonel was, by general consensus, a thoroughly good egg. He was shrewd and well-mannered, ruthless when necessary, but strangely uncorroded by decades of cloak and dagger work. He also had a rather mischievous sense of humour. That was the only reason I could think of for inviting Harry and me this weekend. 'Nothing in the old line, I take it?' he asked the American.

'Not these days, sir,' Harry said. 'I'm more of an independent now. And purely commercial work. Nothing that would interest you.'

'Well, that's something to be thankful for.' The Colonel pulled himself up and gestured towards the hallway. 'Well, come inside, both of you. Make yourselves at home. The lady of the house will be down shortly. Townsend will show you to your rooms.' A servant leapt forward to help Hargreaves with the luggage, though Harry kept a firm grip on his holdall. 'Drinks at six. Dinner at eight-thirty. Remember though, no shop talk. Strictly mess rules this weekend. We've got some games organised for tomorrow and a dance band for Saturday evening.'

Harry caught the look of horror on my face and let out an evil chuckle. He knew how much I hated dancing. I had barely mastered the Charleston, after three years of trying. I didn't have a hope with the Black Bottom or the Five Step. Harry, needless to say, was a master of them all.

'Anyone we know?' I asked, referring to the band.

'We couldn't afford Paul Whiteman,' the Colonel joked. 'But I daresay my chaps have found a decent local substitute.' Another car was pulling up in the driveway. 'Ah, you'll have to excuse me,' he said. 'I think it's the chap from the Daily Mail.'

Drinks were served as promised at six o'clock in the billiard room, to the left of the main staircase. A dozen or so guests were congregating in a room that looked for all the world like a medieval Great Hall in miniature. A solid, multi-arched ceiling and sleek oak panelling created a timeless atmosphere. Only the electric light hanging from the ceiling spoilt the illusion.

Lady Fanny Leon, an elderly but equally solid woman, was busily greeting the guests as they arrived in the hall. The Colonel hovered tactfully to her left, while a couple of servants began serving drinks from a table set up in a recessed arch at the far end of the room. Our hostess, though fearsome in aspect, proved meticulously polite.

The introductions were necessarily elongated. This was not a gathering of old friends. The Colonel had thought it a bad idea to bring together too many old acquaintances from the intelligence community and instead had selected a representative sample of some of the more memorable characters from MI5's first two decades. Most of them were strangers, to me and to each other, but I did recognise one woman: Dorothy Kilbride, who had been a typist in 1911 and was now apparently in charge of payroll. Everyone knew Dottie, though few paid her much attention. Her conversation was legendarily dull. She had been a handsome woman in her day, though her looks had faded now, and she'd always been rather unlucky in love. Her first husband had caught a packet at Passchendaele in 1917 and her second had died of the Spanish Flu. After that, sensibly in my opinion, she had given up trying.

Harry Latimer was a stranger to everyone, apart from the Colonel, but his naturally gregarious nature had soon endeared him to a couple of bright young things. Typical Harry. I could see him turning on the charm, refilling the glasses of a young blonde and a rather pretty brunette over by the door.

I was less fortunate with my own companions. Having only just lit a cigarette, I found myself cornered by a couple of crushing bores, one of whom was the Daily Mail journalist the Colonel had mentioned earlier on. I had thought he was joking. The damn swine cadged a cigarette from my case and introduced himself in one fluid move.

'Anthony Sinclair.' He extended a hand. I recognised the name if not the face. Sinclair was a journalist, a high-profile reporter, though more of a gossip-monger than a serious newsman. Needless to say, my wife adored him. The fact that he was here this weekend meant that he was also a former MI5 man, which was something of a surprise. Mind you, it was not without precedent. There are an awful lot of spies working in the newspaper business, even today.

'You're the fellow who wrote that piece on Mussolini,' I said. Elizabeth had shown me the article over the breakfast table some months earlier, around the time of the General Election. I've always been a staunch Conservative, but even I had wrinkled my nose at that particular piece. Fascism in 1929 wasn't the laughing stock it later became, but I have always disliked idolatry and Mussolini was a brutal thug by anybody's standards.

'I interviewed him last year,' Anthony Sinclair boasted. 'Charming man, in his way. Got his head screwed on, that one. Mark my words, gentleman, fascism is the future. We need strong government in this country, not a bunch of bloody socialists.' It was a common enough view.

'I always thought Mussolini was a bit full of himself, to be honest,' I said, taking a puff of my cigarette. 'Not terribly bright, so I've heard.'

'That's just communist propaganda. You should visit Rome. You've never seen a more peaceful and ordered city. And that's with the Eye-ties in charge. I tell you, he's doing that country a power of good. Not like these damned trade unionists we voted in over here.'

'I don't know,' I said, feeling the sudden urge to be contrary. 'A bit of a shake up every now and then does the country the world of good. And the Tories will be back in charge soon enough.'

'But we can't have communists running the country!' Sinclair exclaimed, in horror.

'They're socialists, not communists. And they're hardly radicals. Rather an ineffectual lot, I thought.'

Sinclair shook his head. 'They should never have been allowed to get in. It's all these women voters.' He glared distastefully across the room at the two girls attending the smiling figure of Harry Latimer. The women had fashionable washboard figures. They wore backless dresses with asymmetrical hemlines that brushed the tops of their knees. Perfectly respectable looking, by the standards of the day, and several decades away from the horrors of the Mary Quant miniskirt. Sinclair was disgusted, however. 'Not a thought in their heads,' he said. 'Damn flapper vote. Should never have been allowed. If something isn't done, we'll end up with women running the country.'

The 1920s was of course the golden age of male chauvinism and Sinclair was one of its most vocal exponents. His regular column in the Daily Mail had half the country fuming. I had learnt to bite my tongue in the face of such antediluvian attitudes. Let the idiot spout his drivel. If I had to challenge every bloody fool who denigrated the fairer sex I'd scarcely have time to brush my teeth in the morning.

'Women, or coal miners,' Sinclair added, with a shudder. 'You mark my words, Sir Hilary. It'll be government by the mob. And all the little oiks will be telling us what to do.'

'Might not be such a bad thing,' I mumbled, 'if it keeps cretins like you out of power. Excuse me. I'm feeling a little parched.'

19

Sinclair stared open-jawed as I brushed past him.

I try to be pleasant on social occasions, but – really – the fellow was unconscionable. This was hardly the time or place for a political discussion and there were limits even to my tolerance. I grabbed a glass of whisky from a passing flunkey, found an ashtray to stub out the cigarette and went over to join Harry with the girls. The American was in his element, surrounded by young women, but he pulled himself away for a moment. 'What did you say to that journalist?' he asked, glancing across at Sinclair on the other side of the hall. 'He looks like someone's just slapped him.'

'Nothing he didn't deserve. How are you getting on with the Mitford sisters?'

'Oh fine, fine. Just a matter of time, old man. I think the blonde might play ball, if I play my cards right.'

I laughed. 'Do you always talk in clichés?'

'I'm an American. It goes with the territory.'

'Yes, of course.' I gulped down the whisky and surveyed the room. It was a fair old mix of people. "Cosmopolitan" I believe is the polite word. One of the girls Harry had his eye on was positively working class. A music hall star, if you can believe it. Her name was Lettie Young. I'd heard her sing a few years before at the Hackney Empire. A pretty little thing, to be sure, with a serviceable singing voice, but not a patch on Marie Lloyd. On the other side of the room, a northern industrialist was making conversation with Anthony Sinclair, in an absurdly booming voice. His wife was over by the window, ingratiating herself with Lady Fanny Leon. How people such as this had managed to inveigle their way into polite society eluded me, but it was happening everywhere. I was all for universal suffrage, but that didn't mean I wanted to *socialise* with such people. There was even – for goodness sake – an Indian gentleman standing over in the corner, talking animatedly to some fat idiot. Secret service work has always by its nature been egalitarian, but this was ridiculous. Even the fat man looked foreign. 'Who's that fellow over there?' I asked Harry. 'Talking to the Maharajah?'

Harry shrugged. 'No idea. Someone said he was a

doctor.'

'The face looks familiar.'

'You've met him before?'

I shook my head. 'I don't think so.'

At that moment, the fat man glanced over at me and for a moment he frowned.

Things picked up over dinner. The dining hall on the north east corner of Bletchley Park mansion was laid out like a medieval banquet and here the mix of people showed its worth. I doubt whether you could have found a more diverse congregation anywhere on Earth. There were doctors, journalists, society girls, even a couple of continental types. Only Dorothy Kilbride, the Colonel's head of payroll, seemed to lack sparkle, though even she had made a remarkable career for herself in a male-dominated world. Her conversation, however, was as dull as the proverbial ditch water. I can attest to this personally, as I had been placed next to her at the dinner table and she spent the entire evening talking about horticulture, a subject which bores me rigid. The two of us had once shared an office, before the war – I even dimly remember taking her out for dinner a couple of times, in the years before I'd met Elizabeth – but that was scarcely any reason to seat us together now.

'Lady Fanny was telling me about the sculpting of the gardens her husband helped to conceive just before the war,' she was droning on. 'I gather there were several articles about it in *The Gardeners' Chronicle* at the time.'

'Fascinating,' I said, struggling manfully to stifle a yawn.

The Indian gentleman to my left seemed a little more animated. He had studied at Oxford a few years before I had and – much to my irritation – seemed to speak better English than I did. What is it about foreigners and grammar? I can conjugate a verb in Latin if circumstances require, but I don't feel the need to demonstrate it in public. What was worse, Professor Singh had actually completed his degree and become a doctor of philosophy. I had been sent down in my second year

21

after getting myself into a spot of bother over a few gambling debts.

'It is most interesting, do you not think,' he said, 'to observe the rituals and hierarchy of the English class system at close hand? An evening such as this provides a perfect opportunity to analyse the strains imposed upon such an antiquated system, when it is clearly struggling to adapt to an ever changing and more complex world.'

I turned back to Miss Kilbride. 'Yes, the gardens are quite impressive. I hear they've even got a maze.'

I was saved from further tedium by Sir Vincent Kelly, who had risen to his feet and tapped his glass. The room quietened and all eyes turned politely to the Colonel. 'I won't keep you long,' he promised. 'The brandy will be here shortly.' That got a brief cheer. 'I really just wanted to thank you all for coming. I was in two minds whether to hold a celebration for our twentieth anniversary. Being such a poor relation to other departments, we could hardly afford the Royal Albert Hall, what?' There were knowing nods from some of the diners. It was common knowledge that the foreign intelligence service received significantly more funding than MI5. 'But I thought it might be amusing to gather together a few chaps...a few of the characters from over the years who for various reasons...'

'National security!' somebody barked good-naturedly.

'...For various reasons have never had the opportunity to meet before and just...well, have a jolly good knees up. I must, of course, thank our charming hostess, Lady Fanny Leon, for allowing us to make use of her home in this quite disgraceful manner. Ha ha! And particularly for allowing our own people to trample all over the kitchens and the servants quarters.' Most of the regular staff had been packed off for the weekend, just to keep everything tidy. Only the housekeeper, a couple of maids and a stable boy had been allowed to stay behind.

Lady Fanny nodded her head graciously. She was sitting at the head of the table, an imperious matriarch, the living embodiment of the spirit of Britain. I wondered briefly if the man from the Daily Mail had realised his hostess had once been a suffragette. She may not have chained herself to any railings or thrown herself under a racehorse, but Lady Fanny had always been a vocal exponent of women's rights. Nowadays she even had a seat on the local council. It made me proud to think of it. I daresay if there had been a few more women like her we would never have lost the Empire.

The Colonel was standing at the opposite end of the table, the *de facto* lord of the manor, if only for the weekend. 'We promise to clear up after ourselves, of course. Ha ha!' He lifted his glass again. 'I would like to propose a toast. To our delightful hostess,' he said.

'To our hostess,' the diners echoed politely.

'And to twenty years of inspired madness on behalf of His Majesty King George V.'

'His Majesty King George V!' we echoed again.

Sir Vincent nodded with satisfaction and gestured to his man to bring on the brandy and cigars. 'Now let's drink ourselves silly and have some fun.'

Chapter Three

Gambling is a deadly addiction and one that has afflicted me throughout my life. Several times I have come close to ruin. More often than not, however, it has proved a pleasant distraction from the dull routine of everyday life. For me the appeal is not so much in the winning – which in my case is probably just as well – it is in the trouncing of an opponent. There is a curious delight to be had in watching somebody else lose an awful lot of money. When the opponent is a man like Anthony Sinclair that pleasure is magnified several times over. It doesn't matter what the sport is – in this case billiards – it only matters that the other person is utterly humiliated.

Unfortunately, Anthony Sinclair was proving to be something of a master at the billiard table. I had barely managed to hit a ball during our match and even the Colonel took something of a thrashing. I'd lost five guineas on each of these games and was now determined to recover them. There had to be somebody in the building who could stand up to Sinclair. 'Any other takers?' the journalist enquired smugly.

It was eleven thirty in the evening and doubtless some people were thinking of calling it a night. The dance band wasn't booked until the following evening and there was no reason for anyone to stay up past midnight, unless they really wanted to.

'I'll give it a whirl,' one young woman volunteered. It was Harry's current favourite, the Honourable Felicity Mandeville Jones. She was a plucky young thing, a slim blonde, full of vim and spirit, not conventionally pretty but with lively eyes and an inviting smile. I could see why Harry was attracted to her. Even her fashionably short hair spoke of centuries of breeding. Her father, Sir Hugh Mandeville Jones, had been a minister under Stanley Baldwin and was tipped as a possible future prime minister.

Harry was confident he could make a conquest. He had played it cool, flattering the girl with just enough attention, complimenting her on her appearance and calling her 'honey' in that nauseatingly over-familiar American way. His speech patterns may have been moderated by many years spent flitting across Europe, but when it came to seducing the ladies, Harry always reverted to his native brogue. 'I figure I'll get to first base this evening,' he declared with irritating assurance, 'and make the home run tomorrow night.'

The terminology was unfamiliar to me. 'I really have no idea what you're talking about. What in God's name is "first base"?'

'Just a bit of canoodling, old man. It's a sporting reference. Don't you follow baseball?'

'Oddly enough, no. I don't hold with these silly American games. Cricket is the only sport for a gentleman.'

'Yeah, well I'm not exactly a gentleman.'

'There at least we can agree. But I'll bet you fifteen guineas here and now even *you* can't charm the bloomers off that particular young woman.'

'Why not? Do you know something I don't?'

'Almost certainly. And it's only fair to tell you, Harry, the wealthiest young bucks in London have been after that little filly for months, and none of them of them have got anywhere near her.' Despite my lack of interest in such things, Elizabeth always insisted on keeping me up to date with the latest society gossip. 'She can have her pick of the men,' I explained. 'She's hardly likely to risk her reputation with a notorious rake like you. In any case, her father's got his eye on some royal, so I hear.'

'Well, if that's what you think, old man...' He extended a hand. 'Then I guess you've got yourself a wager.'

Now another little bet was brewing. I had observed the Honourable Felicity Mandeville Jones as she took up the billiard cue. She looked surprisingly confident. She thinks she can beat him, I thought at once. It may sound ridiculous, but sometimes you can see a person and just know they have an ace up their sleeve (Harry Latimer is not the only one who can talk in clichés). That was good enough for me. I laid down another five guineas.

Sinclair looked rather put out to be challenged by a

woman. He was – as I have already mentioned – a male chauvinist of the worst kind. Not that there's a best kind, come to think of it. In many ways, he reminded me of my father. Sinclair was the sort of fellow who believed women should be allowed to play one round of bridge after dinner and then be packed off to bed.

Dorothy Kilbride had done just that, funnily enough. She had retired early, complaining of a headache, and the rest of the party had then split in two. A few gay souls were having a sing-along in the drawing room. Not everyone was interested in gambling or billiards. Professor Singh was at the pianoforte, accompanying Lettie Young – the cockney songbird – in a succession of cheery ditties. Her rendition of *I've danced with a man, who's danced with a girl, who's danced with the Prince of Wales* could be heard even from the other end of the hallway.

Anthony Sinclair moved back to the billiard table where the Honourable Felicity Mandeville Jones was waiting. The two competitors placed their cue balls down and a quick shot from each had the balls ricocheting off the far side of the table. Felicity's ball covered more ground, almost returning to the near cushion, which gave her the choice of starting or not. 'I'd quite like to break, if that's all right.' She beamed. 'This is all tremendous fun.'

Right from the first shot, it was clear that English Billiards was a game the Honourable Felicity Mandeville Jones knew inside out. It is quite a simple game, really, but it requires some skill to play. There are three balls, two white and one red. The players have to hit the opposing balls with their cue ball, pocketing one or other if they can, and thus acquiring points.

Sinclair looked on in horror as Felicity hit both balls in one shot and had soon lined up the red in the far corner and pocketed it. I gleefully marked down the score on the black board.

Felicity gave her opponent a dazzling smile. 'Sorry darling. Just beginner's luck.' But the luck continued for the next three strokes.

Sinclair's appalled expression was a pleasure to observe as the game progressed. The man could not afford to lose his temper in such a public arena, but he was clearly having difficulty keeping his anger in check. I met Harry's eye and we exchanged a moment of mutual satisfaction. When the time came for him to take his turn, however, Sinclair pulled himself together and focused all his energies on the table. He struck the cue ball with an expert hand and earned his first points with ease.

'Good shot,' the Colonel applauded, even handed as ever. Everyone else was rooting for Miss Jones.

The game lasted half an hour, with scarcely a miss-cue between the contestants. Felicity Mandeville Jones was probably the better player – quite where she had picked up the skills I had no idea – but she was only just nudging ahead as we came in sight of the finish line. Another red ball left her within a single point of victory. Sinclair was breathing down her neck, at 297 to 299, but it made no difference. Felicity had already won. She didn't even need another pot; all she had to do was hit the white ball head on. If that kissed the red, I would be up five guineas and Sinclair would be a laughing stock.

The man was shaking with barely suppressed rage. Felicity gave him a charming smile and bent forward, aiming her cue with slow deliberation. Not a sound could be heard as she sized up the shot. Even the pianoforte on the other side of the house seemed to momentarily hold its breath. There was a loud thwack as the cue struck the white ball with unexpected ferocity. A groan erupted from the crowd. I watched aghast as the ball leapt into the air, thumped the edge of the table and flipped over the cushion. In apparent slow motion, it plummeted to the floor.

For a moment, there was silence. The sing song in the drawing room had broken up and the revellers, coming by to say goodnight, had already been caught up in the drama.

Miss Jones smiled beatifically. 'It looks like you've won after all, darling.' She beamed.

And so it proved. Sinclair picked up the white ball, reset the table and in one swift move took the game.

I could scarcely credit it.

Harry Latimer was chuckling to himself. He'd made

money on Sinclair in the first two games but hadn't bet anything on the third. He always knew when to quit, did Harry.

'Well done,' said the Colonel, amidst a smattering of polite applause. 'Awfully bad luck, there, Miss Jones.'

The lady in question sighed theatrically. 'And I came so close. Well done, darling.' She touched Sinclair's arms gently.

I stared at the two of them. There was an odd look in her eye, a knowing look. And suddenly, the truth hit me. Felicity had thrown the game. She could have beaten Sinclair but she had chosen not to. I gaped at her in astonishment. What possible reason could she have had for doing that? Damn it, was she sleeping with the fellow? Whatever the reason, the bloody woman had lost me five guineas. And the only crumb of comfort was that Sinclair knew he had been allowed to win. He pulled his arm away from her, his face a textbook illustration of public humiliation.

'It's getting late,' he said, collecting his winnings with ill grace from the edge of the table. 'If you'll all excuse me, I think I shall retire. Goodnight everyone.' And with that, he marched off.

'I've heard of bad losers,' Lettie Young laughed from the doorway, in her alarmingly guttural East London accent, 'but he takes the biscuit. Blimey, what a pillock.' The intrusion of such crude vocabulary broke the tension of the room and conversation abruptly resumed

'Actually, Sinclair won every game,' the Colonel pointed out.

Lettie frowned. 'Didn't act like he'd won.'

Professor Singh, fresh from his triumph on the piano, was oblivious to the confusion. 'It looks to have been a most stimulating contest,' he observed.

Felicity Mandeville Jones stretched her arms above her head. 'But jolly tiring, I must say. I thought I had him at the end there.'

Her words were fooling nobody. She had thrown the game and everyone knew it.

The Colonel adjusted his monocle. He was far too polite to say anything. 'Yes, off to bed, everyone,' he agreed. 'Don't want to miss all the fun tomorrow. Ha ha! We've organised a treasure hunt for the morning. Ten o'clock sharp.'

I gritted my teeth. I'd had just about as much fun as I could manage already. Fifteen guineas lost in one evening. And I would probably lose another fifteen tomorrow.

I was in a prickly mood as I prepared for bed in the early hours of the morning. Hargreaves had retired early, so I was forced to undress myself, although he had at least laid out my nightshirt on the four-poster bed. It had been a long and rather frustrating day and I was looking forward to a protracted period of unconsciousness. I changed quickly, keeping my bandages in place underneath the shirt, just to be on the safe side. If a fire alarm was called during the night, I didn't want my bits jiggling about in front of the servants.

The guest room they had given me was serviceable, though it suffered from the same tasteless clash of styles as the rest of the house, aspiring to substance but never quite achieving it. The place was also rather chilly. A cast iron fireplace on one side might have provided some warmth, had anyone thought to light it. But luckily, there were plenty of blankets on the bed.

I wandered over to the window to look out across the estate. The room was south facing, overlooking the rose garden, a pleasant lawn studded with circular flowerbeds. It was the sort of view you expected from the front of a house rather than the side. Bletchley Park had that feel about it. Nothing was quite as it seemed.

A pathway ran along the edge of the building and, looking down, I caught sight of Professor Singh, lighting up his pipe. Great puffs of smoke were already wafting up into the air. Another fellow was standing to his right, a plump little man, with his own small pipe. This was the foreigner Professor Singh had been speaking to before dinner; the doctor. He was a Frenchman, judging by his accent. Or possibly Belgian. There was something oddly familiar about him. I still hadn't caught his name. Why the two of them were up and about at this hour,

I had no idea. Perhaps they were just having a quick smoke before bedtime. Or maybe the doctor had asked the professor some arcane philosophical question and Singh was still giving his reply.

The doctor was pointing to the steeple of St Mary's Church, visible now through the trees only in silhouette, set against the moonlit sky. Perhaps they were having a religious discussion. It wouldn't have surprised me. I wondered idly if the professor was even a Christian.

I pulled back from the window as the doctor swung his head round and looked upwards towards the house. I wasn't sure if he had seen me. I swayed for a moment, a sudden dizziness threatening to overpower me. I had drunk quite a bit over dinner and it was beginning to have an effect. I steadied myself. Nature was starting to make her usual demands and there was no point going to bed without relieving at least some of the pressure on my overworked bladder. A chamber pot had been provided underneath the bed, but I have an aversion to using them and Bletchley Park did at least have the semblance of modern plumbing. There was a water closet at the far end of the corridor.

I unlocked the door and made my way quietly along the landing and up a short flight of stairs. The sounds of snoring could be heard from at least one of the bedrooms to my left. Some lucky beggar was already in the arms of Morpheus. My money was on the Colonel. There was a man with a clean conscience. Surprising, really, given the nature of his job. I heard whispered voices coming from a second room as I passed it by and I wondered briefly if Harry had already reached "first base" with the Honourable Felicity Mandeville Jones.

My ablutions taken care of, I hurried back to my room but stopped halfway when I heard a cry and a sudden thump from one of the other bedrooms adjacent to my own. It had sounded like quite a hard thump. I hesitated for a moment. Probably none of my business, I thought. But better to be on the safe side.

I knocked gently on the door.

'Is everything all right in there?' I kept my voice low, so

as not to disturb the rest of the corridor. 'I thought I heard a bump.' Several seconds elapsed without a response. I knocked quietly a second time.

There was a shuffling from within the room and a few seconds later the door opened and the Honourable Felicity Mandeville Jones peered out through the crack. She was not yet dressed for bed, although her clothes did seem somewhat dishevelled.

'Sorry to disturb you, Miss Jones,' I said. 'I thought you might have had an accident. Are you all right?'

There was a bright red mark on the side of her face.

'Yes, I'm fine,' she said. 'I slipped and banged my head on the bedstead. It's nothing. Terribly clumsy of me. But I'm fine.'

I wasn't sure I believed her, though I couldn't very well call her a liar. 'Well, if you're sure.' A shadow flitted behind her. There was somebody else in the room, but I couldn't make out who. It was hardly any of my business. 'Would you like me to send down for a glass of water?'

'That's terribly sweet of you, Sir Hilary, but I'm sure I'll be fine.' She smiled awkwardly. There were rings around her eyes and I felt sure she had been crying. 'I'm just a little bit tired. All this exertion! Too much excitement for one evening.'

'Yes. Damn shame, losing the game like that.'

'And your five guineas too. Can you ever forgive me?'

'I daresay I'll manage. Well, if you're sure everything is all right?' She nodded. 'Then I'll bid you goodnight.'

And with that, the door closed.

I hovered for a moment on the landing, trying to make sense of what I had seen. A mark on her face and an unknown figure lurking in the background. There was only one conclusion to be drawn: there was a man in the bedroom of Felicity Mandeville Jones. The gossips had been wrong. She was clearly not as Honourable as everyone supposed. And after that last game of billiards, it was clear that the man in question was none other than Anthony Sinclair.

How the daughter of a former cabinet minister had ended up entangled with such an unpleasant fellow I couldn't begin to imagine. She didn't seem the sort to sacrifice her reputation without good cause. And Sinclair, I knew, was a married man. Not that marital infidelity bothers me in the slightest. Many seemingly happy marriages are little more than shells – I speak from personal experience – and if people can get their pleasure elsewhere, good luck to them, I say. But no one could find any pleasure in the arms of a brute like Anthony Sinclair. The man was an unfeeling cad.

I felt a pang of sympathy for Miss Jones. She wasn't the first woman to fall for a blackguard and she wouldn't be the last.

That mark on the side of her face, though.

If Sinclair had beaten her, then he was even more of a scoundrel than I had first supposed. I cannot abide violence against women. It shows a profound weakness of character. Part of me was inclined to break down the door and give the fellow a good thrashing. But if Felicity Mandeville Jones had chosen to get involved with a man like that, it was not my place to interfere. And in any case, there was a real possibility that I would be the one that would receive the thrashing. Knowing my luck, Sinclair would turn out to be an amateur boxing champion. No, sad as it was, I would have to leave well alone. Whatever mistakes the Honourable Felicity Mandeville Jones had made, she would just have to suffer the consequences.

There was one crumb of comfort, though, as I made my way back to the cold darkness of the bedroom, locking my door carefully behind me as I had done every night since I was a child.

At least now I was sure Harry Latimer would lose his bet.

Chapter Four

The treasure hunt the following morning was the kind of enforced jollity that any sane person would do their uttermost to avoid. The Colonel had done his best to spice things up – daringly splitting the guests into mixed couples as we followed a series of cryptic clues – but on a cold October morning, with drizzle in the air, an extended tour of the estate, even in the name of entertainment, was the last thing anyone needed.

I was not the only one with a shocking hangover. Arriving at the breakfast table, I was confronted by a scene of abject horror that would not have disgraced the Somme. Lifeless eyes were staring mindlessly in every direction. Felicity Mandeville Jones did not appear at all, though she sent her apologies, saying she was not feeling well. Only Harry and Professor Singh seemed unaffected by the indulgences of the previous evening. Harry could drink anybody under the table and the professor had made a small sherry last all night. The only satisfaction I could garner, as my head throbbed and my brain threatened to shatter the thin cradle of bone holding my skull in place, was that Sinclair – who had arrived unpardonably late at the table – had been paired off for the morning with the terminally tedious Dorothy Kilbride. The fascist and the dull widow. It could not have worked out better.

The mixing of couples was organised with scrupulous precision. Lots had been drawn and when the one married couple who had been invited for the weekend somehow managed to end up together, chance rather than planning was to blame.

Mr and Mrs Smith accepted their fate with good grace. They were a strange, ill-matched couple. He was a bluff northerner in his fifties, she a hoity-toity home counties girl, adept at looking down her nose at everyone. The Colonel had introduced us the previous evening and insisted that they really were called Mr and Mrs Smith. 'If I wanted to manufacture an alias,' he told us, 'I'd have come up with something a bit more imaginative than that. Ha ha!' It would not have sounded so improbable if one of them had been called Ariadne or Ethelbert, but no, it was plain old John and Mary Smith. It was rare to find a married couple in the Security Service (relationships were frowned upon, for very good reasons) but they had met and fallen in love – goodness knows why – and nature had taken its course.

Sir Vincent was in charge of the morning's entertainment, which happily for him meant he would not be participating in any of it. Lady Fanny Leon had graciously consented to be involved, however. She had drawn a name from the hat just like all the other women and had shown the appropriate amount of pleasure on discovering she had been paired off with Professor Singh.

'It will be a most enjoyable game,' the academic assured her, with a beam of pride.

'I am sure it will,' Lady Fanny agreed.

As for me, I had to make do with the irksome Lettie Young, the "much loved music hall star". 'I hope you've got a brain,' she declared, scanning the type-written sheet the Colonel had handed out to each of the teams. ''Cos I ain't got a bleedin' clue.'

We gathered on the roundabout at the front of the house to begin our quest. The sky was somewhat cloudy, though sadly there was little prospect of precipitation bringing a premature end to our activities. We would just have to see the game through to its conclusion.

Hargreaves was trying to attract my attraction from the doorway but I waved him away. If I *had* to take part in this game, it was better simply to get on with it.

A set of clues had been typed out, leading to a variety of locations across the estate. Letters would be collected from each site and gradually a word would be revealed. That would tell us the location of the treasure and the first one to grab it would be the winner. It was a convoluted and rather silly game, but fully in keeping with the finest traditions of the British civil service. I could just imagine some dullard at Queen's Gate chuckling to himself as he thought it all up. I only hoped the prize was something decent. A bottle of whisky, perhaps.

'That American friend of yours is a bit of a charmer, ain't he?' Lettie Young said, as we set off in search of the first letter. 'Where's he hiding this morning? He disappeared pretty sharpish after breakfast.'

'He had an errand to run,' I admitted, tightly.

Harry was no fool. He had no more desire to criss-cross the grounds of Bletchley Park on a cold October morning than I did. 'I need to borrow your car,' he had announced, bold as brass, over the breakfast table. Typical Harry. 'I've got a bit of business I need to take care of.'

If it had been anyone else, I would have given them short shrift. But Harry could be very persuasive and he had done me quite a few favours over the years. Reluctantly, I'd lent him the keys. Hargreaves had offered to drive him too, but I drew the line at that. Let him find his own damn chauffeur.

Harry was probably meeting up with some dubious contact and the less I knew about it the better. Maybe he was delivering that holdall I had brought up with me from London. I didn't much care. He had promised to be back in time for lunch, which was all that mattered; at which point he would doubtless resume his attempts to deflower the Honourable Felicity Mandeville Jones. He was wasting his time there, of course. The man from the Daily Mail had already beaten him to it. And I doubted Anthony Sinclair would appreciate a rival.

Lettie Young seemed rather taken with Harry. If he had put his money on her, he might have had some chance. Lettie was a "home run" girl if ever I met one. She was dressed in a heavy outdoor coat, with thick gloves and a brightly coloured cloche hat against the cold. Her figure was washboard thin. Whether she was actually that shape or was enduring the fashionable contortions of the age was impossible to guess. I had some sympathy. Although I have always been modestly proportioned, it still takes some effort to disguise my true shape. A couple of coins and a length of bandage were usually sufficient to flatten it all down. It was either that or the Symington Side Lacer, a reinforced bodice all the bright young things were using to disguise their bosom and achieve that fashionable boyish silhouette.

'You want to be careful with Harry,' I warned. 'He's not exactly a gentleman.'

'Well, I ain't exactly a lady.' She laughed. 'Don't you worry, love. I can handle myself. I've been married twice already.'

'Good grief. But you can't be a day over twenty-five.'

She grinned 'They do things differently in the theatre.'

That much was evident.

'Are you...divorced?' I asked incredulously. It was bad enough that a woman of her class had been invited to be part of this weekend at all, but a *divorcee*. What was the Colonel thinking of? I know everyone gets divorced these days, but you must understand – back in the 1920s a divorced woman was about as disreputable as you could get. It smacked of infidelity and it was felt – rightly or wrongly – that there was something just plain wrong with a woman who was unable to keep her husband. The fact that some husbands were of the order of Anthony Sinclair never really seemed to register at the time.

'Divorced and widowed.' She laughed. 'On the lookout for number three, so you'd better beware!'

'I'm already married,' I told her firmly. And had I not been, Lettie Young would have been the last person on my list of potential fiancées.

'I know. I'm only teasing. So what was that clue again?'

I glanced down at the piece of paper in my hand. I was finding it difficult to develop any interest in the game. There hadn't been time to organise a sweepstake. '"*It grows like wheat but puzzles the mind.*"' The answer was obvious.

Lettie wiped her nose with a glove. 'Nope. No idea.'

I sighed. 'It's "maze".' Still she didn't understand. '"Maize" the crop and "Maze" the puzzle.'

'Oh, I get you. That is clever. They got a maze here then?'

'So I've been told.' In fact, the entrance to the maze was only a couple of hundred yards from the front of the house.

Lettie grabbed my arm. 'Well, then, lover boy. Let's go and get lost.'

A succession of clues led us back and forth across the grounds in a frustratingly unpredictable manner. It was not a large estate – acres rather than miles – but there were plenty of awkward nooks and crannies to confuse the unwary. I was puffing with the exertion of it all. Each stop on the treasure hunt provided us with a single letter of the alphabet – thankfully we didn't have to go into the maze to find the first one, or we might have been there all day – and gradually the location of the treasure would be revealed. There were seven clues in all and the first three letters were B, R & Y. 'It's going to be "LIBRARY",' I guessed, with some confidence.

Lettie laughed. 'God, you ain't half clever. They should take you on full time.'

'How on earth did *you* get involved with all this?' I asked, my hand gesturing vaguely in the air. 'With the Colonel, I mean?' The question sounded less polite out loud than it had when it had first formed in my head. But it was still worth asking. How had a music hall star ever managed to get mixed up with MI5?

'Ooh, wouldn't you like to know!' She grinned. 'No shop talk, didn't you hear the Colonel?'

I nodded. 'Quite right.'

On reflection, it probably wasn't so odd. Information was the lifeblood of intelligence work and Lettie was a professional entertainer. Travelling up and down the country, from theatre to theatre, she would doubtless come into contact with a wide variety of people. It was the perfect way to gather information, especially for someone with the common touch. And Lettie Young certainly had that.

I glanced down at the clue sheet. One more letter should do it, I thought, just to confirm "library" really was that all-important final word.

The next clue directed us to a yard on the far side of the mansion. A long row of stables fringed the back of a rudimentary square and a stable boy stood smirking beside a set of large wooden doors. We passed inside and made our way along the rustic stalls. The smell of straw and animals, even in the cold, made my nose turn up. Several large horses stood passively watching us as we made our way to the far end. I regarded them suspiciously. I can ride well enough, but I have never been much of a one for the country. Lettie Young, surprisingly, was in her element.

'I always wanted to own a horse,' she confided. 'You're a handsome devil, ain't you?' Thankfully, at this point, she was talking to one of the horses. She patted its head and the animal nickered happily.

'I think it's a mare,' I said.

Lettie laughed. 'You need your eyes testing, mate.' She gestured to the rear of the animal and I realised, on reflection, that it was actually a rather impressive stallion. Appearances can sometimes be deceptive.

The horse was of far less interest to me, however, than the sheet of white paper pinned to the far wall of the stable. Which poor sap, I wondered, had been tasked with the duty of placing all these silly bits of paper across the estate? Probably that stable boy. It would be beneath the dignity of any of the valets.

Lettie stared happily at the large letter "A". 'Looks like you were right.' She grinned. 'Clever sod.' She grabbed the sheet of clues from my hand. 'So, what's the next one then?'

'Forget it,' I told her. 'We know where the treasure is. We might as well go straight there.'

She smiled mischievously. 'You're a crafty beggar, you are. I don't know if I should be left alone with you, what with all this hay lying around.'

I let out a sigh. The damn woman was flirting with me. 'I assure you, Miss Young, you are perfectly safe with me.' My tone was less than friendly.

She made a pretence of disappointment. 'You don't like me very much, do you?'

'I...haven't formed an opinion.'

'Don't give me that.' Her eyes were gleaming with mischief. 'You think I'm a mouthy little tart who doesn't deserve to be here with all you respectable types. Be honest, that's what you think, ain't it?'

'Very well. If that's what you want me to say, then yes, that *is* what I think. A respectable country house is not the place for an East End girl. It makes everyone feel very uncomfortable.'

'Not me, it don't. It's no skin off my nose what people think. You go on the stage, you're used to dealing with all sorts. But you,' she observed me shrewdly. 'You ain't comfortable anywhere, are you?'

I snorted. 'That's your considered opinion, is it?'

'Yes, since we're being honest. I think you're a stuck up prig who wouldn't know a good time if it bashed you in the face.'

I blinked. And then I laughed. I couldn't help myself. I do admire plain speaking. 'Miss Young, I believe I may have misjudged you.'

'Too bloody right. Now are we gonna win this stupid treasure hunt or what?'

I gestured to the stable door. 'To the library!'

Lettie grinned. 'I'll race you there!'

That was going too far. 'I have no intention of running.'

'Suit yourself.' She bolted from the stable without another word, nearly crashing into the groom before clattering inelegantly across the yard. I stopped in the doorway and watched her go. I didn't have the heart to tell her she was heading in the wrong direction. There was an archway off to the right that led straight through to the back of the house. I could pass under that and arrive at the library in half the time. And *I* wouldn't have to run.

I pulled out my fob watch and checked the time against the clock on top of the arch. It was just coming up to midday. On the far side was a set of garages, running parallel to the rear of the house. The metal shutters were down, meaning all the automobiles were safely locked away. I wondered idly if the Morris Oxford had arrived back yet, but Harry had only been gone a couple of hours, so it seemed unlikely.

Lost in thought, I almost collided with one of my competitors, heading in the opposite direction. It was the doctor, the portly Frenchman who had been out smoking with

39

Professor Singh the previous evening.

'I beg your pardon, Monsieur,' he said, as we nearly crashed head first into one another. He was tubby fellow with a crop of short curly hair and a rather fine moustache. He walked with a gentle limp and had his own sheet of clues clutched tightly in his hand.

The man was unaccompanied. There had been an odd number of participants, with the Honourable Felicity Mandeville Jones unwell, and he had volunteered to be the odd man out.

I stepped back politely. 'Monsieur Lefranc.' I had finally learnt his name. Gaston Lefranc. The name, like the face, had a nagging familiarity. I had only been to France a couple of times and it was not a place I had any happy memories of. The most recent trip had been three years ago to the south of the country and I had barely met a soul during several months of confinement.

The memory of that suddenly collided with the amiable Frenchman standing in front of me. And now I knew where I had seen him before.

Gaston Lefranc observed me with quiet amusement. 'You recognise me at last,' he observed. 'I wondered whether you would.'

My throat began to constrict. 'You…remember me?' I asked, my voice a hoarse whisper.

'I didn't at first. It was your manservant I recognised. I saw him this morning preparing the car for Mr Latimer. I knew him at once, although not by the name of Hargreaves.'

'Listen.' I gestured him away from the arch and over towards the back of the house. 'This is damned awkward.'

'Do not worry.' Lefranc placed a reassuring hand on my shoulder. 'Your secret is safe with me, Madame.'

Chapter Five

Affairs of the heart can be damned difficult when you're leading a double life. I have the same impulses as any normal hot-blooded woman. When I was a child, my tutors had insisted that "female persons" did not have sexual desires. Men lusted, they said, women acquiesced, though only in the devoutly Christian context of the marital bed. When I hear people in the latter half of the century talking nostalgically about "Victorian Values" I always let off a snort of derision. The Victorians, like every other generation, were a bunch of hypocrites. I had desires and, though my peculiar life as an English gentleman did make things difficult, I also had my fair share of romantic encounters.

One particular liaison, pertinent to this story, took place during the General Strike of 1926. I had volunteered to drive a tram – helping to keep London running while the rabble sat around drinking themselves into a stupor, pretending they were being radical. One young man had taken my eye and although I would usually only dally when away from home – where I was less likely to be recognised – he was such a fine looking fellow and it had been such a long time since I had last indulged myself that I was determined to have him.

Hargreaves set me up in a small flat in the vicinity of Sloane Square, and posing as a Mrs Rimington, a respectable widow, I set about seducing the young tram conductor. It wasn't difficult. He was twenty-one and had never had carnal knowledge of a woman. Whether he was saving himself for marriage or had just been unlucky I didn't know. But I was thirty-seven and well versed in the arts of love.

It was a gloriously inconsequential affair and of course it couldn't last.

When I found myself in a state of embarrassment some months later, I realised I had been the naïve one. I'd thought there was little risk of me getting pregnant in my late thirties, but evidently I had been mistaken. An abortion was a possibility – even in those days, there were doctors who were willing to break the law for the appropriate fee – but I'd had an abortion once before, in my university days, and I couldn't face going through that a second time. So I travelled to the south of France instead, for six months, with Hargreaves posing as my husband, and awaited the happy event. I don't think Elizabeth even noticed I was gone.

The midwife we engaged was an astonishingly ugly old crone who can't have been a day under a hundred and three. She didn't speak a word of English and her accent was so thick I wasn't even sure she could speak French. But she knew her job and helped deliver a healthy baby. I think it was a boy, but I was too exhausted to care.

It was Hargreaves who then sent for a doctor, to give the baby the once over before we packed it off to the orphanage.

And it was then, lying flat on my back, covered in sweat, that I had briefly met the man standing before me now in the back yard of Bletchley Park. Doctor Gaston Lefranc.

It was a moment I had feared for so long, it was almost a relief that it had finally arrived. I had had so many narrow escapes over the years, particularly in my Oxford days. And now someone had discovered the truth and my fate was in his hands.

'How much do you want?' I asked, with a frankness born of desperation. Perhaps it might be possible to buy his silence.

'Want?' Lefranc stared at me blankly. 'I'm afraid I don't understand, Monsieur.'

'How much money do you want? To keep quiet?' If I could persuade him to take a bribe, it would make everything so much simpler. But perhaps he intended to blackmail me, to take me for every penny I had. That is what Harry Latimer would have done. This was a disaster.

'I assure you, Sir Hilary, I have no desire to extort money from you. If you choose to live your life as a man, that is your business, not mine.'

'You're…not going to tell anyone?' I couldn't quite believe it.

'Why should I? It is none of my concern. In any case,

we doctors, we are like priests. We respect people's privacy.'

'I was never really your patient, though.'

'The principle still applies. I must admit, however, I am intrigued by this strange life you are leading. I have come across cases of indeterminate sex, but that is a medical matter. I have never heard of a woman choosing to live her life as a man. It is absolutely fascinating. I was talking to Professor Singh just recently and he was saying…'

I blanched at the name. 'Please tell me you're not going to discuss it with *him*!'

'Do not concern yourself, Monsieur. Professor Singh is a very learned and intelligent man, but patient confidentiality must take precedence over everything else.'

'I…I'm glad to hear it.'

Lefranc stared at me thoughtfully. 'But I must confess, I am curious to know why anybody would choose to live in such a way.'

'I didn't exactly *choose* it,' I said, somewhat defensively. 'And it's not as if I'm the only one doing it.' It felt odd to be discussing this so openly. I had never spoken to anyone about it before. It made me feel rather uncomfortable. 'Quite a few women signed up to fight in 1914, you know. Joined the army as men and fought alongside the other Tommies. You won't read about it in the history books, but it happened.'

'You fought in the trenches?' Lefranc was incredulous.

'Good lord, no,' I said. 'I packed my bags in 1914 and went to live in America. But plenty of others stayed behind.'

For the first time, I saw a hint of disapproval in the doctor's eye.

'You must have been with the French army,' I guessed.

Lefranc nodded. 'I was a battlefield surgeon. It was a distressing experience. I am glad I will never have to go through that again. But Monsieur. Madame. Forgive me. I am fascinated by this double life of yours. It must create all kinds of difficulties. Have you lived your entire life this way?'

I nodded. 'It was my father's fault. He couldn't stand women.' Sir Frederick Manningham-Butler had wanted a son and heir, but my mother had died giving birth to me and Sir Frederick couldn't bear the thought of having to marry anybody else. 'He falsified the birth certificate and brought me up as a boy.'

'It cannot have been easy.'

'Lord, no. He couldn't exactly pack me off to boarding school. Not with the rugger matches and the communal showers.' I laughed. 'More's the pity. Nanny Perkins knew the truth, of course, as did my valet. But I was educated privately. Personal tutors, formal lessons. And everybody was kept in the dark. It wasn't until I went off to university that things began to get really tricky.'

'You could have rebelled, Monsieur. You could have revealed the truth, despite your father.'

'Don't think it didn't occur to me. I was quite a reckless young thing. Played fast and loose. Got sent down in the end. But eventually I learned to live with it.'

'And this man of yours, Hargreaves. I assume he is not really your husband?'

'God, no.'

'Or the father of the child?'

'No. There was...another fellow. A brief fling, you understand. Nothing serious.'

'I understand.' There was no recrimination in Lefranc's voice. I suppose a doctor cannot help but be a man of the world. 'What happened to the child I examined?' he enquired.

'Off to the orphanage. Probably put out for adoption. A couple of Frog parents, I daresay. Oh, no offence.'

'None taken.' He smiled warmly. The man was altogether too amiable. It was rather unnerving.

'You won't...you won't breathe a word of this to anyone?' I asked again.

'I have given you my word, Monsieur. And we are all, are we not, experts at keeping secrets?'

'I'll say. A house full of secret agents.' I wondered suddenly how Lefranc had got involved in all that. But if my double life was none of his business, then his life as an employee of MI5 was none of mine. As the Colonel had said, no shop talk.

'Now I must finish the game,' Lefranc declared. 'I am convinced the final word is "library" but I need one more letter to confirm it.' Each team had been given a slightly different set of clues.

I gestured to the stables, just visible through the elaborate archway. 'The far end, by the final stall. Watch out for that black stallion. I think he's getting a bit frisky.'

Lefranc bowed. 'Merci, Monsieur.'

I stood for a moment after he had left, breathing in the cold air. My heart was beating rapidly. The doctor seemed a thoroughly decent fellow, but I was loath to accept his assurances at face value.

I would have to have a word with Hargreaves.

A loud clunk sounded from somewhere nearby. I looked around with concern, but there was nobody in sight.

My secret was safe, for now.

Chapter Six

Lettie Young was attacking the small wooden box with a hat pin. Her face was screwed up in deep concentration as she manoeuvred the pin inside the lock. Professor Singh stood to her left, peering over her shoulder in benign amusement. 'You've just got to tickle it,' she explained to him, her voice peculiarly strained. All at once, there was a gentle click and a sudden round of applause from the assembled guests. 'There you go, professor,' she said. 'Piece of cake.'

The young music hall star stepped back and allowed Professor Singh to open the box. The chest was made of heavily polished wood. It was about six inches tall and almost a foot across. The lid was narrow and as Professor Singh pulled it open a miniature ballerina sprang up and a mechanical device started playing a brief extract from *The Sugar Plum Fairy*. The ballerina danced or rather revolved with little reference to the music being played.

'Most delightful!' the professor exclaimed. He lifted up the box for a moment, examining it in minute detail, and then gallantly presented it to Lettie.

'You're a real gent.' She grinned, holding the box proudly for a moment. Then she saw me standing in the doorway. 'And where the bleedin' hell have you been?' she exclaimed.

All eyes shifted in my direction.

I had dallied for several minutes along the pathway that led around the back of the house. It had taken me some moments to recover my wits after the alarming conversation with Doctor Lefranc. The sheer coincidence of the good doctor being here had seriously unnerved me. Two strangers who met once in the south of France might plausibly bump into each other again a few years later in England, but surely not at the same country house and having belonged at one time to the same organisation? I have always distrusted coincidence and this particular reunion had done nothing to make me reconsider that attitude. Doctor Lefranc's presence at Bletchley Park beggared belief. If someone was playing games, then I for one was not remotely amused.

There was no time for further reflection, however. Having arrived at the doorway, and with all the guests now staring at me, some justification for my tardiness was required. 'I...got side-tracked,' I explained, rather lamely, stepping forward into the library.

The room was an oasis of ordered calm. The book-lined walls would have done the British Museum proud. An oak-framed fireplace dominated the near wall, with a huge mirror hanging above it. Bookshelves filled the remaining space, packed solidly with innumerable worthy volumes, except to the south, where a wide bow window provided a pleasant view of the gardens. Several solid leather armchairs were scattered across the room, helping to create the impression of a gentleman's club in miniature. Not the kind of club I would have wished to join, admittedly – it was a little stuffy for my taste – but the kind that the Colonel and even perhaps (in those progressive days) Professor Singh might have felt at home in.

Lettie Young was standing by a small table, a picture of working class inelegance, her pretty rouged face glowing with enthusiasm (she would not have been allowed to join the club; the days were not *that* progressive). Lady Fanny Leon, by contrast, seemed rather at home there. She was seated comfortably in a heavily padded armchair, observing the proceedings with an amused detachment. She had been partnered with Professor Singh and it was the Indian gentleman, naturally, who had been the first to follow the trail of clues to the music box. The damned fellow was now positively beaming with pride. Lady Fanny, for her part, still looked a little flustered. She was a rather portly woman and was probably not used to the exertion. I knew exactly how she felt.

'Professor Singh just nipped in before me,' Lettie explained. 'If you'd told me which way to go I might have got here first.'

'Alas,' the professor exclaimed, 'I was unable to open the box without the proper key.'

'One final test,' the Colonel declared, from his own leather armchair. 'Capital fun! Ha ha! Where on earth did you learn that trick with the hat pin, my dear?'

Lettie grinned. 'It's amazing what you can pick up, living in an orphanage.' She placed the music box back down on the table and closed the lid. There was only so much of *The Nutcracker* anyone could appreciate in one sitting.

Professor Singh had won the contest, but Lettie had ended up with the prize. It was, I suppose, a satisfactory conclusion to what had proved – aside from my encounter with Doctor Lefranc – a rather lacklustre event. What further delights would the Colonel have in store for us this afternoon? I wondered.

A few of the stragglers from the treasure hunt were still arriving at the library. Mr and Mrs Smith swept in from the hallway, laughing gaily, and behind them came a glum-faced Dorothy Kilbride. She had been partnered with Anthony Sinclair, so it was hardly surprising she was not in the best of spirits.

'Looks like you're the last, Mr Sinclair,' I observed with some relish. 'The clues a bit too difficult for you?'

Sinclair smiled icily. 'Not at all. And I believe Doctor Lefranc is yet to arrive, so we are not quite the last.'

'You're right. Second to last.' I nodded smugly. 'Not quite as bad.'

Sinclair raised an eyebrow. 'It's the taking part that counts, Sir Hilary.'

'Quite right,' the Colonel agreed, pulling himself up from the armchair. 'And now, I believe, it's time for lunch.'

The dinner suit was freshly laundered. It showed none of the alcohol stains I vaguely remembered dribbling over the lapels the previous evening. Hargreaves was hanging it up in the wardrobe. He tensed slightly as I opened the door, his eyes betraying the usual mix of embarrassment and admiration. 'Did you have an enjoyable morning, sir?' he asked, as I moved into the bedroom.

'Passable, Hargreaves, passable.' I flopped down onto the bed and stretched out my arms. 'Didn't win the damn treasure hunt though.'

'I'm sorry to hear that, sir. And how was Miss Young as a companion?'

'Loud and crude. Although I must confess I'm beginning to warm to her.'

'She has a lovely singing voice.'

I grimaced. 'She'll probably be singing again tonight, worst luck. Is the car back yet?'

Hargreaves nodded. He turned and gestured to the bedside table. 'Mr Latimer returned the keys ten minutes ago. I took the liberty of parking the car myself.'

Ever efficient. 'Did you check the milometer?'

'Thirty-five miles, sir, since this morning.'

That was dashed odd. 'He must have been gone nearly three hours. What on earth was he doing?'

'That I couldn't say, sir.'

I lay thinking for a moment. I didn't like this at all. There was far too much going on that I didn't understand. There was all that business with the Honourable Felicity Mandeville Jones as well. Hargreaves seemed unaffected, however. Perhaps he hadn't had the opportunity yet to get a really good look at Gaston Lefranc.

There was something altogether dog like about my valet. I often caught him looking at me with a kind of doey-eyed affection; that mindless adoration only dogs can have, because they lack the sense to see the faults in their masters. Not that I have many faults. I drink like a fish, gamble to excess and have something of a weakness for men in uniform, but such things are hardly unusual for somebody of my class. Hargreaves was a good seven years older than me and I suspected that – in his sad middle-aged way – he was a little bit in love with me. Not that he would ever have admitted it, but he was always a little too keen to scrub my back when I was in the bath. And although I found the very idea of it nauseating, it did at least mean that he was easy to control. There was none of that inverted master-servant relationship between us that PG

49

Wodehouse later parodied so well, though I knew plenty of other people for whom it was true.

'Have you bumped into that Frenchman yet?' I asked. There was no point beating about the bush. 'The doctor?'

Hargreaves tensed again. His shoulders always tended to slope somewhat, so when they hunched together, you really noticed it. 'I...saw him this morning, sir. As I was preparing the car for Mr Latimer.'

'You recognised him, of course?'

Hargreaves nodded, turning towards me apologetically. 'I'm afraid I did, sir.'

I took a deep breath and then allowed myself to explode. 'Well, why the blazes didn't you tell me?!?'

It was Hargreaves' turn to take a breath. 'If you recall, sir, I tried to speak to you just as you were leaving with Miss Young this morning, but you told me not to disturb you.'

That was true enough. I'd been in a foul mood. 'You should have insisted.'

'I...I didn't like to.'

I growled in despair. 'You're hopeless, Hargreaves. Absolutely hopeless.'

'I'm sorry, sir. Did...did the doctor speak to you?'

'He did.' I sat up on the bed. 'He knows everything. The child. You, me. One word from that man and I'll be ruined. A laughing stock.' And what Elizabeth would think I didn't dare contemplate. She would be humiliated and worse still she would lose her title. 'Why couldn't you have kept yourself out of the way?' I said. 'He wouldn't have recognised me. It was you he remembered.'

'I'm very sorry, sir.'

'Stop apologising, damn you!'

Hargreaves was quiet for a moment. 'What are we going to do?' he asked, at length.

I bit my lip and reached into my jacket. My cigarette case was in the inside pocket. 'Nothing we can do. He doesn't seem inclined to tell anyone. Actually, he seems a rather decent sort. But even so...'

'He lives in France, sir. That I do know. I spoke to the

Colonel's man about him this morning. He's heading straight back to Bordeaux tomorrow evening. He has the ferry booked already.'

I lit a cigarette. 'That's something, I suppose.' I took a long drag. Hargreaves and I had stayed somewhere near Bordeaux, during my confinement. 'That farmhouse we rented, a couple of years back. Didn't Harry have something to do with that?'

Hargreaves considered for a moment. 'I believe he did, sir. You sent him a cable, when he was in America.'

'Good lord. So I did.' I had needed to rent a property for six months. I'd asked Harry if he knew anywhere suitable and he had wired back, giving me the name of a friend in the South of France. The friend had provided the farmhouse.

'A bit odd that, sir.'

'I'll say.' Another damn coincidence. Perhaps Harry *did* know Doctor Lefranc. He had claimed not to, when I'd pointed to the fellow the night before, but he might well have been lying. I growled in frustration. 'I wish I'd never agreed to come here this weekend. You should have talked me out of it.'

'Yes, sir. Will you be needing anything this afternoon, sir?'

'What? No, just the evening wear. They've got a dance band coming, can you believe it?'

Hargreaves grimaced. He was a worse dancer than I was. Not that he had any reason to fear. He wouldn't be the one forced onto the ballroom floor. And knowing my luck, I would probably end up spending most of the evening waltzing with Dorothy Kilbride. Perhaps I could tear one of the younger girls away from Harry.

I stood up and walked over to the window. Before the dance, there was an even greater horror to face. A couple of servants were making their way along the side of the house, carrying a table between them laden down with various sporting implements. The afternoon's entertainment was being prepared over by the lake.

I shuddered.

Dancing I could cope with, but croquet...

Chapter Seven

Lunch had been laid out on the edge of the croquet lawn, some distance from the main house. A protective stand overshadowed the tables, in case of rain, and a succession of outdoor chairs had been provided for those of us not directly involved in the game. The lawn itself was elongated, running along the south side of the lake, adjacent to a narrow pathway that circled the water. Half a dozen hoops had been hammered into the grass at regulation intervals and mallets had been provided for the first four competitors. It was a mixed doubles match and with a toss of a coin – the Colonel acting as umpire – it was Dorothy Kilbride and Professor Singh who chose to tee off (or whatever the correct expression is). Lettie Young had joined a frostily polite Anthony Sinclair to form the opposing team and a more ill matched pair you could scarcely have hoped to find. It was a joy to behold.

I had a plate of food in my lap and was sitting back happily, waiting to observe the carnage. It was a little chilly out, but Hargreaves had insisted I dress for a blizzard so there was little chance of me catching cold. A few glasses of whisky and soda, in any case, would provide all the warmth any woman could want.

What had possessed the Colonel to organise a croquet match in late October was beyond me. A hunt would have been more appropriate; a bit of grouse shooting or some such. But the estate wasn't really big enough for that and, in any case, it was not for the likes of me to question the decisions of Major-General Sir Vincent Kelly KMCG. Perhaps, as Harry Latimer had suggested, it was another demonstration of the man's endearingly quirky sense of humour.

My American friend was observing the proceedings with a typically amused expression. Unlike me, he was going easy on the food, though he had cadged a cigarette from my case and joined me in a glass of Scottish nectar. 'So what do you say, old man,' he suggested, watching the two teams moving forward with their mallets. 'How about a little wager?'

I didn't see why not. 'Two guineas. On Miss Kilbride and Professor Singh.'

Harry's brow creased suspiciously. 'Do you know something I don't?'

'Not at all. Just can't bear the thought of Sinclair winning anything.'

That seemed to satisfy him. 'Well, it seems a shame to take your money but...' He reached across and we shook hands. 'Two guineas it is.'

Dorothy Kilbride was just preparing to take her first shot. She lined up the mallet carefully and gave the ball a solid thwack. It flew across the lawn in a perfect straight line. There was a polite ripple of applause. Harry shot me a suspicious glance but I was saying nothing.

The last time I had seen Dorothy playing croquet was at Syon House back in the summer of 1913. She had slaughtered all comers. It was her one great skill. I was surprised Harry didn't know, but then he had never visited the London office. I had lost a lot of money that weekend and it was shortly after that that I had been forced to propose to Elizabeth. No, there was no chance of anybody beating Miss Dorothy Kilbride, not when it came to croquet. Even if her partner was lacking in skill – and given his damnable proficiency at everything else Professor Singh was bound to be good at croquet – Dorothy Kilbride would take up the slack. It would be another well-earned slap in the face for Anthony Sinclair. Perhaps the afternoon might not be a total wash out after all.

There was one small matter I had to attend to, however, now that Harry and I were alone. 'I was speaking to that doctor fellow this morning,' I said, tentatively. 'Doctor Lefranc.'

Harry dropped the end of his cigarette onto the grass and stubbed it out with his foot. 'Oh yeah?'

'You know he lives near Bordeaux?'

'I can't say I did, old man.'

'Near that farmhouse I rented a couple of years back. You remember? The one your friend arranged for me.'

Harry raised an eyebrow. 'Sure, I remember. So I guess you *have* met him before? You said he looked familiar.'

'It's damned odd, but yes, briefly. Hargreaves had a bit of a cold,' I extemporised, 'and Doctor Lefranc came out to the farmhouse to give him the once over.'

Harry frowned. 'Bit of coincidence, old man, him being here as well.'

'That's what I thought. Are you sure you've never met him? You do have friends down there, near Bordeaux.'

'Oh, one or two, one or two,' Harry admitted. 'But I've never come across Doctor Lefranc before.' He drained his glass. 'Leastways, not until this weekend.'

I nodded. When it came to bare-faced lying, Harry was in a class of his own, but he might just as easily be telling the truth. There was clearly nothing more to be got from him on the matter. Perhaps it was just a coincidence after all.

'Oh, thanks for the loan of the car,' Harry said, changing the subject. 'You're a life saver.'

'I hope you didn't damage it.'

'Oh, not a scratch, old man. Not a scratch. I even filled up the gas tank on the way back.'

'That's not saying much. It was full when we arrived.'

He chuckled. 'It's the thought that counts, old man.'

'So where did you go?'

'Oh, here and there. Just a few errands to run. You know how it is.'

'In other words, better not to ask. Oh good shot!'

Professor Singh had taken to the field and had got his ball through the first hoop after a perfect set up from Dorothy Kilbride.

The professor bowed in acknowledgement of the applause. 'You are all very kind,' he called. 'It is a most exhilarating game.'

Harry was mortified. He hated losing money even more than I did, and he hadn't had nearly as much practise.

'It looks like you might lose two bets today,' I teased.

'How do you make that out?'

'Well, you don't seem to have got very far with Felicity Mandeville Jones.' I gestured to the young woman, who was helping herself to a sandwich at the food table. 'I think you must be losing your touch.'

'Now hang on, old man. I thought we said evens on her or Lettie Young.'

'Harry, we said nothing of the kind. It was fifteen guineas to win, on the Honourable Felicity Mandeville Jones.'

'Okay, okay. That's what we agreed.'

'You can pay up now if you like.'

'Oh, I've no intention of conceding defeat.' He smiled. 'I figure I've got a few hours left. And there's still the dance this evening. But what about you, old man? Do you fancy having a go at the delectable Miss Lettie Young? I hear the two of you spent the morning together.'

'I'm a married man, Harry.'

'Of course you are.' He grinned mischievously. My lack of interest in women had always amused him. He often liked to tease me about it. Harry was of the opinion that I was a bit of a Nancy Boy – he knew relations with my wife were non-existent – and I was happy for him to think that way. It was a reasonable cover story and Harry was broad-minded enough not to think any less of me because of it. He wasn't above a bit of blackmail, of course, but as he was never going to catch me *in flagrante* that hardly mattered.

'Do you want another drink?' he asked.

I proffered my glass. That was more like it. 'Whisky and soda. Not too much soda. Actually, just make it a whisky.'

Harry nodded and made off. There was a loud 'ooh' from the spectators. Lettie Young had taken her first shot and had bungled it badly. 'Bleedin' hell!' she exclaimed, with a laugh. 'This is more difficult than it looks!'

Sinclair, needless to say, was glaring daggers at her, but Lettie seemed utterly oblivious. I leaned back in my chair with a rare feeling of satisfaction. Money in the bank at long last.

Harry was deep in conversation with Felicity Mandeville Jones over by the food table. She was smiling warmly at him. That was not such good news. I had fifteen guineas on the line, after all. But there was no need to fret. Harry could not win that bet, not when Felicity was already so thoroughly involved with Anthony Sinclair.

'Do you think it will rain later?' I flinched at the sudden booming voice. Mr Smith had wandered over from the house. 'Looks a bit gloomy, don't it?' He spoke in a loud Yorkshire brogue, as disconcerting in its way as Lettie Young's strangulated vowels.

'We live in hope,' I said. A bit of rain would suit me perfectly. It would put a stop to the croquet before anyone managed to drag me out onto the field. I was happy to sit and watch other people making fools of themselves, but I had no desire to join in.

Mr Smith pulled up a chair and sat down next to me. 'You don't mind us sitting here?'

'Not at all,' I replied, through gritted teeth. Just what I needed, some fat idiot providing me with a running commentary on the game. John Smith was a tall, oddly proportioned man. His face was proud if a little weather beaten and he sported an admirably unapologetic belly. It was a peculiarity of the age that whilst women were expected to look like stick insects, men were becoming ever more rotund. And there could be few more gut-wrenchingly obese than Mr John Smith. The man owned a string of factories in the North of England, and – if the size of his stomach was any indication – he was doing rather well for himself.

Smith had not been in the best of moods when I'd passed him in the main hall on my way out to the croquet lawn. He had been on the telephone trying to get a message through to New York. It was a tricky business at the weekend, and Mr Smith was unpardonably rude to the poor girl on the other end of the line.

'Did you get your message sent?' I asked him now. It was rather bad form making use of the telephone like that. Nobody was supposed to know we were here at Bletchley Park.

'Aye, but lord knows when I'll get a reply. Lazy buggers these telegraph people. Excuse my French. But if I don't hear back from New York by tomorrow I'll be in serious trouble.'

'What is it? Some sort of business matter?' I didn't really care, but it seemed only polite to ask.

'Aye. You must have seen what's happening in the papers?'

'I did glance at the Times over breakfast.' There had been more on the problems in Wall Street. 'They said things had stabilized yesterday.'

'Aye, but I reckon it's just the calm before the storm.'

'Still. Doesn't affect us. If the Americans go to the wall, too bad.' I glanced over at Harry, who didn't seem in any hurry to return with my whisky.

'If only it were just them. But the world's getting smaller. If one part goes under, we all go.'

'You don't have stocks and shares in the US surely?'

'No, I don't. But...er...' He leaned forward confidentially. 'There's an American company I've been in communication with. They're interested in taking over JW Smith. I'm expecting to receive an offer in the next few days.'

'What, for your whole business?'

'Aye. Lock stock and barrel. But if the market collapses over there then it'll all fall through.'

'That'd be a shame,' I said, feigning sympathy. 'But probably just as well, isn't it? Hardly ideal, having British factories bought out by Americans.'

'You don't understand. They're losing a fortune. It's all these bloody trade unions, demanding extra money for their workers. We haven't made a profit in over two years. I want to get out, before the whole thing collapses.'

'And these Americans are willing to pay for a failing business?'

'Oh, they won't pay what it's worth. But they'll pay me and the wife enough to retire comfortably.'

'What about the workforce?'

'Sod the workers. I've done my best for them, but they're an ungrateful bunch. I won't be sorry to see the back of that lot, I can tell you. But if we can't finalise the deal in the next couple of days, well...I dread to think what will happen.'

'Good show!' I called out as Dorothy Kilbride knocked her ball through the "Rover" – the final hoop – and made a start on the return journey. 'I'm sure everything will sort itself out,' I assured Mr Smith. Not that I cared one way or the other. There was something inexpressibly vulgar about the man. I had only known him five minutes and already he was confiding in me about his personal finances. If I wasn't careful, he'd soon be discussing his love life and there I would have to draw a line.

'I hope you're right, Sir Hilary,' he said.

There was a brief lull in the conversation and I took that as my cue to escape. I rose up, empty plate in hand. 'If you'll excuse me, Mr Smith, I think I'll go and get a bit more food.'

Felicity Mandeville Jones was laughing as I moved across to the tables. She was dressed in a brimless cloche hat and a long winter coat. Her face was prettily made up, but the bruise mark on the left side was still visible. Harry was working his customary magic, standing almost too close for propriety, with his eyes locked on her face. A master craftsman in action.

I coughed and Harry turned around to acknowledge me. 'I got your whisky, old man,' he said, proffering the glass at last, having not moved more than an inch from the decanter to deliver it.

I took the glass with an acid glare. 'You're looking much better, Miss Jones,' I observed.

Felicity Mandeville Jones smiled a dazzling white smile. I could see why Harry was so enamoured of her. He wanted to win his bet, of course, but I suspected there was rather more to it than that. 'I'm feeling a lot better,' she said. Her voice was a pleasingly light trill, effortless and unaffected, a pleasant change from the guttural vowels of some of the other guests. 'A bit of fresh air does me the world of good. You must think me an awful bore, missing the treasure hunt, but I had such a splitting headache this morning.'

'You weren't the only one,' I admitted, knocking back the whisky. 'I had a devil of a job getting out of bed.'

Harry laughed. 'You'd think he'd be immune, the amount he puts away.'

'Well, it is meant to be a celebration.'

'You're quite right,' Felicity agreed. 'It's been super fun so far. The Colonel was so kind to invite us all.'

'Well, quite.' There was an awkward pause. Harry

clearly wanted to continue the conversation in private. His efforts were diluted with me standing there. But I wasn't about to make things easy for him. 'Are you joining in the games later?' I asked, gesturing to the croquet lawn.

'Cripes, I don't think so,' said Felicity. 'I wouldn't have a hope. Miss Kilbride is such a good player. Who'd have thought it?'

'Not Harry,' I said. 'I think he owes me two guineas already. Good shot!' I called. Professor Singh was within a few feet of the final hoop. At that moment, a splash of rain fell on my cheek. I put out a hand to confirm the downpour. 'That's a shame,' I said with a huge grin on my face. 'If it rains, I'll have to miss my turn.'

'Too bad, old man, too bad.' Harry twinkled. 'Of course, if they have to abandon the match then all bets are off.'

I wasn't having that. 'I'll see if I can find them some umbrellas.'

By now, the rain was really starting to pour. We would have to retreat to the house to avoid a thorough soaking.

'Damnation!' Anthony Sinclair cried, from the other end of the lawn.

'Just one more shot,' Lettie Young insisted. 'Go on, professor.' She was a good sport, that one, I had to admit.

A final thwack sent the ball through the hoop.

And with that, for the first and only time that weekend, I won a bet with Harry Latimer.

Chapter Eight

The ballroom was situated in the southwest corner of the house, just along from the billiard hall and directly beneath the guests' quarters. By eight o'clock, the sound of music was already beginning to waft up the stairs. Hargreaves was putting the finishing touches to my bow-tie in the bedroom. The orchestra had opened with a lively rendition of *Fascinatin' Rhythm*, which was fast becoming a standard. Hargreaves was tapping along to the melody as he brushed off the shoulders of my evening jacket.

A telephone rang somewhere in the house, instantly destroying the mood. I tutted in irritation. I have always disliked telephones. If it was up to me, the damn things would never have been invented. They are far too intrusive. If you are in the middle of a conversation and some idiot comes towards you ringing a bell, insisting that you talk to him, you would give him short shrift. But if the telephone rings, everything must stop at once. It's the devil's work. Luckily, the phone rang off after two or three loud blasts. A passing servant must have stopped to answer it. But who on earth would be calling at this time in the evening?

I adjusted my bow tie and examined myself critically in the bedroom mirror. I have never been handsome, but like my valet I can scrub up well enough when the need arises. The tight formal wear of the age suited my straight, masculine physique, though I had no particular liking for the starched shirts and cumbersome jackets that were *de rigueur* on such formal occasions.

I took a quick sip of whisky from a glass on the bedside table and headed out into the corridor.

Mr Smith was standing at the far end of the upper landing, looking somewhat annoyed. 'You look fine, woman,' he shouted through to his wife, who was presumably still getting dressed. 'Get a bloody move on!' He acknowledged me with an exasperated nod.

I turned right and made my way down a narrow set of

steps onto the lower landing. There was an archway to the left and, passing through it, I came to a halt at the balustrade overlooking the main stairs.

Anthony Sinclair was by the telephone in the hallway beneath me. The timber staircase snaked down at right angles from the first floor in three short flights and I could see the man's slicked back hair from above, as he stood by a small table, scribbling information down in a blue notebook while holding the receiver awkwardly in one hand. The evening dress he wore was almost identical to my own, though it was perhaps a touch more stylish. Sinclair was the kind of man who paid particular attention to his appearance and – I have to admit – he was handsome enough to make it worth the effort. He must have been near the telephone when it rang, since there hadn't been time for a servant to come and fetch him.

I made my way down the stairs towards him, past the large frosted windows opposite the balustrade. Sinclair stiffened slightly. 'Bit late for phone calls, isn't it?' I observed, as I reached the bottom step. Strictly speaking, he shouldn't have been using the telephone at all. Mr Smith had set an unhelpful precedent.

Sinclair placed the receiver back in its cradle. 'Not really any of your business, is it?' The fellow had abandoned any pretence of civility towards me since the billiard game the previous evening

'Just making conversation.'

He flipped the notebook closed and returned his pen to a breast pocket. 'If you must know, I was on the phone to the office.'

'What, on a Saturday evening?' I snorted.

'There's always somebody there. The news doesn't stop at the weekend, you know.' He scratched his chin idly. 'I've got a little story brewing and I needed to check a few facts.'

I regarded him suspiciously. 'A story? What story?' Everything at Bletchley Park was off limits. It might be a social occasion, but it was still an MI5 affair.

'Oh, rather a shocking one, I'm afraid.' Sinclair smiled maliciously. 'Perhaps not front page material, but certainly something that will raise a few eyebrows.'

I grunted. 'Ruining somebody's life, no doubt. That's what you do, isn't it? All that scandal and tittle-tattle.' The Colonel would have a fit.

'I just report the facts, Sir Hilary. And this one's a corker. Fraud, deception. Sexual deviancy. You name it. Actually, it might be of interest to you. Do you take the Mail?'

'My wife does.'

'Sensible woman. Ah, here comes Felicity.'

The Honourable Felicity Mandeville Jones was a vision of painted splendour, descending the winding staircase with all the grace and confidence that only someone of her class could muster.

'You look delightful, my dear,' Sinclair smarmed.

'Thank you, darling.'

Lettie Young was following behind with considerably less poise but greater enthusiasm. Sinclair made a point of reserving his charm for people of his own class, so it was left to me to pay Lettie the appropriate compliments. 'You look as radiant as ever, Miss Young,' I flattered politely.

'Thank you, kind sir.' She grinned, reaching the bottom step and performing a mock curtsy. 'The bands not half bad, is it?' she said, straightening up. 'The Colonel's done us proud, I reckon.'

The orchestra had already raced through *Yes, We Have No Bananas* and was now moving on, rather appropriately, to *Has Anybody Seen My Girl*.

Sinclair was not so easily impressed. 'That remains to be seen,' he declared acidly.

For an awkward moment, the four of us were stood together at the bottom of the stairs, crammed between the last step and a couple of badly placed marble pillars. Sinclair pocketed his notebook.

'Shall we go in?' I suggested, taking Felicity Mandeville Jones by the arm while her odious lover was momentarily preoccupied.

Sinclair grimaced. That left him with no choice but to escort the other young woman. 'Miss Young,' he said, proffering his arm with ill grace. She rewarded him with a dazzling smile.

We made our way through the billiard hall towards the swirling lights of the ballroom. Sinclair's words were playing on my mind. Which poor blighter did he have in his sights this weekend? It was typical of the man to abuse the hospitality of his hostess and spy on his fellow guests. And there couldn't be anybody here whose behaviour was any more scandalous than his. What right did he have to expose the private peccadilloes of other people when his own life was such an unpardonable mess? Perhaps, I thought, it might be worth having a word with the Colonel. The slightest whiff of scandal would be anathema to an MI5 man, even if it was just a few extra-curricular bedroom antics. Yes, Sir Vincent would put a stop to any scandal on his doorstep. But perhaps now was not the time to broach the matter.

The dance was in full swing. The large oak-panelled ballroom was illuminated from above by several vast candelabras. There were multiple windows along the two exterior walls, dark now of course, and an elaborate coved ceiling. Several guests had taken to the dance floor. Dorothy Kilbride had nabbed Professor Singh and even Lady Fanny Leon had got into the spirit of things, accompanying the Colonel in a quick but elegant twirl. The valets and various ladies' maids accompanying us all for the weekend had been press-ganged into serving as waiters for the evening and drinks were being passed around on silver platters. A set of caterers had been brought in and were slaving away in the kitchens. The Colonel's man, Townsend, was in overall charge, but my man Hargreaves was helping out on the floor, alongside one or two of the other valets.

At the far end of the hall, the Johnnie Hazelwood Orchestra were already in full flow. They were a typically nimble dance band, a tuxedoed octet with a cheery-eyed saxophonist, a manic drummer, and a trumpet player whose enormous moustache would not have disgraced a Mexican bandit. Where the Colonel had found them I had no idea, but they were certainly a jolly bunch. The orchestra had galloped through three songs in a little under ten minutes and, as I grabbed a glass of whisky from a passing Welshman, they struck up anew with the inevitable *Charleston*.

By 1929, anyone with any sense was getting fed up with the Charleston. It had been fun enough for the first couple of years, but the dance required such energy and co-ordination that it was simply impossible to enjoy. The purpose of dancing – as Harry Latimer would attest – is to get men and women as close together as possible, in the hope that a few sparks might fly. If your arms and legs are crashing around all over the place, that is hardly likely to happen. There is certainly no chance of prolonged intimacy. Give me a good waltz, any day. One, two three. One two three. That I can manage.

Felicity Mandeville Jones was observing the proceedings with keen interest, waiting politely as custom demanded for me to make the appropriate offer. Harry Latimer was approaching, fresh from a mad jig with Mrs Smith, and the thought of depriving him of Miss Jones' company for a few more minutes prompted me to do the decent thing. If I could keep her away from Sinclair too, so much the better. 'Would you care to dance, Miss Jones?' I said, proffering my hand.

She smiled sweetly. 'Darling, I thought you'd never ask.'

The Colonel was taking a well-deserved breather and after ten minutes of embarrassing gyrations – mine, not Miss Jones' – I joined him at the outer edges of the hall, grabbing another whisky and catching my breath. 'Capital fun, eh, Butler?' he said.

'Absolutely,' I lied. 'Nothing like a good dance.' And that, I added silently, was nothing like a good dance.

'You're a damn liar,' Sir Vincent asserted good-naturedly. 'You're just here for the whisky. Ha ha!'

I nodded. The Colonel was nobody's fool. 'It's good exercise, I suppose. But I draw the line at the Lindy Hop.' That was one of the most recent dances. It was all right for the *hoi polloi* in downtown New Orleans but scarcely appropriate for

Bletchley Park.

'No stamina, Butler, that's your trouble. Latimer seems to be enjoying himself, though.' There was a hint of disapproval whenever the Colonel mentioned Harry Latimer. 'Quite a good dancer, too,' he observed with distaste.

Harry had grabbed hold of the Honourable Felicity Mandeville Jones as soon as I had deserted her. 'Hey, honey,' he'd said, as I was leaving the dance floor, 'I'll show you how a real man dances.' The nerve of the fellow. Utterly shameless. And the worst of it was, he knew exactly what he was doing. So did Miss Jones, as I had already discovered. The two were now throwing themselves about the dance floor with gay abandon.

'Rather a jolly band, aren't they?' the Colonel observed.

'I've seen a lot worse.' I nodded amiably.

'Not professionals, you know. Just a few friends earning a bit of pin money. But not bad, all things considered.'

The Johnnie Hazelwood Orchestra may not have been in the top drawer but they could certainly hold their heads up in respectable company. Jazz music was all the rage in the twenties, of course, though it wasn't real jazz of the negro kind. Orchestras like this played comfortable middle class dance music with a slightly jazzy flavour and were none the worse for that.

Lettie Young was certainly enjoying it. She was throwing herself across the dance floor like a whirling dervish, in front of a bemused Mr Smith. The fat northerner had two left feet but Lettie didn't seem to mind. She lacked any sense of inhibition – or skill, to be brutally honest – but the sight of her gleeful face darting across the floor couldn't help but make you smile. Against my better judgement, I was really starting to warm to the shameless little minx. For all her lack of education, and impropriety, and atrocious manners, and inability to speak the King's English, she certainly knew how to have a good time.

The same could not be said for all the guests. My eyes rested for a moment on Mrs Mary Smith, the unfortunate wife of the fellow currently dancing with Lettie. She was a queer one, I thought. A home counties bride whose rigid dance style reflected a much less flamboyant character. I'd only spoken to her briefly, the previous evening. She had struck me as rather snooty, but vulgar too. She affected an air of superiority, but years spent married to a Yorkshire man had clearly coarsened her. She wore an elaborate sequinned dress that was dripping with jewellery; the kind of ostentatious baubles more appropriate for the opera than for a dance hall. She was paying little attention to her partner, the amiable Doctor Lefranc.

I avoided the Frenchman's gaze as the mismatched couple swept by. I was itching to ask the Colonel about him. I was still doubtful of the coincidence of him being here this weekend. But – as with Sinclair – this was not the time or place to enquire further. Even if the Colonel did know anything about the man, it was unlikely he would confide in me. For all his jovial exterior, Sir Vincent hoarded information as jealously as a nun guarded her virtue.

I was not the only guest to have abandoned the dance floor. Anthony Sinclair was over by the window, involved in a polite conversation with Professor Singh. His mind was on other things, however. I could see the daggers he was directing at Harry Latimer.

A valet passed by with a tray of food and I quickly snaffled a few mouthfuls. Polite applause greeted the end of another number and for a brief moment the floor emptied. Dorothy Kilbride approached the Colonel. She was looking a little dizzy. 'I can't keep up with these modern dances, I'm afraid,' she admitted.

'Come, my dear, let me find you a chair.' The Colonel was all concern. The two were old friends as well as colleagues. They had known each other since before the war. Dorothy Kilbride had worked her way up from humble secretary to head of payroll, a remarkable achievement in such chauvinistic times, especially given her distinct lack of personality. 'Good woman that,' the Colonel mumbled, when he had properly seated her. 'I hope you'll ask her to dance when she gets her breath back.' It wasn't exactly a request. Evidently, Sir Vincent felt quite paternal towards Miss Dorothy

Kilbride.

'I'd be delighted,' I said.

Three hours later, everybody was feeling a little the worse for wear. The band had taken a short break and there was a healthy buzz of conversation across the dance floor. Food was being consumed to act as ballast against the alcohol and there was a smattering of laughter. Harry was schmoozing with Felicity Mandeville Jones over by the far window. Lettie Young was with them, shrieking away with no sense of shame but knocking back the gin without any deleterious effect that I could see. She was always shrieking away. Lettie could handle her alcohol better than I could. The combination of dancing and whisky had disorientated me slightly – I was not exactly young any more – but though my speech was becoming a little slurred, I was still some way from the fall-down drunk stage that I intended to reach by the end of the evening. There were a few hours of heavy drinking to go before that.

Not everybody would stay the course, however. Dorothy Kilbride was already slumped in a chair, fast asleep. She had perked up on the dance floor, through a couple of quieter numbers, but was now thoroughly exhausted.

I felt a pang of sympathy. 'Should we leave her to sleep?' I asked the Colonel.

'Better pack her off to bed,' he thought. 'You can do the honours, old chap. I'm sure Miss Young will give you a hand.'

Lettie was only too willing to help. 'Come on, love,' she said, waking up the dozing figure with a gentle pat. 'Time for beddie-byes.'

Dorothy Kilbride blinked uncertainly, not quite sure where she was, but the drowsy woman soon struggled to her feet. Lettie and I escorted her from the ballroom, through the billiard hall to the main stairs.

The orchestra were reassembling for the next session behind us. 'This is a brand new song,' the compère announced, in a fashionable but unconvincing American accent. 'Hot foot from the US of A. It hasn't been released here yet but we think it's going to be a big hit. It's called *Happy Days Are Here Again.*' And with that the orchestra was in full swing once more.

Lettie Young laughed. 'I like the sound of that. Here, mind the step.' We were halfway up the staircase now, navigating the second corner towards the balustrade, and from there it was a short but tortuous journey to the guests' quarters on the southern side of the house. The geography of Bletchley Park was difficult to fathom when sober, but slightly tipsy as we were, it might as well have been one of those impossible paintings by Escher.

On the upper landing, confusion rained. There were half a dozen bedrooms in this part of the house, and the only one I knew about was my own. 'Which one is it?' I asked Lettie.

'Search me.' She shrugged. 'Hey, Dottie. Which one's your room?'

The older woman swayed blearily, but gestured nonetheless in the direction of one particular door.

'In here?' I asked again, as we arrived at the door.

Dorothy nodded vaguely. She was starting to hiccough.

I pulled at the brass handle and we entered the room. A rather grand four poster bed formed the centre piece of the chamber. The walls were wood panelled and the décor cod-medieval. The room was a little larger than mine, but looked out onto the same neat lawn. A small fireplace on one wall offered the possibility of warmth, but the fire had not been lit. The blankets on the bed would have to suffice. There was carpet underfoot, however, and the room did not seem particularly chilly. I had managed perfectly well on Friday night and Dorothy Kilbride was too far gone to care.

I helped her over to the mattress and she flopped down in one solid movement. In seconds, she was asleep.

'Ah, bless her,' Lettie said, gazing down at the woman. She certainly looked peaceful, snoring quietly there but with the occasional loud snort interrupting the rhythm of her breathing. The Colonel was right. She was a decent old stick. She might lack sparkle but she had a good heart.

'He's got a real soft spot for her, you know. The

Colonel,' Lettie said. 'She's been with him right from the start.'

'I remember.' Dorothy Kilbride had been the first member of MI5 I had ever met. My father had arranged the interview with Sir Vincent – his last act of kindness towards me after I had been sent down from university – and it was Dottie who had shown me into the great man's office. She had been pretty, then, in a quiet way, and we had got to know each other fairly well over the next couple of years.

'Poor cow,' Lettie said. 'She hasn't had much luck in life, has she? Two dead husbands and a couple of miscarriages.'

'Miscarriages?' I had not heard anything about that.

'It's not exactly something you talk about.'

'No, I suppose not.' It was bad enough *having* a child, I knew from personal experience, let alone losing the damn thing.

'And when her second husband kicked the bucket, that was that.'

'How do *you* know so much about her?' I asked, suspiciously

Lettie grinned. 'Oh, the Colonel and me, we're thick as thieves. He tells me everything.'

'I find that difficult to believe.'

'It's true,' she insisted. 'Going way back. He was a friend of my mothers.'

'Oh, really? A "friend"?' I smirked.

'Nothing like that, you dirty sod. She was a house maid. Worked for him before the war. I mean, well before the war. She got into a bit of trouble. Not with him, some footman or other. And…well, here I am.'

'So you're a bastard, then,' I observed, with some relish.

She grinned. 'Too right. It ain't a secret, neither. I'm proud of it. Take what you can get, that's what I say. But my mum died when I was just a nipper, and the Colonel, he promised to look after me.'

'I thought you were brought up in an orphanage?'

'I was. He could hardly bring me up as one of his own, could he? But he found a decent enough place for me, as far as it goes. And he often came by and said hello. Got me my first job and everything. He's been good to me.'

'So it seems.' Not the typical spy master at all.

'Well, are you gonna stand there gawping or are you gonna sod off and let me get her undressed?'

I started. 'Yes, of course. I'll leave you to it.' I hurried towards the door. A gentleman cannot stand and watch while a woman is being undressed (sometimes I get so caught up in my life as a man, I fail to see the absurdity of it).

Lettie was already searching for some appropriate night clothes. 'You know she's got a bit of a soft spot for you, old Dottie.'

'What do you mean?' I asked, from the door.

'Fancies the pants of you, so I hear.' She grinned maliciously. 'You old devil.'

I pursed my lips. 'Maybe when we were younger. But it's been years since I last saw her. And we've both been married.'

'Still holds a bit of a torch, I reckon. You know it was her what got you the invite.'

I frowned. '*She* invited me? This weekend?'

'Typed up the list. And asked the Colonel if she could add your name, for old time sake.'

I glared at Lettie, unconvinced. 'You're making this up.'

''Course I am.' She winked. 'Shut the door on your way out.'

I stood in the corridor for a moment, a little nonplussed. The idea of Dorothy Kilbride holding a torch for me after all these years was laughable. But she had certainly enjoyed our dance that evening. And she *had* pressed against me rather tightly through the slow numbers. I dismissed the idea. It was just Lettie making mischief.

I needed another drink. I had promised Mrs Smith a dance and I knew I would not be allowed to break my word. It was time to return to the ballroom.

Descending the main stairs, my attention was caught by raised voices coming from the front of the house. A man and a woman. Light was streaming out from the drawing room through the lounge hall. By the sounds of it, quite a serious argument was in progress. Before I could step forward and investigate, the Honourable Felicity Mandeville Jones swept out of the drawing room and across the hallway directly in front of me. Her eyes were wet with tears. I barely had time to register the sobs as she bolted through a side corridor and into the library.

I made to follow her but then stopped myself. There was only one person I could think of who might have upset her in that way. A certain disreputable journalist. I peered through the arches leading back into the lounge. The damned fellow wasn't going to get away with it a second time.

Anthony Sinclair would get a piece of my mind.

Chapter Nine

The lounge room leading off from the main hall was empty when I looked in, its bizarrely shaped glass roof as dark as the sky above it. But lights were burning in the drawing room just beyond and the acrid fumes of a lighted cigar wafted in my direction. I pushed open the door.

Anthony Sinclair was standing between two large wooden pillars on the far side of the room, his back to me, looking out quietly through the windows at the trees swaying in silhouette just beyond the carriage turnabout. There was enough residual light spilling out from the house to illuminate at least some of the driveway. Sinclair took a puff of his cigar and must have caught sight of my reflected image in the window as, at that moment, he turned slowly and regarded my entrance to the room with well-practiced disdain.

The door swung shut behind me.

'Not dancing, Sir Hilary?' Sinclair raised a quizzical eyebrow. He was a good looking man, with shiny black hair and a pencil moustache, but the permanent sneer on his face provided ample warning of his true character.

'Evidently not,' I snapped. The impertinence of the fellow. Alcohol was flowing through my veins and I was not about to pull any punches. 'And neither was Miss Jones, by the look of her.'

I stepped forward. The drawing room was lightly furnished, with barely more than a sofa and a couple of tables. A pianoforte stood abandoned in one corner. The walls were covered in the same oak panelling as the entrance hall and the ceiling was patterned with basic geometric shapes. A wooden fireplace dominated the northern side of the room and there was a blandly functional grey carpet spread out beneath us

Sinclair frowned. 'I think she has danced enough this evening.'

'The woman was in tears,' I said. 'If you've done anything to hurt her...'

'What are you talking about?' Sinclair stared at me, his

face a mockery of perplexed innocence.

'I heard the two of you arguing, just now. And then I saw Miss Jones running away. In something of a state, I might add.'

Sinclair laughed humourlessly. 'You have knack for over-dramatising, Sir Hilary. You ought to be a journalist. It's none of your damn business.'

'A woman in distress is everyone's business, Mr Sinclair.'

He laughed again. 'She was hardly in distress.' He took a puff of his cigar. 'If you must know, I was merely castigating Miss Jones for her inappropriate behaviour this evening.'

'*Castigating* her?'

'You must have seen her dancing with that American... well, I hesitate to use the word "gentleman".'

'Harry Latimer is a friend of mine.'

Sinclair exhaled a cloud of smoke. 'Well, that doesn't surprise me.'

'And you disapprove of a young woman dancing, at a *dance*, with another man?'

'No, Sir Hilary. I disapprove of a woman disappearing into a private room and engaging in a passionate embrace with a man who is not her husband.'

Now it was my turn to be nonplussed. 'What on earth are you talking about?'

'Your friend Harry Latimer. He was in the library, embracing Miss Jones. Kissing her. I saw them together.'

My jaw dropped. It looked like Harry had got to "first base" after all. I couldn't stop myself from smiling. It might be worth losing fifteen guineas, I thought, if it upset Sinclair so much.

'You find it amusing? That Miss Jones would risk her reputation for a scoundrel like that? I'll have you know, her father is a close friend of mine. You have *heard* of Sir Hugh Mandeville Jones?'

I nodded. The man was a prominent Tory MP.

'Sir Hugh would be outraged. But I think the girl just needed a good talking to. I told her to buck her ideas up. She will not be speaking to Mr Latimer again.' Sinclair took another puff of his cigar. I could scarcely believe the hypocrisy of the man. Here he was, pretending to be the protector of Miss Jones' virtue, yet in reality he had already compromised that virtue and in a manner far graver than Harry's harmless flirtation.

'You, sir,' I breathed, 'are a hypocrite.'

Sinclair blinked. 'I beg your pardon?'

My anger could not be constrained. 'You have the effrontery to criticize that poor woman when your own behaviour beggars belief. You present this ridiculous image of propriety, when your own profession takes such pleasure in ruining people's lives. And you yourself behave in the most depraved and scandalous manner imaginable.'

Sinclair reached for an ashtray and stubbed out the remainder of his cigar. 'I don't care for your tone, Sir Hilary.'

'I don't care for you at all, *Mister* Sinclair.'

The man laughed suddenly. 'If I'm a hypocrite, Sir Hilary, then what does that make you?' There was an evil gleam in his eye. All trace of civility had disappeared. 'Tell me, is it possible for a daughter to inherit a baronetcy from her father?'

I flinched. 'What…what do you mean?'

'And is it legal for a woman to enter into matrimony with another woman?'

'I…I don't know what you're talking about.'

'Oh, you know exactly what I'm talking about, Sir Hilary. I overheard your little conversation with Doctor Lefranc this morning. It was most illuminating. Unlike the Frenchman, however, the very idea of it sickened me. You, sir, are a pervert. A sexual deviant. Not only that, you are a criminal. A fraudster. And you have the effrontery to accuse *me* of hypocrisy. You, a middle-aged woman who has spent her entire life pretending to be a man.'

There was a long pause. I was having some difficulty breathing. 'You…overheard everything?'

'Indeed I did, Sir Hilary,' he boasted, with some relish. 'The two of you were out by the tradesman's entrance. I'd gone to answer a call of nature and overheard your conversation

74

through the bathroom window. Then, after the treasure hunt, I put a call through to the paper, just to check a few facts – your title, how long you'd been married, that kind of thing – and they telephoned me back this evening with all the sordid details. It couldn't have worked out better. The perfect garnish for our Monday morning edition.'

This was too much. 'You're…you're going to publish a story? About me?'

Anthony Sinclair smiled cruelly. 'Indeed I am. The woman who lived her life as a man. How she deceived the world and had a love child with a tram conductor during the General Strike. The readers will lap it up.' He patted his jacket pocket. 'It's all in my little notebook. I shall write it up this evening before I go to bed.'

My heart was thumping. Good god, what would Elizabeth say? I would be ruined and she would be a laughing stock. 'I won't let you do it,' I breathed. 'I won't let you destroy my life.' Lord knows, I had never loved my wife, but I couldn't bear to think of the shame and ignominy that would be heaped upon her. Perhaps – my mind was grasping for an alternative – perhaps Sinclair would accept a bribe. He struck me as that type. Not an honest man, like Doctor Lefranc. 'I have some considerable funds,' I said. 'Well, my wife does. Perhaps if I were to…'

He raised a hand to forestall my offer. 'I have no need of your money, Sir Hilary. I am a man of independent means and I take considerable pride in my work. I do not take bribes, not from you or from any man. Or from any little slut, come to that, which frankly, my dear, is exactly what you are.'

'You sanctimonious prig,' I snarled. It was clear that there was no reasoning with the fellow. If he was determined to ruin me, the least I could do was return the favour. 'I'm warning you, Mr Sinclair. If you print a single word about me or my wife, I will make it known to the whole world that you are having sexual relations with the Honourable Felicity Mandeville Jones.'

'I – .' Sinclair stopped. Momentarily, he was lost for words. He hadn't expected me to know any of *his* secrets. The boot was on the other foot now.

'You have deceived your wife and dishonoured the daughter of a former cabinet minister,' I continued, warming to my theme, 'who I'm sure will have your private parts on a platter if he's got any sense when he discovers the truth. And you claim he's a friend of yours!'

Sinclair was glaring angrily. 'How dare you!' he exclaimed. 'How dare you suggest Felicity is my mistress! I would never…'

'Don't try to deny it,' I said. 'I *know* she's your mistress. I saw you in her bed chamber last night. And everyone saw the bruises on her face this morning.'

That hit home. Sinclair flinched, as if I had slapped him across the face. 'Sir Hilary,' he growled, 'you have taken leave of your senses. I have never laid a finger on that girl and she is certainly not my mistress.'

'There's no point denying it. I saw the two of you together. And I saw the marks across her face.' The nerve of the man, to deny the truth in such a bare-faced manner. 'You're a vicious brute, Mr Sinclair. And since journalism is so close to your heart, I'm going to do you a favour and tell the *whole world* exactly what you've been getting up to.'

Sinclair's face was now a fetching shade of beetroot red. 'You little…'

I laughed. 'Now you know how it feels. Now you know what it's like when someone discovers your sordid little secrets and threatens to expose them. Hoist on your own petard, Mr Sinclair. It's not very pleasant, is it?'

The fellow was clenching his fists now. 'I ought to…'

'What? Give me a thrashing? You like hitting women, don't you…?' Let him try it, if he dared.

'You're not a…'

'I may be a fraud, I may even be a liar. But I would never sink as low as you have sunk. And if you lay so much as a finger on Miss Jones ever again I will break your bloody neck, sir.'

Sinclair stared at me for a moment, calculation sharing space in his mind with the reddest of rage. 'Very well,' he said eventually, his voice now unnervingly calm. 'There's only one way to settle this. If you want to live your life as a man, then I'm going to treat you like a man.' He raised his fists. 'And give you a damned good thrashing.'

Before I had time to digest the implications of his threat, a fist had arced through the air and smashed into my jaw.

I careered backwards, nearly stumbling over an awkwardly placed occasional table.

'I have never been unfaithful to my wife!' Sinclair declared, as I recovered my balance and charged at him.

The two of us smacked heavily into one of the wooden pillars supporting the window frame.

More punches flew. I staggered under the ferocious onslaught. It was as I had feared. Sinclair knew how to box. I grabbed at his throat and for a few brief seconds we were locked in an unfortunate embrace. There was no delicate way to break apart. I brought up my knee and fetched him a hefty wallop between the thighs. His face contorted with pain and rage. He fell back towards the windows, but the separation was momentary. All at once, the damn fellow was at me again. Three or four more blows sent me crashing to the ground. My head smacked awkwardly on the floor and I clutched it in pain as the room reverberated around me.

There was no chance of me winning this fight. I was having difficulty now even focusing on my opponent.

Sinclair walked forward and stood over me, contemptuously. 'You really do fight like a girl,' he sneered, turning away. 'Make your accusations, Sir Hilary and I shall sue you for slander. No one will believe a word of it in any case. Not after the story I'm going to print about you on Monday morning.'

It was my turn to shake with rage. I had come to rest near the wooden fireplace. I pulled myself up shakily on my hands and knees and grabbed hold of a metal poker propped up by the side of the hearth. Sinclair had moved over to the window and stood with his back to me now, between the two pillars, as he had done when I first entered the room. I got to my feet, the poker in hand, and ran at him. Sinclair must have caught the movement in the window, but he was slow to react. I smacked the poker across the side of his head and he staggered for a moment, losing his footing and falling towards one of the wooden columns. His forehead struck the pillar with an unpleasant crack and his body thumped down onto the lightly carpeted floor.

I stood for a moment with the poker still raised above my head. Sinclair lay unconscious on the carpet. At least, I hoped he was unconscious. A cold fear suddenly gripped me. There was a bloody mark on his forehead and no obvious signs of respiration. I dropped the poker and moved forward to take a closer look. Crouching down, I turned the body over and took a deep breath. There was another large mark on the side of his head where the poker had struck. Quickly, I grabbed his wrist and searched for a pulse. But I couldn't find one.

Anthony Sinclair was dead.

Chapter Ten

A strange paralysis gripped me as I stared down at the lifeless body. I had been many things in my life – a scoundrel, a thief, a blackmailer and a whore – but never a murderer. My mind struggled to comprehend the enormity of what had just happened. I had killed a man. I had taken a life I had no right to take. Admittedly, the fellow was a villain and the world was probably a better place without him, but that was scarcely the point. I was a murderer and as soon as that fact was discovered I would be arrested, tried and hanged. In an instant, I saw it all and my hands clasped the side of my head in despair. The best I could hope for was a plea of manslaughter and even then, I would probably spend the rest of my life in jail. It may have been callous to think about my own fate when Sinclair was lying there dead but blind panic was starting to seize hold of me. Nobody would believe this was an accident. How could they? It *wasn't* an accident. I had struck Sinclair deliberately, from behind, and even though I'd had no intention of killing him, his blood was on my hands.

I looked down at the body. There was mercifully little blood. A slight dent was visible on the wooden column where Sinclair had struck it and there was a smudge of red on the carpet around his head, but it was not the loss of blood that had killed him.

My mind began to race furiously. Was there anything to be done, any way to forestall the inevitable? Could I blame somebody else? Could I hide the body? I looked up at the bay windows. It was hopeless. The room was a fishbowl and a brightly illuminated one at that.

Anyone who had been looking in from the front of the house would have seen everything. A servant taking the air, having a quick cigarette. An illicit couple, having a crafty fumble in the flowerbed. Almost anybody might have heard the scuffle. And what was true for the exterior of the building was doubly true for the interior. There had to be something like forty people in the house this evening – including the orchestra, the valets and the ladies' maids – and though the majority of these were congregated in the ballroom on the far side of the mansion, there was nothing to stop any one of them wandering about as they saw fit. Even a servant might flit in, to relight the fire or switch out the lights.

I had to get Sinclair out of the house. That much was obvious. But I wouldn't be able to carry the body far on my own. Perhaps my valet could give me a hand. The thought of that familiar, balding head and his pathetically eager expression gave me a moment of hope. I would find Hargreaves and he would help me sort out this mess.

I couldn't leave the body lying here in the open, though, while I went to get him. And I couldn't exactly roll Sinclair under the nearest sofa. At the very least, I needed to drag the body out of harm's way.

The only route out of the drawing room was back through the lounge hall. This led through a triple archway to the main entrance, but the corridor there was visible from the billiard room, not to mention the main stairs. If I dragged the body that way, I was bound to be seen. There was another option, however. Passing into the lounge, there was a large set of doors off to the right. These led through to the dining room. From there, if I remembered correctly, there was a sizeable exterior door, installed by some mad architect, which opened directly on to the front of the house. That was my best chance. If I could haul the body out onto the carriageway, I could arc left over the gravel and perhaps find a bush or something where I could dump it. That would give me a breathing space to go and find Hargreaves. Then the two of us could carry the body away and hide it somewhere more secure. In the back of the Morris Oxford perhaps; or maybe we could weigh it down and throw it into the lake.

I grasped at this dubious plan with all the enthusiasm of a drowning man reaching for a life belt.

Dragging the body through the lounge was the trickiest part. I would be out of sight of the stairs but anyone moving through the hallway would catch sight of me through the arches. The doors through to the dining room were shrouded in darkness, however, and if I was quick I was unlikely to be seen.

I stuck my head out to make sure the doors to the dining hall were open. Then I crouched down and grabbed hold of Sinclair's body. He was a dead lump in my arms, but I managed to drag him awkwardly a little way across the carpet. I stopped at the entrance to the lounge hall, listening for any unusual noise, but there was nothing, save the distant hum of music and the clinking of glasses from over in the ballroom. The hallway itself was empty. In one quick burst, I hauled the body across the lounge and into the dining room. Then I closed the doors behind me.

So far, so good.

The dining room was just as I remembered it, a long white room with a northern exterior wall. Several thick mahogany columns supported the weight of the ceiling and there was an odd bay window framing the north east corner of the house. The place was in darkness, but a large dining table formed the centre-piece of the room, visible even in the dimmest of light. Beyond that were the double doors leading out onto the carriageway.

I left the body in the corner and moved across to take a closer look at the exit. The doors were thick and heavily polished, probably made from the same dense wood as the pillars. An elaborate swan motif on a brass-plated cross decorated the mid-section and there was a small keyhole on the right hand side. I pulled at one of the handles. The door was locked. I growled in frustration. What kind of blithering idiot locked an exterior door from the inside?

I stood for a moment, a hand to my face. There had to be a key somewhere. Perhaps in the servants' quarters. Hargreaves would know. But it would take time to find him. Maybe I could force the doors, take a run at them. But the wood looked very solid. I would probably end up dislocating my shoulder. And even if I did manage to force them open, the noise was bound to attract attention, especially if I damaged the hinges and couldn't close them up again afterwards.

What was the alternative?

I glanced at the dining table. It was long and highly

polished, with a set of chairs lined up symmetrically along each side. Perhaps if I dragged the body under there, that would keep it out of sight, at least for a short while. Of all the rooms in the house, this was surely the one least likely to attract any attention in the next few hours. If I left the body out of the way here it might at least give me a few minutes grace to find Hargreaves and get his help.

It was the best idea I could think of.

Madly, I began pulling back the chairs and then with some effort I hauled Sinclair's body alongside the table. I stuck a hand into his jacket pocket, while I had the opportunity, and fished out the little blue notebook he had been writing in earlier on. Better to be safe than sorry, I thought. There were too many biographical details in there. I slipped the book into my own jacket, then manoeuvred the corpse as best I could underneath the table. Finally, I stood up and glanced around the room, making sure nobody had crept in from the lounge hall behind me, before at last returning the dining chairs to their original positions.

I stood back for a moment. It was hardly expert camouflage, even in the dark. But unless you were crouching down beside the table to look for something, you were unlikely to see the body. With the lights out and the doors closed, it would probably be safe there for half an hour or so.

I moved back through the lounge hall and into the drawing room, closing the door behind me. Was there anything I needed to tidy up, before I went in search of Hargreaves?

The iron poker lay on the ground over by the fireplace. The bloodstain on the carpet had to be cleaned as well. Better to sort that out first. I rushed across with my handkerchief and did my best to soak up the blood from the floor. My hands were trembling and all I succeeded in doing was creating a small purple smudge. I rubbed my shoes across the carpet for good measure, but that just made things worse. In exasperation, I grabbed an occasional table and positioned it over the stain. The table didn't look too out place, and it certainly covered up the damp patch.

What else? Fingerprints! My paws were all over that

damn poker. I'd soiled my handkerchief soaking up the blood, so I couldn't use that to wipe it clean. I pulled down the arm of my jacket instead, grabbing the end of the sleeve from the inside and sliding it up and down the poker, to give it a good polish. That would have to do. I returned the poker to its rightful position beside the fireplace.

Looking around the room one last time, I caught sight of my reflection in the window. I moved closer. Sinclair had given me a thorough beating, but apart from a bloody nose and a slightly bruised lip, I was not too badly off. I would need to find a bathroom, though, just to have a quick wash. I couldn't stumble through the house looking like this without arousing suspicion.

There was a bathroom on the first floor but I couldn't risk the main staircase. The water closets off the main hall were out of bounds for the same reason. In any case, I really needed somewhere with a sink and a mirror. There was likely to be a washbasin in the servants' quarters, however. I could gain access via the servery at the far end of the dining room. That was a far better bet. The back stairs were bound to be quiet, with everyone over at the ballroom.

I flicked off the drawing room light and slipped back into the dining hall, closing the doors quietly behind me.

I would make my way around the north side of the house, clean myself up and then locate my man Hargreaves, and he could help me get the body out of the house. Then we could dump it in the lake, or set fire to it, or bury it or do whatever the hell one does with an inconvenient corpse. Harry would know, it occurred to me suddenly. The American would probably be more useful than Hargreaves in this situation. But given his penchant for blackmail, it wasn't worth the risk involving him.

No, in the circumstances, Thomas Hargreaves was the only friend I had.

I made my way quickly through a narrow corridor running alongside the servery and from there made my way into the servants' quarters. The bloody place was like a labyrinth but, as I had hoped, the area was quiet and dimly lit.

The butler's pantry off to the right was occupied, but the man inside was enjoying a private moment and I was able to skip past unobserved. The kitchens would definitely be occupied, even at this hour, so I skirted left and around the store cupboards. A long, narrow corridor ran the length of the storage area and through a door into the darkened servants' hall. I passed through here, veered right and – at long last – reached the servants' bathroom.

It was a narrow tiled space, with a water closet off to one side and a large sink. This was probably where Sinclair had been when he'd overheard my conversation with Doctor Lefranc. The bathroom was accessible from the dance hall and there was a small window facing out onto the tradesman's entrance at the rear of the mansion. Sinclair had nipped in here to relieve himself during the treasure hunt and overheard everything. Damn the man.

I flipped on a light and moved across to the washbasin. There was a mirror on the right hand side. I gazed at my dishevelled image in the glass. All things considered, I did not look quite as bad as I had originally feared. I ran some water and cleared the blood from my nose. The cut lip had dried and having wiped away the crystallized blood the scar was barely noticeable. I grabbed a hand towel and wiped my face down. My clothes were a little dishevelled but it was the work of a moment to restore some order. Luckily, my bow-tie had not come undone. I would have had a devil of a job refastening that. Hargreaves always took care of the complicated stuff.

The blood stained handkerchief was still in my pocket, as was the notepad I had taken from Anthony Sinclair's jacket. Better to get rid of that now, I thought. I went over to the WC and lifted the toilet seat. The notebook was still in my pocket. I pulled it out and began tearing up the pages, dropping the little bits carefully into the bowl. Then I produced a box of matches from my trouser pocket, lit one of them and set light to the end of the handkerchief. It flared quickly and when I could hold it no longer, I dropped the remnants into the bowl of the toilet and pulled the flush. Thank heavens for modern plumbing.

Taking one last look at myself in the mirror – my eyes

were haggard but that could not be helped – I pulled open the bathroom door.

I was lucky to have got so far without being seen. My luck did not last, however. As I barrelled back down the corridor, past the servants' hall, I all but collided with one of the valets. It was Townsend, the Colonel's man. He was a bluff, ugly fellow, six feet two or three, but immaculately dressed and faultlessly polite. The near miss had been entirely my fault but it was Townsend who offered his apologies. 'I'm afraid I didn't see you there, sir.'

'That's quite all right,' I reassured him as breezily as my shattered nerves could manage. 'I was looking for a lavatory. I had to use the servants' bathroom. I hope that's all right.'

'Yes, of course, Sir Hilary,' he replied, in a mild West Country lilt. He didn't seem at all suspicious. Mind you, the man had one of those imperturbable butlerish faces that wouldn't react even if he'd found you hanging naked from the chandeliers.

'This house is a bit of a rabbit warren,' I said. 'Too complicated for me at this time of night. Had a bit too much of the old sauce, I'm afraid.' I thought it was worth adding that, just to bolster the illusion of my own cluelessness. Actually, it wasn't far off the truth. 'You couldn't show me the way back to the main hall?'

'Certainly, sir. It's just along here.'

He led me through a narrow back hall to an oak panelled door that led on to the main staircase.

'Ah yes, of course. I remember now. Oh, you haven't seen my man Hargreaves, have you?'

The valet thought for a moment. 'I believe he is in the ballroom, sir. Helping to lay out some food.'

'Good show. Well, I'll see him there then. Thank you, Hargreaves. I mean, thank you Townsend.'

'My pleasure, Sir Hilary.' The Colonel's valet withdrew, to complete his own errand, and I made my way through the billiard room towards the dance hall. The majority of the guests were still gathered here, jiving happily away. A waiter was just leaving as I arrived – Sinclair's man, I noted with some alarm –

and I grabbed the one remaining whisky from his tray to steady my nerves as I scanned the floor.

Hargreaves was on the far side of the hall, not far from the Johnnie Hazelwood Orchestra, who were still belting out songs though it was after midnight now. It was entirely possible they would still be here at four or five in the morning. These events did tend to go on rather. Hargreaves was laying out food for the first breakfast. An early hours meal was often provided so that people had the stamina to see the night through.

Harry Latimer accosted me before I could make my way across the dance floor. 'Where have you been skulking?' he demanded. 'You've missed all the drama, old man.'

'I haven't been *skulking*. I was just – what drama?'

Harry looked at me for a moment. 'Are you okay, old man? You don't look too bright.'

'I...I was feeling a bit sick. Had to find a lavatory.' It was as well to stick with the story I had given Townsend.

'Too much lemonade?' Harry sympathised.

'Far too much. I doubt I'll last the evening.'

Harry peered at me critically. 'I don't think you'll last the hour,' he mocked. 'No stamina, you limeys.'

I grabbed a second glass of whisky and knocked it back. I was more concerned with his earlier comment. 'What did you mean, a drama?'

Harry smirked. 'Oh nothing, nothing. Miss Jones and I had a little tête a tête away from the dance floor. A little canoodling, in the library. You know the kind of thing.'

'You filthy swine.' I did my best to laugh.

'Oh, all quite innocent, old man. Just a bit of harmless fun. But then your journalist friend Anthony Sinclair comes in, acting like the jealous husband. All protective. It might have been sweet if it wasn't so absurd. He threatened to thump me.'

'Good lord.'

Harry grinned. 'I talked him out of it.'

'Probably just as well.' Sinclair might have been good with his fists, but Harry fought *dirty*. There were no Queensbury rules in America. I had once seen Harry Latimer fell a man twice his size in New Orleans. It had not been a

86

pretty sight. Not that backing down had done Sinclair any good in the long run.

'But he dragged Felicity away and gave her a good talking to. Said he was friends with her father and wanted to protect her reputation.'

That was the line he had taken with me. It was strange, how vehemently Sinclair had protested his innocence, when I had accused him of sleeping with her. 'I did...I did think I heard raised voices in the drawing room. When I came down,' I said. And if everyone knew about the row then perhaps Felicity Mandeville Jones would be blamed for Sinclair's death, when the body was eventually discovered.

'It was all very predictable,' Harry said. 'Felicity was in tears, of course, and ran off to her room.' He grinned.

'I don't know why you're looking so happy. You've lost your bet.'

'Not at all, old man. It's all to play for.'

I glared at him suspiciously. 'What do you mean?'

'I figure I'll leave it ten minutes and then slip upstairs. Pay the little lady a visit.'

'Miss Jones has invited you up to her room?'

'Well, no, not exactly *invited* me. But I figure if I bring her a bottle and offer some consolation she won't say no.'

'Harry, you're a rogue.'

'Well, fifteen guineas is fifteen guineas, old man. I'd hate to lose two bets in one day.'

I grabbed another glass of whisky.

'Hey, steady on, Hilary,' he warned. 'I don't want to have to carry you to bed as well.'

'I'm fine,' I lied, wiping the dregs from my lips. 'I just need to have a word with my man. Excuse me a minute.' The orchestra was coming to the end of *Let's Do It* – no doubt played for Harry's benefit – and a gap had opened up in the floor. I marched quickly forward to grab hold of my man Hargreaves. Before I got halfway, however, I was accosted by Mrs Smith.

'You promised me a dance, Sir Hilary,' she announced imperiously.

That was the last thing on my mind. 'I...I'm not feeling terribly well,' I said, excusing myself.

'Nonsense! One dance won't kill you.' Mrs Smith was the kind of woman who would not take no for an answer. She was a short, slim-hipped creature with a cold, pretty face and an unfashionably prominent bust. Her dress was dripping with jewellery and she moved with a confidence born of life-long wealth. The band were already skipping on to the next number and the damn woman grabbed hold of me before I was able to protest further.

Hargreaves had seen me now and taken note of my imploring gaze, but there was little he could do.

Lettie Young was at the bandstand. She had just spoken to Johnnie Hazelwood, the moustachioed band leader, requesting a reprise of the new American song the orchestra had played when we had left the dance floor earlier on.

And so, increasingly dizzy, with the alcohol sloshing in my belly and the corpse of Anthony Sinclair lying cold beneath a table less than fifty yards away, I found myself dancing with a gaudily bejewelled Mrs John Smith to the joyful strains of *Happy Days Are Here Again.*

Chapter Eleven

My head nestled comfortably in the groove of a plump white cushion. The mattress was warm and soft beneath me, my torso enfolded in gentle cotton beneath a heavy woollen blanket. It was a rare moment of joy and I would happily have remained there in that blissful slumber, but for an urgent whispered voice summoning me back to the realms of consciousness. As I awoke groggily in bed, the weight of the previous night came crashing down on me. My throat was as dry as the Atacama Desert and my head was screaming in protest at the abuse I had inflicted upon it the previous evening. I did manage to prise open an eye, but then winced at the blinding light emanating from the bedside table.

Hargreaves was leaning over me, immaculately turned out, the yellow glow of the lamp bouncing harshly off the top of his balding pate. He handed me a glass of water and I pulled myself up to take a sip. 'Lord, my head,' I croaked, as I swallowed the precious liquid and coughed my voice back into some semblance of normality. 'What time did I go to bed?' I clutched my face mournfully. The events of the previous evening were – momentarily – a complete blank.

'About half past twelve, sir,' Hargreaves answered smoothly. If I hadn't known better, I would have sworn there was a glint of amusement in those otherwise deferential eyes. 'I brought you up to bed. You appeared to fall asleep on the dance floor.'

I coughed again and took another gulp of water. 'What are you blathering about? Nobody falls asleep on the dance floor.'

'You seemed to manage it, sir,' Hargreaves responded dryly.

I glared at him. 'Hargreaves, I've warned you before about flippancy.'

'I'm sorry, sir. But you *did* fall asleep, on Mrs Smith's shoulder. While the two of you were dancing.'

'Don't be ridiculous!' I snorted. I had never heard

anything so preposterous. 'Fell asleep on her shoulder!'

'I judged it a good time to put you to bed. I hope that was all right, sir.'

I grunted, placing the glass back down on the bedside table. Perhaps it was true at that. I had been somewhat inebriated and it wouldn't be the first time I had fallen asleep in an embarrassing position. At least I had dropped off on Mrs Smith's shoulder and not in her décolletage. 'What time did the party go on to?' I asked.

'A little after three o'clock, sir.'

I wiped my eyes blearily and stretched my arms above my head. My mind really was fogged. I took a moment to collect my thoughts. 'What time is it now?' There was no light coming through the curtains. It looked like it was still the middle of the night.

'It's a quarter past five, sir.'

'A QUARTER PAST FIVE??' I spluttered, in abject horror.

Hargreaves didn't blink. 'Yes, sir.'

'What the blazes do you think you're doing, waking me up at this ungodly hour?'

'Please, sir, if you could keep your voice down. Other people are trying to sleep.'

That was too much. '*I* was trying to sleep, you blithering idiot, before...' I stopped. A sudden shard of memory was stabbing at me from the dark.

'Are you all right, sir?'

There were images flashing through my mind. Disturbing images. But as yet they weren't making any kind of sense. 'I...I think I must have had rather a bad dream.' I frowned. 'So why, Mr Hargreaves, did you think it a good idea to wake me up quite this early on a Sunday morning?'

The valet hesitated. 'I'm not exactly sure, sir. The Colonel asked me to wake you up. He says there's been...some kind of incident.'

And then the full force of it hit me. Anthony Sinclair. The body in the dining room. I let out a strangled cry. A quarter past five in the morning! The corpse had been lying in that dining room for over five hours. An incident? That could only mean one thing. One of the servants must have stumbled across the body. 'What...kind of incident?' I asked, my voice a gravely whisper.

'The Colonel wouldn't say, sir. But I think it must be serious. Doctor Lefranc was speaking to him as I came away.'

Lefranc. That confirmed it. A doctor to examine a dead body. It made perfect sense. The Frenchman was close to hand and obviously he would be asked to make a quick examination while somebody else called the police. 'Hell!' I grasped for the glass on the bedside table and took another swig of water. 'Haven't you got anything stronger?'

'Of course, sir. I didn't have time to prepare your usual...'

I waved my hands at him in exasperation. 'Well pour one now!'

'Yes, sir.' Hargreaves reached for the whisky. I always keep a bottle by the bedside for emergencies, even when I am away from home.

Damnation!

I gulped down the whisky and pulled back the sheets.

The Colonel may have found the body, but unless someone had actually seen me kill Anthony Sinclair there was no reason for him to suspect I had anything to do with it. I had removed the notebook from the man's jacket pocket and destroyed everything he had scribbled down on the telephone. They would check his office eventually and find out that he had been making a few enquiries about me, but that was unlikely to happen for some hours yet. It was still the middle of the night, after all. I had a little time left to brazen things out.

'Pack up my things, Hargreaves,' I said. 'We might have to leave in a hurry.'

'Is something wrong, sir?'

'Nothing at all!' I snapped, wincing at the cold floor under my feet. 'What could possibly be wrong? Now find my damn slippers and help me on with that dressing gown...'

Sir Vincent Kelly was taking tea in the drawing room. A silver service had been laid out and the lights were blazing, though the rest of the house was shrouded in darkness. The occasional table was where I had left it, covering the bloodstain on the carpet. That was the first thing I noticed as I stepped into the room. The bay windows at the front were as cold and black as ever, but someone had stoked the fire in the hearth and a warm glow permeated the room. The Colonel made to rise and gestured to a chair opposite.

'You're looking a bit the worse for wear, Butler,' he observed. 'Some job falling asleep on the dance floor like that. Ha ha!'

No matter what the gravity of the situation, the Colonel always maintained the same jocular tone. It was a mistake, however, to believe there wasn't a calculating mind behind that absurd monocle. You don't get to be head of the British Security Service without a first class brain.

I seated myself down cautiously. The body of Anthony Sinclair may have been discovered, but the Colonel could not yet know that I was responsible for his death. There was nothing to connect the two of us. The fact that the Colonel had woken me to discuss the matter, however, suggested he might have some suspicions. I would have to be very careful.

'Sorry to drag you out of bed like this. You must have a shocking head. Would you like some tea?' he asked, sympathetically. 'Doctor Lefranc's man was kind enough to brew us a pot.'

I demurred. Tea was the last thing I needed. I should have brought down the whisky. The cups and saucers had been laid out on the occasional table. I glanced down nervously, but the bloodstain was out of sight beneath the finely crafted legs. The dining room door had been closed too. Passing through the lounge hall, I had glanced across at it, just to make sure. 'Hargreaves said there had been some kind of incident?'

The Colonel nodded gravely. 'Rather a bad one, I'm afraid. No easy way of putting it, Butler. One of the guests has been murdered.'

I gave myself a moment to register the information.

'Murdered?' I tried to sound shocked.

The Colonel nodded again. 'I'm afraid so.'

'Lord.' I pondered the unexpected news for several seconds, giving the information time to sink in. I have never been much of an actor, but when necessity compels me I pride myself I can fake a reaction as well as anyone. Harry would have been proud of me. 'Are you sure?' I asked, eventually.

'No two ways about it. A bullet through the head. Couldn't possibly be suicide.'

'A bullet?' My jaw dropped open. What bullet? What was he talking about? 'I...I didn't hear a shot.'

'I doubt you'd have heard anything, Butler, the state you were in. Ha ha! But yes. Definitely a gun shot to the head. I discovered the body myself.'

My mouth opened and closed without uttering a sound. A *gunshot*? Surely someone hadn't put a bullet in Anthony Sinclair? Not after I'd bashed him across the head. I struggled to regain my composure. I had to be very careful. I hadn't asked the obvious question yet. 'Who...who was the victim?'

Here at least there would be no surprises.

'Dorothy Kilbride.'

'Do –?' I wish someone had taken a photograph of my face at that moment. It would have been the definitive portrait of blank incomprehension. I cannot think of any other time in my life when I have been taken so completely by surprise.

The long pause that followed did not need to be faked.

Dorothy Kilbride? 'Good lord,' I whispered at long last.

The Colonel sighed. 'Poor old Dottie. Been with me for years,' he said. 'Irreplaceable. Absolutely irreplaceable.'

'But...but...' I stammered. I could barely begin to register the news. 'Who...who on earth would want to kill Dorothy Kilbride?' It was unbelievable. The fact that one person had been killed that evening was shocking enough. But two people, by two different murderers? No, it wasn't possible. It must be some sort of joke. The Colonel was playing games with me.

But I could see from his expression that he was not.

Another, even more preposterous idea flickered across

my mind. Was it possible the Colonel *hadn't* discovered the body of Anthony Sinclair? My heart skipped a beat. If he had woken me to talk about the murder of Dorothy Kilbride then… was it conceivable that Sinclair's body hadn't yet been found? No, I didn't dare to hope that.

But the house was quiet and the dining room was closed up.

It was maddening not to know the truth. And I couldn't exactly get up and have a look.

'That's what we have to find out,' the Colonel said, in response to my question. 'Whoever did it must have used a silencer.'

That at least was true. An ordinary gun shot would have been heard right across the house. Even with a silencer there would have been some noise, though perhaps not enough to be heard beyond the adjacent rooms. 'A professional, then?' I suggested, trying to concentrate on what the Colonel was saying.

'It would have to be. Unfortunately, we've got a house full of professionals this weekend.'

'Not professional *assassins*, though.'

'No, but people who know how to handle firearms.'

That was also true. Harry Latimer had a small hand gun, that much I did know, and I had a couple of pistols locked away in a cabinet at home. Doubtless, other people had access to similar weaponry. Harry's revolver, of course, had been in the holdall I'd brought up with me from London. But Harry could have nothing to do with the murder of Dorothy Kilbride. He had never met the woman and was not the type to kill in cold blood. Besides, a Newton .32 was hardly the weapon of choice for an assassin; and a revolver like that wouldn't work with a silencer in any case.

'Have you called the police?' I asked. That was the most important question, from my point of view.

The Colonel shook his head. 'Doctor Lefranc is upstairs, giving the poor girl a preliminary examination. My man Townsend is up there too. He was a police sergeant during the war. He'll make sure nothing's tampered with. He's going to take a few photographs as well. We were lucky enough to find a camera in the servants' quarters. And I'll get some men up from London to examine things properly this afternoon.'

'What, from Scotland Yard?'

'God, no. The last thing we want is Special Branch crawling all over the place.' The Colonel had a well-known antipathy towards that particular organisation. 'They're not exactly reliable these days, Butler. Been leaking like a sieve the last couple of years.' There had also been disturbing rumours of a takeover bid for MI5. The two organisations had long been rivals. 'No, we need to keep this quiet, if possible. It'll have to be an internal matter. Otherwise we'll be a laughing stock. Egg all over our faces.'

'But surely the most important thing...'

'The most important thing, as always, is to discover the truth. But don't fret, old chap. Townsend knows his stuff. And I give you my word: justice will be served. We'll find the devil who did this. But quietly, behind closed doors.'

I was still having trouble believing Dorothy Kilbride was dead. The news hadn't really sunken in. She had been such a harmless creature. It wasn't her fault she was a little dull. 'No one could have anything against Dottie,' I said.

'Nothing personal, certainly. But she *was* in charge of payroll.' The Colonel had had more time than me to think through the implications. 'She handled all the wages. Plenty of scope for abuse. Not by her, of course, but some of the case officers. Maybe a chap on the ground. It does happen.' He leaned forward. 'There is another possibility, though. That's why I got you up, Butler. I needed to ask you something.'

'Of course,' I said, trying not to sound wary.

'You put Dottie to bed, didn't you?'

'Er...Miss Young and I did, yes. You surely don't think...?'

The Colonel laughed. It was his full-bodied Labrador laugh. I pitied the person trying to sleep in the room above us. Nobody had thought to fit the Colonel with a silencer. 'Don't be daft, Butler. I know you had nothing to do with it. We could all hear you snoring away. Ha ha! But why did you put Dorothy

95

to bed in someone else's bedroom?'

I didn't understand. 'I...I wasn't aware that I had.' Dorothy Kilbride had pointed to the room. It was the one next door to my own. There had been a dress hanging on the door of the wardrobe. 'Whose bedroom was it, then?'

'Felicity Mandeville Jones'.'

My mouth opened and closed. 'Good lord.'

'You didn't know?'

I shook my head. 'That was the room Dorothy indicated to us. But she was a bit dazed. Perhaps she made a mistake.' I jolted as the implications came through. 'You don't think the murderer might have been intending to kill *Miss Jones*?'

'It's a possibility. I gather there was some kind of brouhaha last night between her and that Daily Mail chap, Sinclair.'

I nodded. 'There was an argument. You don't think Mr Sinclair...?' I had to stop myself from laughing.

'We have to consider every possibility.'

If I knew one thing for certain, it was that Anthony Sinclair had nothing whatever to do with the death of Dorothy Kilbride. However, the fact that the Colonel was even considering the possibility was proof positive that he was unaware of the journalist's death. The body was resting unobserved in the dining room, after all this time. And with a second murderer on the loose, I might even be able to pin the blame for Sinclair's death on somebody other than me.

'Goodness knows how Miss Jones will react when she realises she might have been the intended victim,' the Colonel said. 'I'm going to let her sleep on for an hour or two. The rest of the household as well. Don't want to cause unnecessary alarm. The servants are in bed already, apart from Townsend and Hargreaves. Oh and the Doctor's man. The orchestra have packed up too. They should be heading off about now.'

'You're letting them go?'

'No reason to keep them here They were still playing until well after three o'clock. And the time of death was shortly after that, according to Lefranc. Between half past three and four, anyway. No, the fewer people who know what's going on

96

here the better. Townsend and I will get to the bottom of it. And our chaps from London will make sure we haven't missed anything.'

If the police were not involved, there was at least some chance that I might get away scot-free. This fellow Townsend was an unknown quantity, however. 'Has he been with you long, your valet?' He wasn't the man I remembered from before the war.

'A few years. Since twenty-two, I think.'

'And he was a policeman before that?'

'A sergeant yes. Don't worry, Butler. He's as solid as a rock. We'll get all this sorted out soon enough. Are you sure I can't tempt you to a cup of tea?'

Hargreaves was coming down the mains stairs as I took my leave of the Colonel. Ostensibly I was returning to my room to get properly dressed. Sir Vincent had remained in the drawing room, making notes of events so far, as was his wont. I was determined to get into the dining hall while the house was still quiet. There was at least another hour to go before it got light and it might still be possible to dispose of Anthony Sinclair's body. If he could be made to disappear completely, there was a chance Sinclair would be blamed for the murder of Dorothy Kilbride and I would be in the clear. That would mean the real murderer went free, of course, but that was a small price to pay if it saved me from the hangman's noose. Sinclair would have to disappear forever, though, and that would take some doing. Hargreaves would have to help.

The hallway was in darkness as my valet arrived at the bottom of the stairs. 'I've packed away most of your clothes, sir,' he said. 'Would you like me to prepare the car?'

I shook my head. 'Change of plan. I need your help with something.'

'Of course, sir.'

'Is there another way into the dining room? I mean, apart from the lounge hall?' I couldn't go through there without the Colonel seeing me.

If Hargreaves was perplexed by the question, he was enough of a professional not to show it. 'We could head through the servants' quarters, sir, via the back hall.' He gestured to a faceless wooden door to the left of the main stairs. I recognised it at once. This was the door I had come through after my first trip into the less salubrious parts of Bletchley Park mansion.

'Get to it then!' I snapped. We would have to carry the body out of the house through the double doors at the front of the dining hall, as I had originally planned

Hargreaves led the way into the back hall. The place was even darker than the main entrance, with only the bland silhouette of the servants' staircase visible in front of us. Hargreaves reached to switch on a light, but I stayed his hand. It wouldn't do to advertise our presence.

'Do you have a set of house keys?' I asked, my voice an urgent whisper.

'Keys, sir?'

'To open the main doors at the front.'

'I believe there's a set hanging up in the butler's office.'

That was in the opposite direction. I grunted. A detour was unavoidable.

'It's this way, sir.'

I followed my man through a second door and then right, towards the kitchens.

'The servants are all in bed, aren't they?' I didn't want to bump into anybody while we were creeping about like this.

'So I understand, sir.'

We arrived at the butler's office without incident. Ordinarily, the room would have been locked, but the butler was away for the weekend with the rest of the staff and he had kindly left it open for us. All the important documents were secured in a small bureau, but a set of house keys had been left on a hook just above the desk.

Now, though, the hook was empty.

'That's a bit queer, sir. I'm sure they were here earlier.'

'Never mind.' With a sense of trepidation, I retraced my steps to the back hall. Hargreaves followed quietly behind as I opened a door and fumbled along another short corridor, this one adjacent to the servery.

'Sir, may I ask...?

'No you may not!' I hissed. 'Now be quiet. I don't want the Colonel to hear us.' I opened the narrow door and together we crept into the unlit dining hall. It was just as I remembered it. My head was clearing now. It's amazing how quickly a hangover can disappear when one's life is at stake. I gestured to the row of chairs along the right hand side and pulled a couple of them back from the table. Hargreaves dutifully followed suit. I crouched down to look for the body and the valet did likewise, though Hargreaves of course had no idea what he was looking for. We both peered at the underside of the table, identical quizzical expressions on our faces. I stood up and strode over to the exterior doors. They were shut, as they had been before, but the door handles had both been pulled down. When I had last been here, they were horizontal. On the carpet, too, there were scuff marks. Someone must have taken the keys from the office and opened the exterior doors.

It wasn't possible. I stared at Hargreaves in disbelief.

The doors had been opened and the corpse of Anthony Sinclair had disappeared.

Chapter Twelve

There was more blood than I'd expected. It had oozed out to cover the pillows and splattered across the blanket and the headboard. Dorothy Kilbride lay motionless in bed, her head turned to the left, the gaping wound in the back of her neck a shocking sight even in the half light of the table lamp. I brought a hand up to my mouth and had to make some effort to stop myself from retching. This was a woman I had known since my early twenties, though we had not clapped eyes on each other in over a decade. She may not have been the most vibrant human being ever to walk the earth, but Dottie was honest and polite and diligent in her work. It seemed impossible that she was dead; monstrous even. The murder of Anthony Sinclair at my own hands had not provoked anything like the same response.

Standing awkwardly in the doorway, observing her lifeless body, I was hard pressed to make sense of it all.

The guest rooms on the first floor spanned the southern side of the house, an upper and lower landing accommodating the different heights of the billiard hall and various others rooms on the ground floor. Lady Fanny Leon had a suite in the eastern corner and there were further rooms at the front of the mansion, to which most of the male guests had been relegated.

I had returned to my own room from the dining hall, in an understandable state of agitation. Reality seemed to be warping around me. Nothing made sense. Corpses were walking, old friends were dying and I was slowly losing my mind.

I stood silently as Hargreaves fussed, getting me dressed. The valet was doubtless bursting with curiosity – not to say concern – after my peculiar behaviour downstairs, but he knew better than to ask anything while I was so obviously preoccupied. I needed time to think, to straighten things out in my own mind before I could confide in Hargreaves. Above all, I needed to think *rationally*.

The body of Anthony Sinclair was not under the table where I had left it. Either somebody had moved the corpse, for reasons unknown, or Sinclair had not been dead and had simply got up and moved himself.

The latter possibility was terrifying. If Anthony Sinclair had somehow survived my assault with the poker – and I didn't believe for a minute that he had – surely he would have caused a fuss, woken the household, phoned the police. He wouldn't have just got up, fetched the keys to the exterior doors, tidily replaced all the chairs along the side of the table and then walked out of the building. The man was dead. There was no doubt about it. I am not a doctor (as you may have realised) but these things are obvious even to a layman. I had checked his pulse and placed my hand over his mouth to confirm that he wasn't breathing. Sinclair could not have survived the battering I'd given him.

The other option was equally troubling. If someone had stumbled across the body accidentally, there should have been a similar degree of fuss. A scream, a shout. Some kind of confusion, as there had been when the Colonel had discovered Dorothy Kilbride. Alarm bells ringing, sirens sounding. No one in their right mind would simply move the body and not tell anybody else.

Unless, unless…

I stopped. My head was beginning to throb. There was no making sense of it Perhaps it was better not to try. I sighed. Poor old Dottie, I thought, lying dead in the room next door. It was time to pay my respects. Standing in the frame of the doorway, a few minutes later, I was having second thoughts. My knees were starting to give way beneath me. I grabbed the frame of the door to steady myself.

'Are you all right, Sir Hilary?' Townsend enquired, keeping his voice low. The Colonel's rock-like manservant had been tasked with documenting the crime scene. He had finished taking photographs of the body with a flashbulb camera and was now packing up all the clothes from the wardrobe. Everything in here, of course, belonged to Felicity Mandeville Jones.

That was my fault too. This was meant to be her bedroom. Another cock up. Perhaps if I had managed to steer

Dottie in the right direction she would still be alive now.

The flashbulb camera was lying temporarily discarded on the floor alongside the bed. Doctor Lefranc had made his examination of the crime scene and departed some minutes before, to report his findings to the Colonel. I was alone with Townsend. And with Dottie.

'It is something of a shock,' I breathed.

'Had you known Miss Kilbride long?' the valet asked sympathetically.

'Lord, yes. Dottie and I went way back. Since before the war.' She had seemed a permanent fixture in that outer office. There were always flowers over by the window, I recalled. That had been her influence. She'd been interested in horticulture even then. 'You must have known her yourself for quite a few years.' The Colonel had said Townsend had been with him since the early twenties.

The valet nodded, closing up the suitcase. 'It's a bad business, sir.' He rose to his feet. He did look rather like a policeman, I thought, though definitely a sergeant rather than an inspector.

'Do you think she was the intended victim?'

Townsend considered for a moment. 'It's difficult to say, Sir Hilary. Judging by the wound on the head, the bullet was fired from the doorway where you're standing. With the light off, you wouldn't be able to see who was sleeping in the bed.'

'But you'd check, wouldn't you?' What kind of blithering idiot would fail to make sure they had the right victim? At least afterwards, if not when they actually took the shot.

'You'd have thought so, Sir Hilary.'

Townsend bent over to pick up the camera, then lifted the suitcase and moved towards me. The household would be waking in an hour or so and Miss Jones' maid would need access to her luggage in order to dress her. 'I'm going to lock up the room now, sir,' the valet said, as I hovered uncertainly in front of him. 'We'll put the suitcase in the Colonel's room for now.' There was no point disturbing the Honourable Felicity

Mandeville Jones. She was probably still asleep. 'Would you like a moment alone?'

I shook my head. It would serve no purpose. 'No. I'm finished here.'

'Very good, sir.'

I backed out of the door and stepped onto the landing. Townsend placed the suitcase outside, in the corridor, then returned to the room and switched off the bedside lamp. I watched as he pulled the door closed and locked it firmly; then he picked up the suitcase and made his way down to the lower landing.

I hovered for a moment, listening quietly from the top of the stairs as the valet deposited the case, locked up his master's room and continued downstairs to rejoin the Colonel.

Alone now, on the upper landing, I looked back along the corridor. There was something here I didn't quite understand. Actually, there was quite a lot I didn't understand. Random facts were sloshing around inside my head like sweets in a glass jar and I was having a devil of a job keeping track of them all. But one thing in particular struck me now, as I gazed at the long row of brass doorknobs.

According to the Colonel, Dorothy Kilbride had been put to bed in a room that by rights should have belonged to Felicity Mandeville Jones. This was the room next door to mine, the one Townsend had just locked up. But when I'd left my bedroom on Friday evening to answer a call of nature, I had heard a thumping noise coming from the next door along. The middle room, not the one where Dottie had met her end. And it was this door that I had knocked on to see if everything was all right. Felicity Mandeville Jones had popped her head out, with tears in her eyes and a bruise on her face. So not only had Miss Jones been forced to sleep in somebody else's bedroom tonight – because of the mix up with Dorothy Kilbride – she had also gone to bed in a different room the previous evening. Curiouser and curiouser.

Any chance I might have had to reflect on the peculiarity of this was disrupted by a noise coming from the fourth door along. This was the bedroom towards the back of the house that should have belonged to Dorothy Kilbride, but which was now occupied by the supposedly sleeping Miss Jones. The door was being opened from the inside.

It was far too early for anyone to be up and about and – whoever it was – I knew instinctively that I didn't want to be seen. Luckily my own room was a few paces away. I slipped back inside, but left a small crack open in the doorway. A tall figure was moving furtively along the landing towards the stairs. I waited a beat, then stuck my head out and observed the silhouette descending to the lower landing. I came out of my room, closed the door behind me and watched him from behind as he moved along the lower corridor towards the front of the house.

The figure was not difficult to identify. Even from behind, in the half light, Harry Latimer's bear-like frame was easily recognisable. He was wearing trousers and a dishevelled shirt. His jacket was slung loosely over his shoulder and his braces were hanging down beside his legs. I followed him down the stairs and across the lower landing, tip-toeing behind him at a discrete distance. Most of the men had been billeted at the front of the house. Harry veered left into the narrow eastern corridor and by the time I'd turned the corner he had already slipped into his own bedroom. If my geography served me right, this was just above the drawing room, where the Colonel was probably still sitting writing up his notes.

I didn't bother to knock. I flung open the door and stepped inside. The interior light blinded me momentarily.

Harry spun around. 'Hilary!' he exclaimed, doing his best not to sound surprised. 'Didn't expect to see you again any time soon. The state you were in last night.'

'I couldn't sleep,' I lied. 'What were you doing, skulking about on the landing at this time in the morning?'

'Oh, you know, this and that. Winning a bit of dough from an old friend.' He grinned happily. 'You owe me fifteen guineas, old man.'

Some people are born lucky. While I had spent the last few

hours navigating dead bodies, clutching my head and trying to avoid the hangman's noose, Harry Latimer had been merrily debauching the daughter of a former cabinet minister; a young woman who was universally respected for her integrity and common sense. It beggared belief. Harry had a huge smile on his face; the proverbial cat that got the cream. 'I'll tell you one thing, old man,' he crowed, his eyes sparking with delight, 'you were wrong about Anthony Sinclair.'

He nodded his head to the far wall. The two men shared adjacent bedrooms. Harry, of course, knew nothing about the journalist's death.

'Wrong?' I asked. 'What do you mean wrong?'

'Like I told you at lunchtime. There's nothing going on between Anthony Sinclair and Felicity Mandeville Jones. Take my word for it. She can't stand the sight of him.'

'What are you talking about? Of course there's something going on between them. I saw them together.'

Harry shook his head. 'I don't know what you saw, old man, but you must have got the wrong end of the stick. Felicity isn't having an affair with Sinclair. She's never had an affair with anybody. Not until tonight.'

My jaw dropped. 'Good grief. You don't mean...?'

Harry nodded. 'Pure as the driven snow. Untouched by human hands, at least until a few hours ago.' He smirked lecherously.

I was at a loss for words. So Anthony Sinclair had been telling the truth after all. He had intervened for the sake of the girl's reputation and not out of jealousy. His indignation at my accusations of impropriety had been entirely genuine. And I had killed him. My God.

My legs started to wobble beneath me for the second time in less than half an hour.

Harry was more focused on his own triumph. There were times when I secretly admired Harry Latimer, but this wasn't one of them. There are few things in life less attractive than a man crowing about the latest notch on his bedpost.

'You're a scoundrel, Harry,' I said. 'Taking advantage of that poor girl.' I had thought Sinclair was the rogue.

'She was all for it, old man,' Harry pointed out, defensively. 'She's an adult. And it does take two, you know.'

'Yes, but doing it for a bet...'

'That was your idea.'

'But damn it, Harry, I'm thinking of her reputation. If this gets out, the poor girl will be ruined. She'll be an outcast from all decent society. And her father will be a laughing stock. He's been trying to marry her off to some minor royal, so I hear.' Another piece of gossip Elizabeth had floated before I left home.

'Relax, old man. It won't get out. I'm not about to blab to anyone. Now pay up like a good sport and let's forget all about it.'

I growled and extracted my wallet. Almost every penny Harry had paid me to deliver his damn bag was now back in his own pocket. It was always the way. 'Well, I'm glad you've enjoyed yourself. While you were busily fornicating with the fair Miss Jones, I was dealing with a rather more serious matter elsewhere.'

'What kind of matter?'

This would wipe the smile off his face. 'Dorothy Kilbride has just been murdered.'

It was Harry's turn to be astonished. I felt some relish at delivering the bad news. The man prided himself on always being ahead of the game – he was rarely if ever taken by surprise – but this was certainly news to him.

'This is some kind of joke, right?'

'I wouldn't joke about a thing like that.'

Harry considered this for a moment. 'Jesus.' He sat down on the bed. I pulled up a chair opposite him. 'But I was in her room,' he volunteered. 'A few hours ago.'

'In her *bedroom*?'

He nodded. 'I went up there with a bottle. You remember? A bit of consolation for Miss Jones? I must have gone up there about half past twelve. Just after you were carted off. But I guess I got the wrong room. Felicity told me she was next door to you, but I knocked real hard and there was no answer. Well, you know me, the door was unlocked, so I crept in anyway...'

'Harry!'

'Fortune favours the brave, old man. Anyway, I was halfway to the bed before I figured out it was the wrong room. Jeez, that little lady can snore. Could snore,' he added, awkwardly.

I couldn't help smiling at the image of Harry Latimer tip-toeing across the room towards the wrong woman. It served him right, the devil. 'There was a bit of a mix up when we put her to bed. You had the right room, Harry. It was Miss Young and I who got it wrong.'

'I figured it was something like that. I tried the next door along but there was no one home. They were all down in the ballroom. All except me. Anyhow, finally I hit the jackpot. And the rest you can imagine. Jesus, Hilary, I can't believe she's dead. Do you want a brandy?'

I nodded. Harry reached over to his medicine cabinet. I took out my cigarette box and produced a couple of sticks. I passed one to the American.

'What time was she killed?' he asked, lighting up.

'I'm not sure. Some time after the party broke up, so I gather. Before four, anyway. Someone put their head around the door and shot her.'

Harry nearly choked on his brandy. 'Wait a minute, did you say...*shot* her?'

I nodded again.

'Jesus. That can't be right. I didn't hear any shooting.'

'The Colonel thinks somebody must have used a silencer.'

Harry bit his lip. 'Makes sense I suppose. But even a silencer would have made a noise.'

'Perhaps. But after that rum punch they served last night, I don't think anyone would have heard it.' I certainly hadn't and I had been in the room next door. 'Though who would want to kill a harmless old widow like Dorothy Kilbride is beyond me.'

Harry put down his brandy glass and took a drag of the cigarette. He thought for a moment. 'I don't think it'd be

107

anything personal. She was head of payroll, wasn't she? That's an awful lot of dough passing through her hands. Easy enough to make enemies. Hey, perhaps she was cooking the books and somebody found out.'

'Not Dottie,' I said firmly. 'She wasn't the type. But she might have spotted somebody else doing it.' I scratched my chin. 'Nobody had anything to gain by killing her. That's what I don't get. None of us are short of a bob or two.'

Harry puffed at his cigarette. 'That's not exactly true, old man. Mr and Mrs Smith aren't doing too well, so I hear.'

That was true. I remembered the dreary monologue John Smith had forced upon me the previous afternoon. 'Lord, did he tell *you* all about his finances as well?'

'The sparklers, old man. The diamonds. I got a good look at them, dancing with Mrs Smith last night.'

'And?'

'They were fakes. You could tell at a glance. Or at least, anyone who knows could tell.'

'Do you thinks Mrs Smith knows?'

'I doubt it, the way she was flaunting them.'

'Still doesn't provide a motive for murder. And it might not have been Dottie they were after. The rooms were mixed up, after all.'

'That's a point,' Harry admitted. 'If I hadn't been serenading Miss Jones two doors along someone might have come in and blown her brains out.'

'Harry, is that you trying to justify your appalling behaviour?'

He grinned. 'You can't blame a guy for trying. If someone *was* aiming for Felicity, she probably shouldn't be left on her own.'

'The Colonel's seeing to that. He's going to send someone up to keep an eye on her. You were lucky to get away when you did.' I stood up and reached over to the bedside table, to tap some ash from the end of my cigarette. 'We've all been lucky, if someone's walking around the house with a loaded weapon. And it's obviously someone who knows what they're doing.'

Harry nodded, finishing off his brandy and placing the glass back down on the table. 'Jesus. Murder at Bletchley Park. Who'd have believed it?'

'You had a revolver in that holdall of yours,' I reminded him carefully.

Harry flinched. 'Now hang on a minute. You're not suggesting…'

'I'm not suggesting anything.' I didn't believe for one minute that he had anything to do with Dottie's death. For a start, he had the perfect alibi, even though I doubted the Honourable Felicity Mandeville Jones would stand up in court and testify on his behalf. 'You're a scoundrel, Harry, but you're not a murderer. And in any case, you can't fit a silencer to a revolver. Even I know that.'

'Oh, you can do anything if you put your mind to it.'

I frowned. 'What do you mean?'

'The Newton .32 has a sealed firing mechanism. It's based on a Russian design; specially adapted.' Harry spoke with worrying authority.

'You mean…you *can* attach a silencer to it?'

'Sure you can. It doesn't get rid of all the noise, but it dampens it.' He grinned. 'It's a useful little toy.'

'Right. And…does it *have* a silencer? Your revolver?'

Harry nodded.

'But…I checked your bag. I didn't see anything in there.'

'There's a second pocket, sewn into the lining. You wouldn't make much of a thief if you didn't see that, old man.' He took another drag of his cigarette.

'What's going on with you, Harry?' I was fed up with secrets and coincidences. 'The Colonel didn't invite you here by chance. There's something else going on.' The time had come for an explanation.

Harry considered for a moment. 'It's complicated.'

'I'm listening.' A couple of large triangular trees were visible through the windows, sprouting out of the carriage turnabout below. Behind them, I could see, the sky was beginning to lighten. 'It's a good half hour until dawn. That gives you plenty of time to explain.'

'It's nothing to do with Dorothy Kilbride. Just the Colonel and me, you understand. A bit of private business.'

'Let's hear it.'

Harry took a deep breath. 'Look. I have some... associates over in France, and they sometimes have – well, let's just say, certain requirements. And some American friends of mine like to help them out. For a fee, of course. Purely business, if not exactly above board. I occasionally act as a middle man.'

'Go on.'

'The plain fact is, these people were looking to buy a few...military artefacts. And I was in a position to help.'

'Military artefacts? You mean *weapons*?' I almost choked in surprise. 'Who are these people?'

Harry hesitated. 'They're an off-shoot of the PCF.'

I blanched. 'Communists?!? You've been selling guns to communists?'

'*French* communists, old man. Not the real deal. And it's all the same to me. Communists, fascists. I wouldn't want to discriminate on ideological grounds. If they've got the dough, then I'm their man.' Harry could see the disapproval in my eyes. 'They're a pretty harmless lot,' he insisted. 'The thing of it is, though, the French Intelligence Service knew all about it. I guess they must have been watching the farmhouse for years.'

'The farmhouse? You mean the one *I* stayed in, near Bordeaux? The one *you* recommended to me?'

'Yeah, that's the place. A useful little bolt hole. They don't use it that often. They've got a few safe houses in the region and most of them are left empty for months at a time. Only it turns out this one wasn't quite so safe and the French authorities knew all about the deal. They sent a list of names to London, to see if the British had anything on any of the people involved, before they moved in. My name was flagged up, the Colonel heard about it, and he sent me an invitation to Bletchley Park.'

I blinked. 'An *invitation*?'

110

'Sure. Just a friendly little note. A kind request. In my interests to reply etc. You know the kind of thing.'

'Why would the Colonel do that?'

'The guns were due to be delivered this weekend.' Harry glanced at his wrist watch. 'The French police are going to raid the farmhouse and catch everybody red-handed. I only wish I could be there to see it. Solidarity and all that.' He grinned. 'The old dog saved my neck, got them to hold back until I was out of the country.'

That made no sense. 'Why would the Colonel help you? He can't stand the sight of you. Not after what you did to his niece.'

'That was personal, old man. This is business. The Colonel understands that. And he owed me a favour.'

'He would have to.' And a pretty big one, I would guess. 'So he pulled you out of the frying pan to pay off some kind of debt?'

Harry nodded. 'That's about the size of it.'

'Lord. And all that nonsense when you arrived – "what are you up to old chap?" – that was all play acting.'

'Afraid so. Although we did have a proper talk later on. Jesus, you should have heard him. You limeys, there's nothing you like more than giving someone a dressing down.'

'Only when they deserve it, Harry.' A sudden thought struck me. 'Was Doctor Lefranc involved in all this?' It had irked me for some time, what his connection with the Security Service might be.

'Oh, sure, sure,' Harry agreed. 'He works part time for the Deuxième Bureau, the French intelligence service. He used to be the MI5 liaison in France. Had an English mother, apparently. Now he's semi-retired, but he helps them out from time to time, keeping an eye on the odd bit of real estate.'

'You told me you'd never met him.'

'Oh, I hadn't. I wouldn't lie to you, old man. But he was with the Colonel when I was given a dressing down on Friday evening. The old man wasn't happy. Can't say I blame him. "Think yourself lucky," he said. "The next time you get yourself into a fix, Latimer, you're on your own."'

'Quite right too,' I thought. 'And what were the French Francs in the holdall for?'

Harry smiled enigmatically. 'That's a separate bit of business. The Colonel doesn't know anything about that.'

I was tired of equivocation. 'Well?'

He shook his head. 'A gentleman's entitled to keep some secrets.'

'You're not a gentleman, Harry. As poor Miss Jones has just had the misfortune to discover. Oh, and if you want to keep the contents of that holdall away from the Colonel I'd hide it now if I were you. They're bound to organise a search. And if I know the Colonel, he'll probably do it when we're all down at breakfast. You don't want anyone finding that revolver of yours.'

Harry shrugged, stubbing out the dying embers of his cigarette. 'It wouldn't matter if they did. That gun hasn't been fired in years.'

'You're sure you've still got it?'

'Yeah, of course.' All at once, though, there was a trace of doubt in Harry's voice.

'When were you last in here?'

Harry frowned, looking around the room. 'I came up to change just before the dance. But come to think of it, I don't think I've checked the bag since lunchtime.'

He stood up and crouched down by the bed, pulling the holdall out from underneath the mattress. He unlocked the clip and ferreted inside for a moment. It did not take him long to complete the search. He looked up and I could read the truth on his face.

The Newton had disappeared and so had the silencer.

Chapter Thirteen

The front doors of Bletchley Park mansion were standing wide open. The house was east facing and the light of dawn was filtering through the trees on the far side of the carriage turnabout. All I could make out from the hallway was the bright glare shimmering through two sets of double doors, obliterating all detail from the notoriously gloomy entrance hall. I had come down the main stairs in search of the Colonel, to tell him about Harry's revolver, but the open doors at the far end had immediately attracted my attention. In the middle of the afternoon it would have struck me as odd. At seven o'clock in the morning – and a clock above the stone fireplace in the lounge hall was chiming the hour as I passed it by – it was damned peculiar. Only the servants would be up this early after a grand ball and none of them would use the front door. Perhaps Sir Vincent had stepped outside for a moment.

There was a small vestibule between the hallway and the outer doors. I passed through it and under the archway into the bright morning light. It took a moment for my eyes to adjust to the glare. A plump figure was standing to my right, his legs obscured by one of the stone griffins standing guard either side of the porch.

Doctor Lefranc bowed politely. 'Good morning, Monsieur.' I had forgotten the doctor was up and about. He had a lit pipe in his hand and a cordial smile on his face.

'Good morning,' I replied automatically. 'I...saw the front door open.'

The doctor exhaled a puff of smoke. 'I came out to watch the sunrise. It is beautiful, is it not?'

I gazed out across the lawn. 'I don't often get to see it.' The lake was just about visible through the trees and the low sunlight was glittering across the surface. 'I'm not really a morning person,' I admitted, rubbing my hands together. It was a trifle chilly out this morning, though that was hardly surprising for late October.

'It is the best time of day,' Lefranc asserted amiably. For

a man who had been awake all night and who had just had to examine a mutilated corpse he seemed remarkably chipper. He didn't even look tired. 'I needed a little fresh air,' he added.

That was understandable. I almost felt sorry for the fellow. It can't have been much fun, being dragged out of bed to examine poor old Dorothy Kilbride. If he had managed to get to bed at all.

'I was looking for the Colonel,' I explained. 'I thought he might have wandered outside.' It didn't take a genius to work out that Harry's revolver had been used to murder Dorothy Kilbride and it was only right that Sir Vincent should be informed.

'I believe he is in the servants' quarters,' Lefranc said, 'talking to the staff.'

'Ah.' Harry hadn't wanted to tell anyone about the Newton, but I had persuaded him to come clean. Better that than being found out and immediately suspected of something far worse. And it wasn't as if Sir Vincent's opinion of Harry could drop any lower. I had left the American upstairs, having a quick shave.

'Has the Colonel spoken to you about Miss Kilbride ?' Doctor Lefranc asked.

I nodded unhappily. 'I've just had a look at the body.'

The Frenchman grimaced. 'It is a bad business.' He took another puff of his pipe and gazed out across the trees.

I shivered again. It really was dashed cold out here.

'I was thinking of walking down to the lake. It might help us to clear our heads. Would you care to join me?'

I only just managed to stop myself from laughing. I didn't want to offend the fellow, but going for a walk in the freezing cold at this time in the morning sounded about as attractive as a dose of syphilis. That said, I was curious to learn more about Harry's trip to France, now that he'd told me about it, and Lefranc might well be the man to fill in the details. 'Why not?' I agreed, with the closest approximation of a smile my haggard face could manage. I would leave Harry to confess his sins to the Colonel. 'Just give me a minute,' I said, nipping back into the vestibule to grab a hat and coat.

Lefranc waited politely for me to return.

'Poor old Dottie,' I said, reappearing in the porch way and buttoning up an overcoat. 'I can't quite believe she's dead.'

Doctor Lefranc took another puff from his pipe. 'It comes to us all, alas. At least she did not suffer.'

I stepped forward and we set off across the lawn towards the lake. The doctor walked with a slight limp, but he moved with the confidence of an educated man.

'Can we ever be sure of that?' I wondered.

'In this case, Monsieur. Her death was instantaneous. She would have known nothing about it.'

That was probably true. Fast asleep and then a bullet through the brain before she'd even heard the shot. Not that there was much of a shot. 'That's hardly a consolation,' I muttered. A sudden anger gripped me. 'How could anybody do that? How could anyone put a bullet through the head of such a harmless, timid creature?'

'Human nature is a perplexing thing,' Lefranc said. 'Professor Singh believes there is no underlying logic to human behaviour. I am inclined to agree with him.'

I snorted. Philosophy I could do without just now, particularly the arcane viewpoint of some jumped up foreign academic.

Lefranc could see my distress. 'The Colonel will find out the truth, Monsieur.'

'I damn well hope so.' I shivered again. Even with the great coat on, it still felt bloody cold. What was it, forty-five degrees? Not much more than that, I reckoned. How the doctor was managing in nothing more than a jacket I had no idea. He didn't seem to feel the cold at all. 'You say he's over in the servants' quarters?'

We had reached the trees and moved on to the gravel path which fringed the south side of the lake.

'Talking to the staff. They will be having breakfast about now,' the doctor explained. 'The Colonel will send them up to rouse the guests in the next half an hour. It will need to be handled delicately.'

'I'll say. A few sore heads this morning, I shouldn't

wonder. And they won't be in the best of moods, being dragged out of bed. Some of them didn't get upstairs until half past three, so my man said.' I had been lucky to get as much sleep as I did. 'Is the Colonel going to make an announcement? About Miss Kilbride, I mean?'

'I believe so. At breakfast. But he wishes to speak to Lady Fanny first, before making a general announcement.'

'That's decent of him.' The lady of the house deserved the courtesy, though I didn't envy the Colonel having to pass on the news. What would Lady Fanny think, to know that her house had been the site of such horrific events? The house her late husband Sir Herbert Leon had spent so much of his life designing and building. The poor fellow was probably spinning in his grave.

A bench loomed ahead of us. We moved towards it and sat ourselves down, looking out across the lake. There were several trees overhanging us and frogs were ribbiting in the foliage.

Lefranc produced a box of matches and relit his pipe. For a moment, we gazed out in silence across the water. It was not a large lake – the size of a rugby pitch perhaps – but I could see a host of brightly coloured fish streaming beneath the surface. A few ducks were swimming across the water too and a couple of geese sat quietly preening themselves on the far bank. The whole place had a pleasantly rustic feel.

'What about Miss Jones?' I asked suddenly. Felicity Mandeville Jones was the unknown factor in all of this. If she really had been the intended victim in the second murder then there was a chance the assassin might have another go. And the Colonel could hardly broach that particular possibility without warning the girl first. How would she react? I wondered. Was it better to be suspected of murder or to be considered a potential victim?

'I believe he will speak to her too, in private.'

'There was nothing going on, you know. Between her and Mr Sinclair.'

Lefranc's eyes narrowed. 'How do you mean, Monsieur?'

'Well, thinking he might have something to do with the murder. A lovers tiff or whatever.' That was what the Colonel had seemed to suggest.

'There were reports of an argument between the two of them.'

'Yes, but I was speaking to Harry – Mr Latimer – and he's convinced there was nothing going on between them.' Anthony Sinclair had not been romantically involved with Felicity Mandeville Jones, despite the evidence to the contrary, a fact which unsettled me more than a little. The man might have had some rather unsavoury opinions, but he was not the monster I had taken him to be. An unscrupulous journalist, to be sure, but not a woman-beating cad. I had lost my temper with Sinclair for no good reason and now he was dead.

The awful image of his head hitting that wooden pillar was replaying in my mind over and over again.

And now somebody had shifted his body. That was the most difficult part to understand. Someone had moved the corpse and was keeping quiet about it. Could that somebody also be the murderer of Dorothy Kilbride? It was always possible. One thing *was* clear, however. If the guests were being woken then Sinclair's absence would soon be noticed. His valet, Mr Jenkins, would find an empty bedroom and then things would get really tricky. I would try to deflect attention from that for as long as I could. Better for now if everyone focused on the identity of Dorothy Kilbride's murderer. There at least, as the Colonel had confirmed, I was clear of any suspicion.

Doctor Lefranc was thinking about Anthony Sinclair and Felicity Mandeville Jones. He sucked at his pipe, considering Harry's assessment of their relationship. 'That may be true, Monsieur,' he conceded, 'but it may not be. I am sorry to speak out of turn, but I do not think your friend is wholly reliable. I am not sure I would take his word in this matter.'

I nodded. Harry had been telling the truth – Sinclair and Miss Jones had never been an item – but I could not blame the doctor for doubting Harry's word. And I couldn't exactly tell him how the American had come by the information. The less people who knew about *that* little tryst the better. 'From what I hear, you have good reason to distrust him. He's told me all about France,' I added, curious to learn more. 'About his communist connections.'

Lefranc smiled quietly. A fish flipped up on the surface of the water and then disappeared from view. 'Ah yes. Your friend certainly likes to play with fire. Luckily for him, the Colonel is a very forgiving man.'

I laughed. 'Typical Harry, getting involved with that kind of thing. But I was surprised to hear about your connection with the Deuxième Bureau.' I was not sure how much the Frenchman would be willing to tell me, but it was worth a try. He already knew everything about me, after all.

'It is not much of a connection now. I am semi-retired, but I help out where I can. I am a patriot, Monsieur. The French communists are harmless, for the most part, but it helps nobody if arms are sold to the more extreme elements. There are always "young Turks" taking things too far. Thankfully, that issue has now been settled. I do not believe it reflects on the current matter.'

'Lord, no. At least I hope not. Except for one thing.'

'Monsieur?'

If I couldn't tell the Colonel, I might as well tell Doctor Lefranc. He had examined the crime scene, after all. 'Harry brought a small revolver with him, this weekend. You know what Americans are like. They always carry guns. But I was up in his room not a quarter of an hour ago. And it's gone missing.'

Lefranc raised an eyebrow. His moustache twitched slightly but he did not seem overly surprised. 'So we have a murder weapon, then.'

'It looks like it, though lord knows where it is now. Good grief,' I said, the absurdity of it all suddenly striking me. 'A murder weapon and a house full of suspects. It doesn't bear thinking about.'

The doctor nodded. 'And the murderer could be any one of us.'

'You speak for yourself. I was fast asleep at the time.'

'Of course. But anyone else.' He tapped out the end of his pipe on the arm of the bench. 'Mr and Mrs Smith. Lettie Young. Your friend Harry. Even the Colonel is not above suspicion.'

Now that was going too far. 'The Colonel? You can't be serious!'

'He worked very closely with Miss Kilbride for many years,' Lefranc insisted, wiping the end of his pipe and pocketing it quietly. 'Who knows what jealousies or awkwardness existed between them.'

'That's ridiculous! The Colonel is the most honourable man I know.'

'People can do the most terrible things, Monsieur, given the right circumstances. Professor Singh was saying…'

'I don't give a damn what Professor Singh was saying!' I was adamant. 'The Colonel had nothing to do with any of this.'

Lefranc raised his hands. 'I have offended you. I apologise.'

'No, no, I'm…I'm just a bit on edge.' And shouting at a man who already knew far too much about my own life was not a good idea. One word from Lefranc and my reputation would be in tatters. 'It's me who should apologise. You're…quite close to Professor Singh?'

'I have corresponded with him for some years. Alas, we rarely have the opportunity to meet in person. You surely do not suspect him?'

'No, but I was thinking. He's in the room next door to Harry's.' On the other side from Anthony Sinclair. 'There's an adjoining door between the two. He could quite easily have slipped in and stolen the revolver.'

'If he had known it was there. And there are several of us on the same landing.' Most of the male guests were sleeping in the old family rooms, at the front of the house.

'I suppose so. You don't think the professor might have some reason for wanting to kill anybody?'

'It is difficult to think of one.'

I wasn't going to let the idea go that easily. If Lefranc

could suspect the Colonel then I could damn well suspect his friend. 'Do you know what Professor Singh does? For the Colonel, I mean?'

The doctor nodded. 'He does nothing now. He is retired from intelligence work. But he was active in India for a couple of years, I believe. And not that long ago. 1926 and 27.'

'Do you know what he was doing in India?'

'We have discussed the matter.' The Frenchman was hardly likely to tell me, however.

'Need to know, I suppose.'

Doctor Lefranc shook his head. 'It is not a particularly sensitive subject. The Colonel and I have talked about it at length. It is in the past now and the Colonel assures me you are a man to be trusted.' He glanced back along the pathway, just to make sure no one was else around. 'Professor Singh was a case officer,' he said. 'He was running a small network of agents, infiltrating the Independence movement on the sub-continent. It was a joint MI5/DIB operation.'

'DIB?'

'The Delhi Intelligence Bureau.' India was part of MI5's remit, as it was still British territory, but the DIB handled a lot of work on the ground. 'There were concerns that the Russians were trying to stir up trouble with the movement. Professor Singh was tasked with discovering the truth.'

'And did he?'

'That I do not know, Monsieur.'

I sat back against the hard wooden bench. All these people, all these possible connections. It was too much to take in. I was suddenly feeling very tired.

Doctor Lefranc stretched out his arms above his head. 'It is a little chilly this morning,' he said, only now beginning to notice the cold. It was the wooden bench that did it; it cut straight through the fabric of one's trousers. 'Shall we return to the house?'

I nodded. We rose up and slowly began to make our way back along the pathway towards the mansion. A breeze was blowing through the trees, adding to the coolness of the air. Clouds were gathering in the sky, not quite blocking out the sunlight, but it looked as if it might rain later on. It had certainly been a wet October so far.

'Do not worry, Monsieur,' Lefranc reassured me. 'These situations always resolve themselves in the end.'

I wondered for a moment just how many murders the good doctor had been involved with. Then I remembered he had been a battlefield surgeon. This was probably a walk in the park for him. I smiled at the appropriateness of the phrase. It was *literally* a walk in the park at the moment. Lefranc must have seen some dreadful sights in the trenches. No wonder he wasn't flustered by a little case of domestic murder. Or even a severe case of sexual deviation. I have never much warmed to Frenchmen, but I had to admit, Doctor Lefranc was one of the better Frogs I had met. In the entire time we had been together he had made no reference to our own prior meeting and his unfortunate knowledge of my physiognomy. The man had impeccable manners. He was a gentleman through and through.

Up ahead of us, as we moved from the pathway onto the lawn, I saw the Colonel's valet coming out of the house, his great granite bulk dominating the porch way and rather putting the griffins to shame. 'Doctor Lefranc,' he called, as we came near enough for him not to have to bellow, 'the Colonel asks if you could join him? He's about to speak to Lady Fanny.'

The doctor nodded, heading towards the arch. 'Excuse me, Monsieur,' he said. I waved a hand good-naturedly and the Frenchman disappeared inside. Townsend acknowledged me with a polite nod and then followed Lefranc back into the house.

I lingered in the driveway for a moment. One of those griffins was giving me the eye. Damned ugly thing, with elaborate wings and a head like an eagle. There were two statues in place, standing guard either side of the porch, like Cerberus protecting the gates of Hades, albeit with one head rather than three. It might just as well be the entrance to Hell, I thought, with all that had been going on in that house over the past few hours. The screams of the damned were notable by their absence, however. The place was too damned quiet.

I glanced across at the bay windows to my right. The

121

sun had disappeared behind the clouds and the windows were shrouded in darkness. If the Colonel was heading upstairs, as Mr Townsend had said, there would be no one looking out from the drawing room just now. I could skip past the windows and take a look at the ground outside the dining hall. Curiosity was bursting inside me. I couldn't help thinking of Anthony Sinclair's body being dragged out through those large exterior doors. How anyone could have managed that on their own I had no idea. Perhaps it was more than one person. Whatever the truth, there was bound to be a trail. And it wouldn't hurt to have a quick look.

I shuffled across to the far side of the house. There were no scuff marks on the gravel here that I could see. The dining room doors were overhung by three archways supported by marble columns. The two doors, I noticed with some surprise, had completely different handles from the ones on the inside. These were circular and much easier to grasp.

I stood for a moment with my back to the entrance, trying to imagine what might have happened here during the night. What would I have done, if I had succeeded in opening the doors? Where would I have dragged the body? There would have been too much light spilling out onto the carriage turnabout to risk dragging him towards the lake. Better to move left, I thought. There was a path around the side of the building, leading to the garages where all the automobiles were parked. But that would also be too exposed. Another path ran parallel to the front of the building, heading roughly north, towards the maze and the stable yard. That might prove a more attractive proposition for any prospective body snatcher.

I pulled out my pocket watch. It was just gone twenty past seven. The guests were probably being woken around now but it would be a few minutes yet before anyone came down for breakfast.

I took a chance and strode a little way along the northern path. A row of trees were planted to my left but within a minute I was on the outskirts of the stable yard. I ignored the rather impressive hedgerows of Sir Herbert Leon's maze up ahead and instead looked west along the short track leading into the square. The horses were stabled at the back of the enclosure and several small buildings stood between the pathway and the far side of the yard. There was a cottage at one end, next to the tack and feed house, and nearer to hand, a large fruit store on the left hand side. The estate had several glass houses and a fair bit of produce was grown over the course of the year. With most of the staff away for the weekend, however, the buildings surrounding the yard would be empty right now. A single groom had remained behind to look after the horses and, as he had been roped in to the festivities the previous evening, it was likely he would have joined the rest of the staff at breakfast.

The stables would be a good place to hide a body, I thought. There was an awful lot of hay in there. I had seen it first hand during the treasure hunt the previous morning. Lord, that seemed like a lifetime ago now. But a corpse might go unnoticed for days buried underneath a large stack of hay.

I hesitated at the corner of the yard. Should I have a look at the stables, or head back to the house and get myself to the dining room before any of the others arrived? It might look suspicious, me wandering around here on my own at this time in the morning. But I was not feeling particularly sensible just now.

A noise from the cottage robbed me of any choice. I ducked back out of sight behind a large tree.

A door slammed and I heard footsteps across the yard. I waited a couple of beats, then took a chance and peered around the edge of the tree trunk. A man was making his way across from the cottage towards the clock tower at the far end. His back was to me, but I recognised him nonetheless. It was Anthony Sinclair's valet. What was his name? Jenkins. Samuel Jenkins. A rather lanky Welshman in his mid twenties. He had helped serve the drinks in the ballroom last night. He'd made a better job of it than the regular servants, I recalled.

The young man disappeared under the archway. From there he could pass the garages and enter the servants quarters from the back of the main house. But what on earth had he been doing out here in the first place?

I glanced around carefully before stepping out into the

yard. The square was empty now. There was no reason for anybody else to be about, but it was as well to be careful.

I hurried across the yard towards the cottage. It was a small two storey building in red brick, dull and functional, with a black door set back behind a small wooden porch. It had been built to house the head coachman, although I doubted whether Lady Fanny kept any coaches now. Perhaps the building had been given over to one of the chauffeurs. There were still horses in the stables, however, so perhaps a head groom remained on the payroll.

A set of net curtains lined the window at the front of the cottage. They were rather tatty looking, but provided a comfortable screen for anybody on the inside. There was certainly no point trying to peer in through the glass. I tried the door instead and to my surprise found it was not locked. Cautiously, I entered the cottage.

A short hallway fed into one large room to the left of the front door. The place was little more than a hovel. A few chairs and a rudimentary table provided the bulk of the furniture.

My attention was immediately drawn to a long white sheet draped across the living room floor. I stepped forward to take a closer look at it. A body was lying underneath.

Chapter Fourteen

I recognised the black brogues sticking out from beneath the shroud. It is surprising how somebody's shoes stick in your mind. I had seen them before, when I had dragged the corpse into the dining room some hours earlier. But I had not expected to see them here. I flipped back the other end of the sheet, just to be sure. The pallid face of Anthony Sinclair stared back, oddly reassuring after the many surprises I had endured over the last few hours. Two murders in one day was more than enough to be getting on with. How he had come to be lying here in the cottage I had not the faintest idea. Well, no, in fairness, it was obvious how he had come to be lying here. The body had been carried from the house, presumably by Samuel Jenkins himself. The question was, why?

When I'd first seen Sinclair's valet crossing the stable yard my initial thought had been that the master himself was still alive but injured, and was intending to come back to the mansion later on to expose me in the grandest and most theatrical way imaginable. That possibility had thankfully proved unhinged. But if his valet had discovered the body, why would he keep it to himself and drag Sinclair over here on his own? Assuming, of course, that he was acting alone.

It was possible that some of the other servants were involved. Perhaps they were *all* involved. It might be some kind of grand conspiracy. My head was suddenly filled with cartoon images of sinister Russians trying to infiltrate the catering staff…

I shook myself. I was losing my grip on reality. In all probability, Jenkins had discovered the body on his own, by accident. The valet might then have informed somebody, or he may have moved the body on his own, for reasons as yet unknown. From a practical point of view, I wondered, would he have been capable of shifting Sinclair without help? I knew from experience what a great lump the man was, and Jenkins was not exactly muscular. In fact, he was a rather slender fellow, perhaps five feet eight or nine in height. But if there was a pressing reason, I suspected even he would be able to drag his master a few hundred yards. There weren't any scuff marks outside the dining room doors, however, which meant that the body had been *carried* rather than dragged. Could Jenkins have lifted the man across his shoulder, like a fireman?

I pulled the sheet back over Sinclair's face. The bruise on his forehead seemed, bizarrely, to be on the mend. Perhaps the valet had cleaned it up, as a last gesture of respect towards his master. Who knows what goes on in the mind of a servant in a situation like that. Maybe they act like dogs, refusing to leave their masters' side. I could just imagine Hargreaves standing sadly over my grave, digging his heels in and refusing to go home.

I pulled out my pocket watch. It was just gone half past seven. High time I headed back to the house.

Nobody saw me as I slipped quietly between the griffins and through the front door. I had taken the scenic route around the front of the building, using various trees for cover so that I was not easily visible from the dining room, in case some of the guests had arrived early for breakfast. I stowed my hat and coat in the vestibule (I say "my" hat and coat, but in truth I had just grabbed the first ones I could find from a hook) then closed up the outer doors and made my way through to the main hall.

A murmur of puzzled conversation wafted through from the dining room. As I had feared, some of the guests were already at breakfast and by the sounds of it they were not terribly happy being up and about at this time in the morning. A quarter to eight may not sound like the crack of dawn – and indeed it wasn't – but on a Sunday morning, after a late night of drinking and dancing in the ballroom (not to mention the odd bit of debauchery) it might as well have been the middle of the night. As someone who had *actually* been woken in the middle of the night, I knew just how they felt.

The chatter from the dining room was not the only sound I could hear. There were footsteps clomping across the first floor landing, heading for the main stairs. Some of the guests were obviously slower off the mark than others. I ducked quickly into the hallway between the library and the morning room. No need for anyone to know I had been outside all this time. The footsteps thumped down the stairs with such an inelegant clatter that I knew at once who they belonged to. My suspicions were confirmed as I reappeared in the main hall and made my way forward, for all the world as if I had been coming out of the library.

Lettie Young was heading towards me. She let out an extravagant yawn and raised a hand in greeting. 'Morning, Sir Hilary!' she exclaimed, far too loudly for this time of day. Her yawn was infectious. I was suddenly feeling very tired. I rubbed my eyes and did my best to stifle a yawn of my own. My cheeks were a little flushed too, coming in from the cold.

'Gawd, you're looking rough,' Lettie said.

'And you're looking delightful, Miss Young,' I parried sarcastically.

She laughed. 'If you say so. How's your head?'

'Not too bad, all things considered. Just a bit groggy.'

Lettie patted me on the shoulder sympathetically. 'Nice cup of tea'll sort you out.'

I nodded. Oddly enough, the outside air had already acted to clear my head. My hangover had all-but disappeared, though I was still feeling a little tired. But it was as well to maintain the illusion.

'So what's the Colonel doing, getting us all up at this hour?' Lettie asked, as we moved through the lounge towards the dining hall. Daylight was flooding in from the glass roof above us and Lettie had to shield her eyes. 'Last time I was up this early on a Sunday the Kaiser was still on the throne.' She laughed. The woman clearly had as much of an aversion to early mornings as I did. I wondered briefly what time she had got to bed. Quite late, I would imagine. Lettie was not the kind of girl to leave a party early. 'It's not another one of Sir Vincent's games, is it?' she asked.

Croquet at seven forty-five in the morning. That might have sounded worryingly plausible, but for the murders. But no, it was not a game. As the rest of the guests were about to discover.

'I think perhaps it's best you hear it from him.'

The remainder of the party were already gathered around the dining room table. Breakfast had been laid out. There was toast and eggs, huge pots of tea. Servants were scurrying around but the guests were all helping themselves. I swallowed hard, seeing them all together. Mr and Mrs Smith, the Professor, Doctor Lefranc, Harry. The Colonel himself was sitting at the head of the table, having presumably finished his talk with Lady Fanny Leon. Which one of these people, I wondered as I sat myself down, had murdered Dorothy Kilbride? And which of them, if any, had helped Samuel Jenkins to move the body of Anthony Sinclair? Did anyone here even know about that first murder?

A few of the guests had made a start on the food. Harry had a plate full of scrambled eggs and was chomping away merrily. He probably needed to refuel after his extended antics in Miss Jones' boudoir. Mrs Smith was nibbling rather delicately on a slice of toast.

Lettie Young plopped herself gracelessly to my left and immediately started filling her plate. She was a girl who liked her food, though you wouldn't have known it from her figure. All that singing and dancing probably helped to keep her fit, though I was sure her torso was just as constricted as mine underneath that dress of hers.

A low mumble of chatter filled the room, vaguely resentful. The servants fussed, replenishing the food, but allowing us to serve ourselves, as was the custom.

I poured some tea from the pot. In the absence of anything stronger, it would have to do. I was still feeling damnably tired. Sometimes, a few hour's sleep is worse than no sleep at all. I added three spoonfuls of sugar. Perhaps that might help to wake me up a bit.

My man Hargreaves was hovering in the doorway. I had not seen him arrive. 'That's everyone, Colonel,' he said.

'About bloody time,' John Smith grumbled, in his bluff Yorkshire brogue. His plate was already empty. He had bolted down his entire breakfast before I had even arrived. 'So what's the meaning of getting us all up at this ungodly hour? On a Sunday? We didn't get to bed 'till gone three and the wife and I were looking forward to a nice lie in.' The expression on Mrs Smith's face was equally sour, though the precise appeal of a lie-in with Mr Smith eluded me. The two of them seemed such an improbable couple. Mind you, the same could just as easily have been said about me and Elizabeth.

The Colonel rose to his feet, arching his back and placing his hands on the table to steady himself. The man had been up for twenty four hours straight, but you wouldn't have known it to look at him. He had a reputation as a workaholic and it had been well earned. He adjusted his monocle. 'I can only apologise to you all. There must be a few sore heads this morning, what?' How he maintained his good humour in these circumstances was a mystery to me. The man positively thrived on adversity. Mind you, this was probably not the worst crisis in his long career.

Lettie Young was glancing across the table and had noticed a few empty chairs. 'Hang on a minute,' she said. 'Felicity ain't down yet. Nor Dottie.' I wondered briefly how well Lettie had known the deceased. "Dottie" indeed!

Harry Latimer was finishing off his plate of eggs. He wiped his mouth with the back of his hand. Americans can be so uncouth, sometimes. 'Sinclair isn't here either,' he observed.

The Colonel nodded. 'Miss Jones is with Lady Fanny Leon,' he explained. 'They'll be along shortly. As to the others…. I'm afraid I have a bit of bad news.'

'We're listening,' Mr Smith said, bluntly. An unspoken "get on with it" lingered in the air.

'There's no easy way of saying this. I apologise to the ladies in advance. But to put it bluntly, chaps, ladies…there is a murderer among us.'

A moment of silence fell across the table, followed by several sharp intakes of breath. Mrs Smith almost choked on her toast.

'What the bloody hell are you talking about?' John Smith demanded.

'Last night, my secretary Dorothy…Miss Dorothy

Kilbride was brutally murdered.' The Colonel paused to let the shocking news sink in. A brief silence descended upon the table. Even Lettie Young had put down her fork and stopped eating. 'By person or persons unknown,' he added. 'Unfortunately, that's not the end of it. A few hours before that, unbeknown to any of us at the time, there was another incident. Mr Anthony Sinclair, the journalist from the Daily Mail, was also brutally killed; bludgeoned to death with an iron poker at around midnight last night.' The Colonel paused again momentarily, allowing everybody time to digest the news.

I was having difficulty breathing. My throat was feeling suddenly and understandably constricted.

'And I think,' the Colonel added, with just a hint of menace, 'that the person who did it may well be one of us sitting here this morning.'

Chapter Fifteen

A hush had descended on the dining room of Bletchley Park. The full import of the Colonel's words would take some time to sink in. Jaws were hanging slack in every corner of the room. Eyes were wide open in astonishment. And pins could be heard dropping throughout the land. For some, the news of the murders was a sudden smack in the face, coming out of nowhere. For others, it was a confirmation of what they had already suspected; a grim affirmation of news hitherto only whispered furtively in private. For me, it was the terrifying realisation that Sir Vincent Kelly had known about the murder of Anthony Sinclair from the very beginning. That, and the sudden frightening possibility that he might suspect my involvement in the man's death. Why else would he have withheld the information for so long?

I sucked in a huge gulp of air, wondering if it might be possible to brazen things out. The Colonel had not accused *me* of anything; the accusation had been aimed at the table as a whole. 'One of us,' he had said, so it was possible he didn't yet know who was responsible for Sinclair's death. However, the fact that he had been aware of it all along and said nothing....

There was no time to reflect on any of this properly. The hush that had enveloped the room for what seemed like several hours lasted in fact for only the briefest of moments.

It was John Smith whose voice shattered the silence. 'If this is another one of your bloody silly games, Sir Vincent.'

An outraged Mary Smith nodded vehemently in support of her husband. 'It would be in very bad taste.'

The Colonel did not take offence. 'I assure you, Smith,' he responded politely, 'Mrs Smith. This is not a joke. Two people have been killed in this house. Two guests we were dancing and laughing with just a few hours ago have been brutally murdered.'

Off the top of my head, I couldn't remember anyone laughing at anything Anthony Sinclair had said, but that was probably beside the point.

'It is true,' Doctor Lefranc confirmed, leaning forward in his chair. 'I have examined both of the bodies. There can be no doubt it was murder.' He spoke with the calm authority of a medical man.

Mrs Smith let out a cry, bringing a hand up to her mouth. The talk of bodies over the breakfast table was disconcerting for everybody. Her husband put a rough, comforting arm around her shoulder.

'Bleedin' hell,' Lettie Young exclaimed. She placed her tea cup back down on the table. 'I can't believe it.'

'There's no need for coarse language,' Mrs Smith admonished half-heartedly.

Harry at least seemed to be taking the news in his stride. Mind you, I'd already told him about one of the murders. 'Have the police been called?' he asked. The thought of the men in blue crawling all over the house would doubtless be as alarming to him as it was to me. He had almost as much to hide as I did.

'Not yet,' the Colonel admitted. 'I'm afraid this'll have to be an internal matter. I have a small team coming up from London. They've just set off and should be here by half past ten at the latest. In the meantime, I've asked my valet to organise a complete search of the house. Servants quarters, bedrooms, everywhere. My man Townsend is a former policeman, so he knows the form.'

'You're going to search our rooms?' said Mr Smith, somewhat alarmed. 'What, now?'

The Colonel nodded.

'You don't have anything to hide do you?' asked Harry, with a smirk. He, of course, had been given advanced notice of the search. Actually, I was the one who had given it to him.

'Course I bloody don't. I just weren't expecting...'

'Has to be done, Smith,' the Colonel said. 'Townsend will be very circumspect. You have my word.'

'Aye. Well.' Mr Smith raised no further objections.

Harry was eager to learn more about the first death. 'So let's get this straight. You're telling me Anthony Sinclair was *battered to death*?

'That's right. With an iron poker across the back of the head.'

'Jesus. I didn't exactly like the man, but....Jesus.'

The room fell silent. Mrs Smith had gone very pale.

I did my best to disguise my own reactions. It seemed the Colonel hadn't just found the body, he knew exactly how the man had died. 'You didn't mention anything about Sinclair to me,' I said, 'when we spoke earlier on.' The Colonel had been sat slap bang in the middle of the crime scene. Lord, did he notice me glancing down at the blood stain on the floor?

'Yes, I'm sorry about that, Butler. But I hope you understand the necessity. Sinclair's death needed to be kept quiet until I'd had a chance to speak about it to Miss Jones.'

Professor Singh leaned forward before I could formulate a response. 'Perhaps, Colonel,' he said, in his maddeningly over-elaborate English, 'you might take us through the events of the last few hours. It may help to facilitate a greater understanding of such surprising occurrences.'

'Surprising!' John Smith snorted. 'Bloody appalling, I'd say.'

The Colonel inclined his head. 'Capital idea, Singh.' He cleared his throat. 'But where to start? Well, it was Townsend – my valet – who first alerted me to the death of Mr Sinclair, although in point of fact it was Sinclair's man Jenkins who stumbled across the body.'

Jenkins! It *had* been Jenkins who discovered the corpse. One fact at last that I had managed to deduce correctly.

'Apparently, he hadn't seen his master for some hours. On duty in the ballroom and so forth. But he wanted to make sure the chap got to bed safely. Might have had too much to drink and fallen asleep somewhere awkward. Happens to the best of us, eh, Butler?'

I coughed with embarrassment, trying not to look at Mrs Smith.

'Anyway, he made a quick search of the front of the house, but there was no sign of Sinclair, so at about four am he decided to head back to the servants' quarters. He passed

133

through here, heading for the servery, and being a solid chap, he noticed one of the chairs on the dining room table was misaligned. Naturally, he went over to straighten it out, but when he did, it banged against something underneath the table. And when he looked down he found the body of Anthony Sinclair. Which was something of a shock, I should imagine.'

'I'll say!' Lettie Young agreed.

Mrs Smith was aghast. 'The body was under the dining table?' She looked down in horror. '*This* table?'

'I'm afraid so, my dear.'

'It's a bit bloody much, serving breakfast on it if some poor bugger's been killed in the same room,' Mr Smith thought. ''Scuse my language dear,' he apologised to his wife.

It was Doctor Lefranc who answered that. 'Ah, but he wasn't killed in this room, Monsieur. We believe Anthony Sinclair died in the drawing room on the other side of that wall.' The doctor gestured across to a mahogany fireplace just to the right of the exterior doors. It had a shared chimney stack with the fireplace in the drawing room on the opposite side. 'Mr Townsend found a small dent on one of the wooden pillars in that room. He also uncovered some traces of blood in the lounge hall. We believe the body was dragged from there to here. Judging by the wounds on Mr Sinclair's head, it seems he was struck by an iron poker from the fireplace and then fell against the pillar. Examination of the cranium suggested that it was the second blow that proved fatal.'

Mary Smith let out another cry.

'Pardon me, Madame,' Lefranc apologised. 'I did not mean to be so graphic. Perhaps, Colonel, Mrs Smith should retire to her room? This may be a little too distressing for her.'

'No, no,' Mrs Smith insisted, wiping her eyes. 'I am perfectly capable of dealing with a little unpleasantness. My husband is from Yorkshire. It's just rather shocking when it's on your own doorstep.'

The Colonel was all concern. 'If you're sure, my dear?'

She nodded unhappily.

Lettie Young was impatient to find out what had happened next. 'So what did you think, when you'd found him?'

'Well, Miss Young, it was a bit of a blow. Dashed awkward, I have to say. It looked like it might have been some kind of accident. Bit of a row that got out of hand, you know the sort of thing. And I remembered Latimer here telling me that Sinclair had had a blazing row with Miss Jones just before midnight.'

Harry confirmed this with a nod.

'You don't think Felicity had anything to do with it?' Lettie asked. 'She wouldn't say boo to a goose.'

'Perhaps not, my dear,' the Colonel admitted. 'Nonetheless, it was my first thought. It was the amateurishness of the crime, more than anything. I mean to say, dragging the body from one room to the next and then hiding it under the dining room table. Damn queer thing to do.'

'Aye, you're right there,' Mr Smith agreed. 'What kind of bloody fool batters someone to death and then leaves their body in plain sight for any idiot to stumble across?'

Of all the many things I had expected to hear around the breakfast table that morning, criticism of my disposal technique was not one of them. But I was hardly in a position to contest Mr Smith's evaluation. I was lucky I had even managed to maintain my composure, with things the way they were. There was one question, though, which I desperately needed to know the answer to.

'If you found the body under the table, why has it been moved?' I kept my voice calm. It was a reasonable question to ask, but I didn't want to seem over-critical. 'Why not leave it here? Surely interfering with a crime scene is a crime in itself? Shouldn't everything be left untouched?'

The Colonel scratched his moustache. 'In the ordinary course of things, Butler, that would be true. But you must understand. I was concerned about the possible ramifications. Miss Jones is the daughter of a prominent ex cabinet minister. If she had attacked and killed someone as well known as Anthony Sinclair and the news became public, it would be the biggest scandal of the decade. A journalist murdered by a politician's daughter! Our involvement couldn't be kept out of it.'

Harry grinned. 'You were going to cover it up.'

'Don't be bloody daft,' John Smith said. 'You can't cover up the death of someone like that.'

'Not his death,' the Colonel agreed, 'but perhaps the circumstances of his death. MI5 cannot afford a scandal, not with the government we have just now. The Labour Government,' he added. Ramsay MacDonald, the new Prime Minister, had already proved deeply suspicious of the security services. 'After Doctor Lefranc had examined the body, we had Sinclair shifted to one of the workers' cottages.' And put him underneath a shroud for me to find. Now I understood. 'We didn't want any of the other servants stumbling across the body. Would have been a bit tricky to explain.'

'My valet helped Mr Jenkins and Mr Townsend to move the deceased,' Doctor Lefranc added, by way of explanation.

They had unlocked the exterior doors and carried the corpse out onto the carriage turnabout, just as I had intended to do.

'And then I went upstairs,' the Colonel continued, 'to have a quiet word with Miss Jones.'

Suddenly, things were beginning to fall into place. And so far, there was no indication that the Colonel had connected me with the first murder.

'That, of course, was when I stumbled across the body of Miss Kilbride. I knocked on her bedroom door, but there was no reply. Given the seriousness of the situation, I had no choice but to enter the room unannounced.'

Mrs Smith was confused. 'I thought you said you were looking for Miss Mandeville Jones?'.

The Colonel nodded. 'That's right. Bit of a mix up over the rooms.'

'That was our fault.' Lettie Young laughed. 'Me and lover boy here. We were putting Dottie to bed, but we got the rooms the wrong way round. We put Dottie in Felicity's bedroom.'

'That's right,' I admitted, with some embarrassment. 'We were all a bit tight, I think.'

'I didn't have a clue we'd got it wrong,' Lettie confessed. 'Not until I bumped into Felicity – Miss Jones – when I was coming back out. "What were you doing in my bedroom?" she said. I said "I thought it didn't look right."' The woman laughed again. 'I never could tell me left from me right. One room either side, what do you expect?'

It was my turn to frown. 'Wait a minute. Your bedroom's the one in the *middle*?'

''Course it is. All girls together. Three in a row with Mr and Mrs Smith just round the corner at the far end.'

Mary Smith pursed her lips with distaste.

Harry had already grasped the implications of this rather trivial mix-up. He had made the same mistake, after all. 'So you must have knocked on Felicity's door,' he guessed, addressing the Colonel, 'but found Dorothy Kilbride.'

'Bleedin' hell!' Lettie exclaimed, also catching on. 'That must have been a right old shock.'

'Rather,' the Colonel agreed. 'My poor secretary, lying dead there, in bed. Shot with a revolver of all things.' That got another gasp from those who were not in the know. 'I called up Doctor Lefranc, of course, and he put the time of death at between half past three and four o'clock. Probably only a short while after most of you went to bed.'

'What time did you find the body?' Harry asked.

'About a quarter to five. Still warm, sad to say.'

'Hang on a mo,' said Lettie. 'I was in the room next door to her. I'd have heard a shot.'

'We believe a silencer may have been employed.'

Harry tried not blink while the group took this in. *What silencer*, his face seemed to say.

Professor Singh had been following the conversation carefully. 'This is most perplexing,' he said, displaying his usual gift for understatement.

That was too much for Mr Smith. 'Perplexing? That poor bloody woman's shot in the head and you call it *perplexing*?'

'I was merely reflecting on the peculiarity of the situation. It is most strange, do you not think?' Professor Singh clasped his hands together. He seemed to regard the whole affair as some kind of intellectual exercise.

'Nothing bloody strange about it,' Mr Smith responded. 'Some bloody madman breaks in here, batters Sinclair then goes up and shoots Miss Kilbride. It was probably a burglar.' He glanced at his wife. 'Have you checked your jewellery, love?' She shook her head.

'There was no sign of a break in,' the Colonel countered. 'The doors were all locked and the murders took place about four hours apart, which makes it rather unlikely that anybody from the outside could have been responsible. A chap couldn't wander about the house for four hours without being seen, not even at that hour. No, I'm pretty sure it was somebody already on the premises.'

'Perhaps one of the staff?' I suggested. What had Jenkins really been doing, creeping around the house at four am?

'Aye.' Mr Smith liked that idea. 'Or one of them band members. That trumpeter with the moustache looked right peculiar.'

'Don't be daft,' laughed Lettie. 'They were playing all evening. They couldn't have killed anyone.'

'Is it perhaps possible,' Professor Singh asked, 'that we are dealing with two entirely separate incidents here? The death of Mr Sinclair could well have been an accident. As you have said, it does not seem to have been premeditated. Whereas the murder of Miss Dorothy Kilbride, it seems to me, demonstrates a degree of calculation which renders it quite unlike the first killing.'

A short silence descended while everyone attempted to digest the professor's words. The man spoke like a walking textbook.

'There's certainly something in that,' the Colonel agreed. 'If Miss Jones was somehow involved with Sinclair...'

'Felicity wouldn't harm a fly,' Lettie protested. 'She wouldn't have battered him to death with a...what was it?'

'A poker,' Doctor Lefranc chipped in.

'A poker. It's not her style.'

'I wasn't aware that you knew her,' Mrs Smith observed coldly. 'So I hardly think your opinion of her character carries much weight.'

'We've got to know each other, these last couple of days.'

That would certainly be true, I thought, if Lettie really had been sleeping in the room next door.

'Anyway,' the Colonel concluded, 'it's a damned queer business all round, but we will sort it out. I've asked my chap to search all the rooms, as I've explained. See if we can find the murder weapon. And in the meantime, I'd ask everyone here if they can stay put for the next few hours.'

'Confined to barracks?' Harry asked with a grin.

'Until this afternoon at least. Feel free to wander the grounds, though. Don't feel like you're imprisoned.'

'Mr Smith and I were planning to attend the local church service at half past ten,' said Mary Smith.

'Of course, my dear. Feel free. Just so long as we know where you are. Don't want anyone deserting us just yet. Townsend and I will want to have words in private with everyone, just to determine where you all were at the time of each murder. So if you can make sure we know where to find you?' He shook his head. 'A bit of a rum do, this. But don't concern yourself, ladies, gentlemen. We'll catch the blighters. You have my word on it.'

The Colonel's valet arrived from the lounge hall and cleared his throat. 'We've searched the rooms, sir,' he announced solemnly. 'And I believe we may have found the murder weapon.'

Chapter Sixteen

A state of confusion pervaded the breakfast table as the Colonel departed to consult with his valet and one or two of the other servants who had helped conduct the search. I had no idea whether they had uncovered anything else of significance, or indeed where the murder weapon had been found, but doubtless we would find out in time. I was more concerned about the ease with which the Colonel had managed to deceive everyone, particularly regarding the discovery of Anthony Sinclair's body. He had known about the corpse under the dining room table when I had spoken to him at half past five in the morning, but he had said nothing. His assertion that he wished to speak to Felicity Mandeville Jones before making the news public had some credibility, if he really thought she might be responsible for Sinclair's death. But the fact that the Colonel had managed to deceive me so completely was a little dispiriting. I pride myself I am usually rather good at detecting falsehood. But I suppose if the head of MI5 doesn't know how to keep a secret, then nobody does. It wasn't just the Colonel, however. His valet Townsend had known about Sinclair, as had Doctor Lefranc. And if the three of them had managed to keep quiet about that, what else might they be hiding? Had someone observed me killing the journalist? Had the Colonel noticed my nervous glances at the carpet underneath the occasional table when we'd had our little chat in the drawing room? And even if the man hadn't suspected me initially, might I have done something since then to give myself away? If not with the Colonel, then perhaps with Doctor Lefranc. The Frenchman, I knew, was a shrewd judge of character and he was already aware that I had secrets to hide.

It had been a mistake for me to stay at Bletchley Park this long. Better to abscond now, while I still had the chance. It would mean going into hiding, of course, but that was a small price to pay to avoid several decades in prison. Elizabeth wouldn't mind, so long as there was no scandal. Hargreaves could fetch the car from the garage and we would be off before anyone even noticed. He had already packed the luggage, after all.

The luggage! Lord, even that would look suspicious. The Colonel had ordered the valets to search all the bedrooms. In the ordinary course of events, it would have been perfectly natural for me to have my belongings packed up ready to leave, but not before breakfast, in the aftermath of a murder, when it would be quite clear that no one would be going anywhere any time soon. If the Colonel did have any suspicions of me, this would only serve to strengthen them.

That decided it. I would cut and run at the earliest opportunity.

One small matter had been eating away at me, though, since I had first found out the truth about Anthony Sinclair. If Sinclair had not been involved with Felicity Mandeville Jones, then who was the shadowy figure I had seen lurking in her bedroom on Friday evening? And, come to that, which damned blackguard was responsible for those injuries to her face? Only one person could answer these questions, and she was sitting next to me at the breakfast table.

Lettie Young pushed back her chair. 'I'm going to pop up and check on Felicity,' she announced, rising to her feet. 'Poor little bleeder. What she must be thinking…?'

'I'll join you, if I may,' I said, brushing a few breadcrumbs from my shirt before I stood up so that I didn't seem too eager. 'I wanted to have a word with Lady Fanny,' I added, by way of explanation. That wasn't strictly true, though I was curious to know how the grand old dame had taken the news. If anyone could cope, it would be Lady Fanny. She was that kind of woman. But it was Lettie I really wanted to talk to.

She gave me her arm and we swept out of the dining room together, with Mrs Smith's disapproving glare burning into our backs.

'You don't think Felicity had anything to do with the death of Mr Sinclair, do you?' she asked, as we made our way through the lounge hall.

'I doubt it,' I said. 'Though I did hear them arguing when I came down the stairs last night. And Harry told me there'd been a hell of a row.'

Lettie dismissed that with a shrug. 'He was just playing the father figure. Him and her dad are as thick as thieves. There was nothing going on between them two, believe me.'

'Oh, I do believe you. But do you think Miss Jones might have been the target for the second murder?'

'I dunno.' Lettie frowned. 'Nobody knew about the mix up over the rooms, did they? Apart from you and me. And Felicity.'

'And Harry,' I added.

'Oh, you heard about that, did you?' She laughed. 'Dirty buggers, the pair of them.' We were in the hallway now, moving towards the main stairs. 'The bedsprings were still going at six o'clock this morning.'

I stopped. 'You're in the room next door to her, aren't you? The middle room.' It was as well to get straight to the point.

'That's right. Should have heard everything last night. But the walls are pretty thick and I was out like a light.'

I was more concerned about the previous evening. 'So when I knocked on that door the night we arrived, that was your bedroom, was it?'

Lettie grinned. 'It certainly was.'

'Even though it was Miss Jones who answered the door?'

She beamed. 'We were having a bit of a night cap. That's when I first got to know her, really.' Lettie moved onto the stairs and I followed behind. 'The two of us started chatting on the way up to bed. Rather like now.' She smiled again, a warm lopsided smile. 'I was teasing her about throwing that game of billiards. You remember?'

'I should say. The damn woman cost me five guineas!'

We had paused midway up the staircase. The balustrade on the first floor stood opposite and a large frosted window spanned the wall to our left.

'It was worth it just to see Sinclair's face. Anyway, Felicity came into my room and we had a right old chin-wag. You know her dad's trying to marry her off to some middle-aged sod she can't stand?'

'I'd heard something about it. Some minor royal, wasn't it? A cousin of Prince Edward. I can't remember the details.' Society gossip was Elizabeth's forte, not mine.

'She was quite upset about it. Sinclair was taunting her during the drinks. Him and Sir Hugh go way back, but she can't stand the sight of him.'

'So that's why she humiliated the fellow on the billiards table?'

'One thing he didn't know she could do. Served him bleedin' well right. Oh. I suppose I shouldn't speak ill of the dead.'

'It's all right. I didn't like him either. So when I heard the bang, on Friday evening?'

'She'd had a bit to drink. There were a few tears. She got up to refill her glass and she tripped up. Banged her head on the bedstead. Simple as that.'

'And that was all it was?'

Lettie nodded. 'Course. Why, what did you think had happened?'

'I thought...I thought someone had given her a good hiding,' I admitted sheepishly. 'Actually, I thought there was a man in her room.' I had obviously got the wrong end of the stick right from the start.

Lettie laughed. 'You've got a filthy mind!' She pushed my shoulder playfully. 'No, it was nothing like that. Mind you, she'd already taken a shine to your mate Harry. That was why she was in such a state. She knew she couldn't flirt with him while Sinclair was watching her. It was like her father was in the room. Anyway, he'd invited her out for a drive on Saturday morning and she wasn't sure if she should accept.'

'A drive? With Harry?'

'Yes. Nice drive out into the country. I told her to go for it. You only live once. If she's going to be chained to some poxy minor royal for the rest of her life, she might as well have a bit of fun first.'

'So she went off with Harry on Saturday morning? In *my* car?'

'Oh, was it yours? Nice set of wheels you got there. Yes, they went off together. You didn't really think she had a headache, did you?

That damned American. The insolence of the fellow. It wasn't enough to seduce the twenty-one year old daughter of a former cabinet minister, he had to do it in *my* Morris Oxford. If he had damaged the upholstery, I would swing for him...

'I think she must have slipped down the back stairs with her maid and met up with him outside. Ducked down in the back of your car and off they went into Aylesbury for a few hours. And good luck to them, I say.'

Aylesbury. That didn't sound terribly romantic. And it wasn't a particularly long drive, either. It was clearly more of a 'getting-to-know-you' trip than a '*really*-getting-to-know-you' trip. Harry had shown remarkable restraint, by his standards. He had waited until after dark before making his final move. The fellow was a romantic at heart. I smiled quietly at the thought, but my good humour was cut short. Mrs Smith was tripping up the banisters behind us.

'Do you have to block the whole of the stairs?' she muttered angrily.

'We don't have to, love,' Lettie replied, pushing herself back against the window, 'we just thought it would be a good laugh.'

Mrs Smith glared at the two of us as she squeezed past. 'I would expect this of *her*,' she grumbled, 'but I thought rather better of *you*, Sir Hilary.' Having made her disapproval abundantly clear, she disappeared up onto the landing.

'Toffee nosed cow,' said Lettie, not bothering to keep her voice low.

I laughed. 'Miss Young, you're unbelievable.'

She grinned, placing a hand on my arm to steady herself as she pulled herself upright from the window. 'Call me Lettie.'

'Very well, "Lettie".'

She looked away for a moment. 'You're all right, you are.'

I raised an eyebrow. 'You mean I'm not really "a stuck-up prig who wouldn't know a good time if it smacked me in the face"?'

'Oh you're that too.' She grinned. 'But I'm not fussy. Shame you're married really. I could quite fancy you.'

I coughed in surprise. 'This is hardly the time or place for flirting.'

'There's never a right time, lover boy.' Her eyes were mocking me now. She leaned in close, to prevent anyone overhearing. 'You never been tempted to stray?'

The unexpected line of questioning had me flustered. 'I...have, once or twice,' I admitted, speaking more honestly than I had intended. 'But not...with girls,' I added.

'Oh.' Lettie blinked. 'Blimey.'

I'm not quite sure why I chose to confide in her at that moment. Harry had always assumed that I was a closet homosexual and I doubted the idea would come as a surprise to Lettie, even if it wasn't exactly true. 'You're not shocked?' I asked her.

'Gawd, no. Get all sorts in the theatre. You just don't look the type.'

If only she knew the truth, I thought. But it was flattering to know that she liked me. Perhaps her taste in men wasn't quite as vulgar as I had first supposed.

'Come on, let's go and see how Miss Jones is getting on.'

Lady Fanny Leon had a private suite in the south east of the house. I knocked gingerly on the door. I wasn't quite sure what I was doing here now. A five minute conversation with Lettie had answered more questions than I had managed to figure out for myself in the last thirty-six hours. I doubted there was much more Felicity Mandeville Jones could tell me. Except perhaps why somebody might want to murder her. That might be worth another few minutes of my time, I supposed, before I finally leapt into the Morris Oxford and made my escape.

A maidservant answered the door. She was a plain thing with a helpful face set against a dowdy grey dress. At sight of us, she gave a quick bob. 'May I help you?'

'Yes. I was wondering if we might have a word with Miss Jones,' I said. 'I gather from the Colonel that Lady Fanny has been looking after her.'

'She's not here, sir,' the maid replied. 'Miss Jones, I mean. Begging your pardon, sir. She went back to her room five minutes ago.'

'She ain't on her own, is she?' Lettie asked, with some concern. It would be madness for the girl to be left unsupervised with a murderer on the loose.

'No, miss. Her maid was with her. The Colonel said she wasn't to be left on her own.'

'Quite right,' I agreed. 'How is Lady Fanny coping with it all?' I peered past the maid, through the doorway, but there was no sign of our hostess. Not that I had a particularly good view.

The maid glanced back nervously. 'She's a bit shaken, sir. We all are. This is a quiet house. Nothing like this has ever happened here before. She says the Colonel wants it all covered up.'

'Probably for the best,' I agreed. 'We don't want any gossip. You understand?'

'Yes, sir. Of course. Sir Vincent made that very clear to all the servants.'

I nodded. 'Good girl!'

'Daisy! Come here!' Lady Fanny was calling from the depths of the bedroom.

The maid jumped. 'Yes, miss!' She bobbed her head at us again, apologetically. 'I've got to go. Lady Fanny's getting ready for church.' The door closed quickly, before we had the chance to reply.

I pulled out my fob watch. 'What time did they say the service was?'

Lettie couldn't remember. 'Half past ten? Not for ages yet, anyway. Why, you thinking of going?'

'Hardly. I'm not exactly the church going type.'

Lettie took my arm again. 'You and me neither,' she agreed.

We made our way back along the lower landing and

146

reached the steps leading up towards my room. Mary Smith was heading in the opposite direction, along the upper hallway, having doubtless ascertained that her bedroom had not been inappropriately ransacked by the servants during their recent search. Her scandalized look when she saw Lettie and I arriving arm in arm at the top of the stairs forced the adoption of an innocent expression on both our faces, at least until she had passed us by. This time, the "toffee-nosed cow" refrained from comment as she descended the stairs.

We continued along the upper landing and came to a halt outside one of the bedrooms at the far end. This was the room that now belonged to Felicity Mandeville Jones.

I took a deep breath and knocked.

It had been a strange twenty-four hours for the young debutante. Goodness knows how she was coping with it all. The poor girl had gone for a drive with a man she barely knew, been dragged into a row with a prominent journalist, surrendered her virtue in a night of ill-advised passion with a dubious American, before finally being suspected of murder. And now it appeared she was a possible target for assassination. Her weekend away had been almost as disastrous as my own. Perhaps the joy of her first sexual encounter had mitigated the horror of events somewhat, but I doubted it. Even with a seasoned professional like Harry, it was bound to have been a little bit clumsy. It was her first time, after all.

There was no reply to the knock on the door. Lettie and I exchanged worried glances. I couldn't quite bring myself to enter Miss Jones' boudoir uninvited, but Lettie had no such qualms. She grabbed the handle of the door and pushed inside.

I followed behind apprehensively.

The room was empty. There was no sign of Felicity Mandeville Jones or her maid.

Chapter Seventeen

The bedroom was in a state of some disarray. The sheets were scattered across the bed, untouched since before breakfast, and there were two crystal glasses on the bedside table, with the dregs of whatever Harry and Felicity Mandeville Jones had been drinking. That was careless, I thought, to leave it in full view like that for the servants to see. Ordinarily a chamber maid would have been in here by now to change the sheets and clean the room, but with most of the staff away for the weekend the handful of remaining servants were having a difficult job coping. The valets and ladies maids considered changing sheets to be beneath their dignity and the valets in any case had been far too busy searching the rooms to even think about tidying them up.

I strode across to the window. 'Where did she go?' I wondered aloud, gazing out across the lawn to the steeple of St Mary's church in the middle distance. 'She didn't pass us on the landing.'

'She must have slipped down the back stairs,' Lettie suggested, coming over to stand next to me by the window. 'Like she did yesterday morning.' The servants had their own set of stairs running down the back of the house. The footmen and chamber maids could clomp up and down there all day without disturbing the guests.

'Stupid girl,' I muttered. 'She shouldn't go wandering off on her own.' I glanced across at Lettie. 'I suppose we'd better find out where she's got to.'

'You don't think she's scarpered?'

'Lord, I hope not. But why the devil would she?'

Lettie gave a face. 'Wouldn't you, if you thought someone might be trying to blow your head off?'

'I suppose so.' There was always a chance the murderer might have a second go. I looked back at the dishevelled bed and noticed a small bottle of sleeping pills lying on the bedside table next to the decanter. Perhaps they belonged to Dottie. A dribble of wine was left in the glass decanter, but not much.

This was not Harry's usual tipple but he was always prepared to make concessions if it served his ends. 'Back stairs, then, I suppose?'

Lettie nodded. 'Back stairs.' We headed for the door.

I hoped to goodness Miss Jones was still in the house, and hadn't made a break for Bletchley rail station. It wouldn't look good if she'd fled a murder scene, especially if she were to blab about anything that had happened here. I growled. This was all we needed. I had enough problems of my own, without worrying about some silly girl taking fright. No, that was not fair. Lettie was right. The Honourable Felicity Mandeville Jones had good reason to be afraid.

We closed the bedroom door and Lettie directed me along the hallway. There was another, shorter corridor at the far end, off to the right. This led to Mr and Mrs Smiths' bedroom and I was half tempted to stick my head inside to see what the married couple had been so worried about the Colonel's search uncovering. Unfortunately, there wasn't time. Actually, I needed to visit the bathroom too, but there wasn't time for that, either.

The back stairs were rather less impressive than the ones at the front of the house. There were no grand archways or heavily decorated marble pillars in this part of the mansion, just a narrow wooden staircase with a functional banister painted a dull beige. It is often the way. No matter how grand the house, the servants' quarters are always painfully utilitarian.

The bottom of the stairs led through to the servants hall, not far from the bathroom I had used to clean myself up the night before. A door off to the right led to an alcove intersecting the ballroom and the billiard hall. Lettie was ahead of me. She swept into the billiard room, but I saw a flicker of movement the other way.

'Hang on a minute,' I said.

Lettie glanced back. I gestured to her and she moved across to take a look.

Felicity Mandeville Jones was standing over by the window in the far corner of the ballroom, her body enfolded in the protective embrace of a rather large American. Harry

Latimer had his back to us and the couple were stood silently together, Felicity with her eyes screwed shut, sobbing gently. The two of them had not seen us arrive.

Lettie and I exchanged looks.

For some people, it would have been a shocking sight, an unmarried man and a young girl locked together like that. Anthony Sinclair had certainly been shocked; enraged even. But this was not some illicit assignation, as it had been the night before. There was no money riding on the outcome of this event. It was simply one human being giving comfort to another. I would never have believed Harry capable of it. He had already won his wager and had nothing to gain from this. But he had nothing to lose either and even my American friend would not refuse comfort to a damsel in distress. This was one of those rare moments when I *did* admire Harry Latimer.

Felicity Mandeville Jones had bolted from her room, dismissed her maid and sought comfort in the arms of her new lover. She had been given firm instructions to remain with Lady Fanny Leon, but it was understandable that she would feel the need to seek out Harry Latimer. The American could provide the kind of reassurance that nobody else would. It was still something of a risk, however, to be caught in such a firm embrace, when anyone might walk in and jump to precisely the right conclusion.

I was about to clear my throat and announce our presence, but Lettie caught my eye and shook her head. *Let them be*, she seemed to say, without actually voicing the words. I nodded. Nothing untoward was happening here and Felicity Mandeville Jones deserved her moment of consolation.

It had been a trying night for everyone.

My man Hargreaves was hovering on the upper landing as I returned to the first floor via the back stairs. My bladder felt like it was about to burst and the guest facilities on the south side were much more comfortable than anything the servants quarters had to offer. Hargreaves had seen me, however, and scurried over to accost me before my hand had even reached the handle of the WC. 'Sir, may I have a word?'

I waved him away with my hands. 'Not now, man. Can't you see I'm busy?' My bladder was on the point of rupturing.

'It is important, sir.'

I sighed. If Hargreaves was finding the nerve to insist, it probably *was* important. Nature would have to wait. 'Oh very well.' I gestured along the corridor.

We were not far from my bedroom. I pulled out the key from my pocket but was irritated to find the door was already open. The servants had been searching, of course, but they might have locked up after themselves. 'Well, what is it?' I said, passing through. 'This had better be important, Hargreaves.'

The valet followed me inside. 'Perhaps if we could close the door, sir?'

'Oh, for goodness' sake.' But I could see the fellow was in earnest. 'Very well.'

I let him close the door and we moved towards the bed. I had tidied the bed sheets myself but there was no sign of any other cleaning up. The chambermaids had not been near the place, even if the valets had. I sat down on the bed and crossed my legs tightly. There was a suitcase over by the wardrobe. Hargreaves had done as I'd instructed and packed everything neatly away. The servants had probably searched the case since then, but they had at least locked it up. Shame they hadn't bothered to be so conscientious with the door.

Hargreaves was hovering awkwardly.

'Well, what is it, man?'

The valet swallowed hard. His hands were shaking. It really was something important. 'It's about…the dining room table, sir.'

I grunted. 'Yes, what about it?'

Hargreaves took a deep breath. 'The Colonel said that that was where they discovered Mr Sinclair's body. Underneath the table, sir.'

'Yes, I know. I was there.' I glared at the manservant. His face was as white as a sheet. And all at once I understood.

Hargreaves and I had crept into the dining room together, a couple of hours before breakfast. We had tip-toed in quietly, at my behest, and had taken a quick look underneath that very table. My valet could sometimes be a bit dense, and damnably obsequious too, but he wasn't a fool. He could put two and two together. And now that he had heard about Sinclair, he had done just that.

Hargreaves was beginning to stutter. It was painful to watch. 'I…I was wondering, sir…if…if…'

I closed my eyes. There was no point in denying it. I had been meaning to tell him anyway. If Hargreaves was to help me escape from Bletchley Park it was better he knew the facts. And if he had guessed the truth on his own, there was no harm in confirming it. At least I knew I could count on his discretion, though it was still rather galling, having to *confess* such a crime to an employee.

'There was an accident,' I said, as matter-of-factly as I could manage. 'Sinclair and I had a bit of an argument. He overheard my conversation with Doctor Lefranc and was threatening to expose me.'

'I see.'

'So then I accused him – wrongly, as it turns out – of having an extra-marital relationship with Felicity Mandeville Jones. He blew his top and there was a bit of a fight.'

'I thought you looked a little dishevelled, sir, yesterday evening. And that cut on your lip...'

I brought a hand up to my mouth. It was barely noticeable. I had checked in the mirror. But that was exactly the kind of thing Hargreaves *would* notice. 'Very observant.'

'And you…hit Mr Sinclair with the poker, sir?'

'I was just trying to hurt him. I wasn't trying to kill the fellow. He fell against one of those wooden pillars. Banged his head. And that was that.' Hargreaves nodded. 'It was an accident,' I insisted. 'Could have happened to anyone.'

'Of course, sir.'

Briefly, I outlined my efforts to get the body out of the house and the reasons for leaving it under the table. None of it sounded remotely sane in the cold light of day. I let out a sigh.

'Dreadful mess, isn't it?'

'Yes, sir.'

There was an embarrassed pause. I didn't know quite what else to say. 'I'm thinking of running,' I managed eventually, heaving another long sigh. 'It might be my only option.'

Hargreaves considered this for a moment. 'It wouldn't be easy, sir. There'd be no going back. Your life could never be the same again.'

'I know that! But what choice do I have? I don't want to go to prison.'

Hargreaves sat down on the bed. Ordinarily, I would have chastised him for his effrontery, but I didn't have the energy to complain. 'It might not come to that, sir. Perhaps if you were to speak to the Colonel. Tell him the truth.'

'Don't be ridiculous. He couldn't let something like that go.'

'If it was an accident, sir...?'

'It makes no difference, Hargreaves. A crime is a crime.'

'But as I understand it, the Colonel is keen to avoid a scandal. That's what he said to the servants, sir. He wouldn't want a public trial.'

I shook my head. 'There were two murders, man. If he lets me get away with one, does he let the other murderer go free?'

'That's different, sir.'

'Is it? I'm not so sure that it is.' I sighed again. 'I think I may just have to cut and run. Do you fancy another trip to France?'

'If that's what you want, sir.' Hargreaves did not sound enthusiastic, though I knew he would do whatever I asked.

I glanced at the bedside table. 'Pour me a drink, will you? I could do with one.' My bladder was full, but my throat was suddenly feeling rather parched.

Hargreaves reached over and poured out some whisky from the bottle on the table. He passed the tumbler across and I gulped it down in one.

'You're a good fellow, Hargreaves.' I coughed.

'I…try to be, sir.' He placed a gentle hand on my leg. It was an attempt at reassurance, but it was going too far. I growled at him and he removed the hand at once.

'I will need to speak to the Colonel before I go.' I stood up and handed the tumbler back. 'See if we can't shed some light on this other matter, before I head for the hills.' I was too involved now not to want to find out what was going on. I could probably afford to stay at Bletchley for another half hour, at least until the men from London arrived.

'He's down in the morning room, sir. The Colonel. With Mr and Mrs Smith.' So the interviews had started already.

'I'd better get down there,' I said. 'And you'd better see to the car. Get the luggage packed away. Make sure Harry really did fill up the tank.'

'Of course, sir.'

Another thought struck me as I headed for the door. 'You don't think I had anything to do with the murder of Dorothy Kilbride, do you?'

My valet was unequivocal. 'No, sir. Definitely not.' There was a ghost of a smile on his lips. 'I put you to bed myself. You were in no fit state to murder anyone.'

Chapter Eighteen

As I came down the stairs – with my bladder now blissfully relieved – my attention was caught by the shrill warble of the telephone in the hallway. I ducked back into the entrance hall and pulled out my pocket watch. It was ten past nine on a Sunday morning. Who on earth could be phoning at this time? I let the telephone ring for a moment, but then a horrible thought struck me: it might be Anthony Sinclair's people. They could be calling back with more details about my private life. I would have to answer it and put them off.

I hurried across and lifted the receiver. 'Hello, Bletchley Park.'

There was a nervous voice on the other end of the line. 'Good morning. May I speak to Mr John Smith, please?'

I breathed a sigh of relief. Nothing to do with me. Now where the hell was Mr Smith? Ah, yes. He was in with the Colonel. 'Who's calling please?' I asked.

'Mr Butterworth. Sidney Butterworth. His chief clerk.'

'All right. Just a moment, Mr Butterworth. I'll see if I can find him.' Taking a message on the telephone would normally put me in a foul mood. Having to deliver it to some fat idiot might make me lose my temper altogether. But this was a good excuse to interrupt proceedings in the morning room and I wasn't going to waste it. I placed the receiver down on the table and made my way along the hall.

The morning room was off to the right, along a short corridor that also gave access to the library. Lady Fanny Leon's suite was directly above it. I knocked politely on the door, but entered without waiting for a reply.

The Colonel was sitting with his back to the window. The morning room was a bright, cluttered space, smaller than the library, but lined with book-filled cabinets and various items of decorative crockery. Edward Townsend, the Colonel's valet, was sitting to his master's right, scribbling notes in a small black book. Mr and Mrs Smith were opposite them, in front of the door.

I brought a hand up to my face, to shield my eyes. There was far too much light flooding into the room. A set of large bay windows had been installed deliberately to catch the morning sunlight. The Colonel had the right idea, I thought, sitting with his back to the damn things.

'Sorry to disturb you,' I said. 'There's a telephone call for Mr Smith. A Mr Butterworth?'

Smith nodded. 'I'd better take it, Sir Vincent.' He rose to his feet.

The Colonel waved a hand. 'I think we're finished with you for now. Thank you for your time, Smith. Mrs Smith.'

I stood back from the doorway as the married couple departed.

The Colonel smiled at me. 'As you're here, Butler, you might as well be next.' He gestured to the recently vacated seats. 'Close the door, will you? Take a chair.'

I did as I was instructed. The Colonel's man looked up from his notes as I settled myself down, his face an unreadable block of stone.

'Bad business, this,' the Colonel observed.

'I'll say.'

'Townsend and I are just going through the times, working out where everybody was when the murders took place.'

I nodded. That seemed a sensible thing to do.

'Let's start with Sinclair. Now most of us were in the ballroom when he was killed. Mr and Mrs Smith. Professor Singh. Doctor Lefranc. Lady Fanny Leon, of course. And the band. And most of the servants. The only exceptions were yourself, Latimer, Miss Young and Miss Jones.'

I blanched. 'And Dottie. Er...Miss Kilbride.'

The Colonel's expression darkened. 'Yes, and poor Dottie.'

'Miss Young and I were helping her up to her room. Or what we thought was her room. That was at about, what, half past eleven? A quarter to twelve?'

'Something like that,' the Colonel agreed.

'I had a bit of a chat with Miss Young. Then I came

downstairs and was heading back to the dance floor when I heard a bit of an argument going on in the drawing room. A man and a woman.'

'Did you hear what was said?'

'No. I was just passing by.'

'But you think it was probably Miss Jones and Anthony Sinclair?'

'I believe so.'

'What did you do then?'

'Well, I was feeling a little sick, to be honest. I'd had a bit too much to drink and I needed to visit the little boy's room. Unfortunately, the cloakroom was occupied, so I snuck through the house to the servants' quarters and used the facilities there. Then I bumped into your man Townsend on the way back to the main hall.'

Townsend acknowledged the truth of that. 'You were a little bit the worse for wear, Sir Hilary, if you don't mind me saying.'

I glared at the valet for a moment. It was hardly his place to comment. But given the circumstances I decided to let it go. 'I had drunk quite a lot,' I confessed.

The Colonel laughed. 'I'll say! Poor old Mrs Smith. Ha ha! Didn't know what hit her.'

'Yes, well...' I coughed with embarrassment.

'And of course you were fast asleep at the time of the second murder. Heard you snoring away when I found the body,' the Colonel explained. 'And you'd hardly have woken up, killed her and gone back to bed, now would you?'

'Er...no.'

'But the first murder. Have to be scrupulous here, Butler. There were a few minutes there where you might have got into a fight with Sinclair.'

'You surely don't think...?'

'Have to explore every possibility. Nothing personal, old chap. You didn't see Latimer at all?'

'Not until I got back to the ballroom. But Harry wouldn't kill anybody. Except perhaps in self-defence.'

The Colonel frowned. 'I'm not so sure, Butler. He's

157

always been a rather shady character. Of course, the girls have no real alibi either. But I spoke to Miss Jones at some length before breakfast and I don't think she can have had anything to do with it. She's quite a child, that one. Don't think she could have faked her reactions.'

'No,' I agreed. 'She does seem rather wet behind the ears.' Felicity Mandeville Jones was barely twenty-one years old. 'Seems a bit young to be involved with the Security Services,' I observed. 'What does she do? A bit of typing?' MI5 had always made a point of placing young aristocratic women in junior roles. It was a standing joke that most of the organisation's typists were of a higher social status than the people they reported to.

'Translation, actually,' the Colonel replied. 'Speaks fluent German. Can be jolly useful. Her uncle was the British Ambassador to Berlin.' He adjusted his monocle. 'And as for Miss Lettie Young…well. I've known her since she was a baby. She's a little minx. No better than she ought to be, as Mrs Smith would say. Ha ha! But I don't believe she would bludgeon someone to death, even in anger. So that just leaves Latimer and you.'

I nodded quietly. I had been so busy defending Harry and the others that I had all but laid the finger of suspicion on myself. Perhaps Hargreaves was right. Maybe now was the time to confess and throw myself on the Colonel's mercy. Then at least we could concentrate on the identity of Dorothy Kilbride's murderer. I clenched my hands uncertainly, but the moment passed before I could bring myself to say anything.

'The thing of it is, Butler,' the Colonel continued. 'You don't have any motive that I can see. But Latimer, well, I could quite see him getting into an argument with Sinclair about Miss Jones.'

'Did she tell you about…?'

'About Latimer spending the night with her? Oh, she told me. In the strictest confidence, of course. Foolish girl. Letting herself be led astray like that.'

'Harry can be very persuasive.'

'Yes. It's him I blame. He could charm the legs off a

billiard table, that one. Ha ha! I suppose he boasted about it to you, did he?'

'We're...old friends.'

'Hardly an excuse. He's a bit of a devil, that one. No two ways about it. And I'm sorry to say it, Butler, but he *is* the most likely suspect, at least where Sinclair is concerned. But innocent until proven guilty and all that. I'm rather more concerned about the second...' A knock at the door cut the Colonel off in mid sentence. 'Seems rather a morning for interruptions,' he said. 'Come!'

To my surprise, it was Thomas Hargreaves. 'What are you doing here?' I demanded. He was supposed to be smuggling my luggage out to the Morris Oxford. But perhaps he had been side-tracked.

'I'm sorry, sir, but Lady Fanny sent me. She's about to address the servants down in the kitchens and she wondered, Sir Vincent, if you would be able to spare Mr Townsend for a few moments?'

'Of course,' the Colonel replied, gesturing to his valet. 'Capital idea. I said she ought to have a word with them. Make sure there's no gossip. Got to keep a lid on things.'

'What time are the regular staff due back?' I asked.

'Not until this evening, thankfully. We'll have to get Sinclair moved before then. Don't want the head groom stumbling over the corpse when he returns to his little cottage. Be a bit of a shock, what?'

'I'll say!'

Townsend rose to his feet. He handed the notebook to the Colonel. 'I'll be back shortly, sir,' he said, following Hargreaves out the door and closing it politely behind him.

Sir Vincent and I were left alone in the morning room.

'Useful fellow that,' the Colonel declared, glancing down at the notebook. 'Awful handwriting though. '

'You said he was a policeman during the war?'

'That's right. Left under a bit of a cloud, actually. Trade unionist, you know. Got the sack for going on strike.'

I laughed. 'And you think he's the right man to investigate a murder?'

'Oh, he's as solid as a rock. Been with me for years. None finer. And everyone's allowed the odd mistake.'

'What happened to the other fellow?' I asked. When I'd first known Sir Vincent, before the war, another man had served him as valet. 'Cameron, was it?'

'Oh, yes. Sad story. Got blown to bits, poor chap. May 1915.'

'In the trenches?'

'No. He was visiting his mother in Stepney. A Zeppelin came over and flattened the house.'

'Good lord.'

'Awful bad luck. Mind you, he was always unlucky, that one. Had a leg blown of at Mafeking.'

'I remember he had a limp.'

'That damn tin leg.' The Colonel laughed. 'Could hear it a mile off. Useless for cloak and dagger work. Ha ha! Had another chap working for me through the rest of the war, but he retired in 1922. And Townsend's been with me since then. Actually, we're lucky to have him this weekend. By rights he should be visiting his sister. She's a bit poorly at the moment, so I gather. But he didn't want to let me down, what with the reunion.'

'Does Townsend have a set of house keys?' I asked.

The Colonel nodded. 'The butler left him all the keys on Friday afternoon. And there's another bunch in the office. Why do you ask?'

'I was just thinking...you heard about Harry's revolver?'

The Colonel's expression darkened. 'Yes. From Doctor Lefranc. Another matter I need to raise with our American friend.'

'The revolver was kept in a holdall in Harry's bedroom and the door was always locked. So whoever stole it and shot Dottie must have had a key to get in.'

'Doesn't follow. Anyone could pick a lock, Butler. You're not suggesting my man had anything to do with it?'

'No, of course not. I'm just saying...we can't rule out the servants. Any one of them could have grabbed those keys from the butler's office.'

'Even your man Hargreaves,' the Colonel suggested.

I laughed at the idea. 'He's no more a murderer than I am.' It was only after I had said this that I realised the absurdity of it, but I managed to cover my embarrassment. 'Mind you, none of the servants would know about the mix up over the rooms.'

'That's true. Or about that revolver. But you're right,' he agreed. 'Have to consider these things, Butler. No one is above suspicion.'

Even the Colonel was a legitimate suspect, according to Doctor Lefranc. 'So where were you at half past three,' I enquired, 'as a matter of interest?' I couldn't resist asking, though I no more suspected Sir Vincent of murder than I did my own valet.

The Colonel chuckled. 'A fair question, Butler. Ha ha! As it happens, I was in the ballroom at half past three, talking to the Johnnie Hazelwood Orchestra as they were packing up. Then I went down to the kitchens to make sure the caterers had left a bit of food out for them before they headed off. The band came along and we had a bit of a chinwag there. An extended night cap, you know the sort of thing. I was just about to head off to bed when the whole Sinclair thing kicked off.'

'You didn't get any sleep at all?'

'I can do without sleep. I'm not going to rest until this business is cleared up.'

That I could believe. 'Your man Townsend said at breakfast that Harry's gun had been found.'

'That's right. And the silencer that went with it. Never seen one attached to a revolver before.'

'And you're sure it's the weapon that was used to kill Dottie...Miss Kilbride?'

'No doubt about it. Two shots fired within the last few hours and one of the bullets recovered from the headboard matches it precisely.'

'Have you tested the gun for fingerprints?'

'Not yet. But we've got it under lock and key. When my chaps get here from London, they can examine it properly.' He glanced at a clock. 'They should be here within the hour.'

'You didn't say where the gun was found.'

The Colonel frowned. 'No. It was a bit tricky with everyone there at breakfast. Didn't want people throwing accusations around. I can trust you not to blab, though.' He leant forward. 'It was found underneath a pillow in Professor Singh's bedroom.'

'Good lord. *Professor Singh*?'

'I'm afraid so.'

I blinked. That was the last place I'd have expected to find it. 'So…do you think *he* was the murderer?'

'Difficult to say. Singh's an intelligent chap. Seems a bit daft, leaving a weapon for someone to find in your own bedroom. As the man himself said, this second murder was obviously premeditated. The killer must have had some plan to dispose of the weapon.'

'Perhaps it's a double bluff,' I suggested.

'He's not *that* clever, Butler.'

'But would he have any motive? For killing Dottie, I mean. Doctor Lefranc said he did some work for you in India.'

The Colonel nodded. 'A case officer. Not a terribly good one, it has to be said. Bright chap, but academic, not good with people. And the intelligence he provided was distinctly low grade. Called it a day after a year or two.'

'You don't think he might have been faking some of it? The intelligence, I mean?'

'It's possible. It does happen.' The Colonel leant back in his chair. 'We had one chap who invented a whole roster of agents. None of them existed at all. Ha ha! He compiled his reports from newspaper clippings. We found him out in the end, though. We have ways of checking these things.'

'Perhaps Dottie found the professor out. If he was claiming money for phantom agents.'

'Maybe. It's all a bit thin, though. Singh just doesn't strike me as the murdering type.'

'Is there a type?'

The Colonel shrugged. 'No idea. Murder's not really my forte.'

'And I suppose the professor wouldn't have known about the mix up over the rooms.'

'No. Or about the revolver. I hate to say it, Butler, but the most likely suspect is your man Latimer. He brought that revolver here. No one else could have known about it beforehand. And a silencer too. You don't carry one of those for self defence.'

'But Harry's no assassin,' I insisted. 'And he's one of the few people here who'd never met Dorothy Kilbride. In any case, he spent the night...' I stopped myself, but the Colonel already knew about Miss Jones so there was no harm in repeating it. 'In any case, he spent the night with Felicity Mandeville Jones.'

The Colonel sighed. 'Yes. That does give him something of an alibi. Miss Jones confessed the whole contretemps to me this morning. According to her, they were together from half past midnight until about six thirty.'

I nodded. That fitted with what I knew. 'Unless one of them fell asleep for a few minutes.' Or had been put to sleep, I thought suddenly, remembering the sleeping pills on the bedside table.

'What, you think he might have crept out for ten minutes, grabbed the gun, shot Dottie and then crept back into bed?'

'Not Harry,' I thought. 'It's not his style.' And murder would have been the last thing on Felicity's mind.

The Colonel yawned suddenly. 'I don't know, Butler. A bit of a rum do all this. Hell of a way to celebrate an anniversary.' All at once, just for an instant, Sir Vincent looked very tired. But he recovered quickly. 'The timing couldn't be worse,' he said, leaning forward confidentially. 'We can't afford a scandal right now. This new Labour government, they really don't trust us. Even the Prime Minister won't talk to me directly. We have to communicate through intermediaries. Mind you, I can't say I blame him, after that cock-up with the Zinoviev letter.'

I nodded. I remembered the scandal. It was old news now, but the wound still festered. The Labour Party had lost a general election back in 1924, after a letter had been leaked to the press connecting the party with an international communist organisation. The correspondence had been authenticated by the secret service, but it had turned out to be a forgery. Now Labour had won an election, they had every reason to bear a grudge.

'If there's a scandal, they could well shut us down altogether. Hand everything over to Special Branch.'

'Lord,' I said. That didn't bear thinking about. Scotland Yard were famed for their incompetence. Most of the arrests they did make were as a result of intelligence received from MI5.

'I'm not going to let that happen,' the Colonel insisted. 'Don't worry, Butler. We've been through worse affairs than this and come out the other end. And I daresay there'll be others in the future.'

Out in the hallway, the telephone started to ring.

The Colonel flipped shut his notebook. 'I think that's everything for now.' He sat back in his chair. 'I suppose you'd better send in your chap Latimer next. I think we need a very long talk.'

Chapter Nineteen

Professor Singh was dozing serenely in a leather armchair. He looked peaceful resting there, his head dipped down into his chest, his dreams no doubt full of arcane philosophical theories rather than anything actually useful, but a benign figure nonetheless. It is difficult to think badly of anyone when you watch them sleeping, even a know-it-all like the professor. And despite the incriminating evidence of the Newton .32 under his pillow, I couldn't really believe he was capable of murder.

I moved into the library and poured myself a whisky from a handily placed decanter left over from the previous evening.

John Smith was sitting at a small table nearby, quietly reading the morning paper. He was an altogether less attractive figure than the professor. His over-sized belly congealed unpleasantly in his lap, but the man seemed ill at ease. He was dressed as smartly as he could manage, waiting for his wife to come down a second time so that the two of them could head off for church.

I wondered if the telephone call he'd received had riled him. He did seem somewhat agitated.

A second call, twenty minutes later, had been answered by Doctor Lefranc. I was on my way to the billiard room at this point, to summon Harry for his interview. 'It is the Colonel's men,' the doctor explained, placing a hand over the receiver. 'Their vehicle has broken down and they will not be here until at least midday.' That was one piece of good news, anyway. I left Lefranc to pass the message on to Sir Vincent while I provided the summons for my American friend.

Harry was in the games room, watching with some amusement as Felicity Mandeville Jones tried to teach Lettie Young to play billiards. The variety star was absolutely hopeless. She laughed as the end of the cue slipped out of her fingers and scraped across the green, missing all three of the balls.

'Bleedin' hell!' she exclaimed. 'I'll never get the hang

of this!'

'Darling, you just need to keep your other hand steady,' Miss Jones explained patiently. 'Don't grip the cue too tightly.'

The impromptu lesson was providing a useful distraction.

I caught Harry's eye and drew him away from the table. 'The Colonel wants you,' I said.

Harry grinned. 'How'd it go with you?' he asked, as we left the billiard room and walked together through the main hall.

'All right, I think.' I breathed deeply. 'He's not too happy with you though, after your shenanigans with Miss Jones last night.'

Harry chuckled. 'Hey, a guy can't help being popular.'

'This is serious, Harry. Be careful what you say to him. I think you're his main suspect.'

'Don't worry, old man. I can take care of myself.'

That I had no doubt of.

In the library, Mr Smith had looked up from his copy of the Sunday Times. 'Sir Hilary,' he acknowledged, as I poured myself that whisky. 'What a bloody mess, eh?'

'I've had better days,' I admitted.

'I thought this weekend would be a nice break for the wife, away from all the usual worries. But it's been a bloody nightmare. I wish I'd never got involved with the Security Service.'

'I know the feeling. Are you still involved with them, then?' It was an impertinent question, but I couldn't resist asking. 'Or did they pension you off?' Most of the guests were former MI5 employees, but a few of them remained on the payroll. 'Sorry. None of my business really.'

Smith shrugged. 'It's no big secret, son. Aye, I'm still active, just about. But I don't do anything important. I'm just a middle man.' He lowered his voice slightly and leaned forward. 'We've got people working undercover, in the trade union movement. Informers, you know. Keeping an eye on the reds.'

'Yes, so I gather.' I had handled a few trade union reports myself, back before the war.

'They send their reports to me and I pass them on. I don't even read them half the time. I'm just another layer of deniability.' His nose wrinkled with distaste. 'Anything I can do to stop those buggers bringing the country to a halt every five minutes. Not that's it done me much good.' He sighed. 'Things are going from bad to worse.'

'That phone call. Was it bad news?'

'Aye. The office got a telegram from New York yesterday evening. You remember that company I were telling you about? The American one.'

How could I forget, after he had droned on all that time, while I had been trying to watch a game of croquet.

'They have a director, Mr Muldoon. Well, apparently he had a heart attack yesterday afternoon. He'll be in hospital for weeks and there'll be no decisions on anything; not for some time, any road. And by then it'll be too late. I'll be bloody ruined. And I tell you, son, it's all down to those bloody unions.'

I gulped down the whisky. 'That's too bad, Mr Smith.'

'Oh, it don't matter for me. I can do without. Self-made man, I am.' There was a hint of pride in his words. 'I know how to look after myself. But the wife, she's used to a proper standard of living. And I'm her husband. I should be providing it for her.'

'You might be able to salvage something. All those factories, must be worth a bit.'

'Not when the creditors move in.' He sighed again. 'I'll be lucky to get out with the clothes I stand in. I've already pawned all the jewellery. The wife doesn't even know. Me sending her up there to check they hadn't been stolen and they're not worth two ha'pennies. We've got nothing left to sell.'

'Something's bound to turn up.' I insisted. The fellow was getting maudlin. 'Got to look on the bright side, eh?'

'I suppose.'

Our conversation had roused Professor Singh. He rubbed his eyes and looked past us to the doorway. 'Mrs Smith.' He smiled. 'You are looking most radiant this morning.'

167

My head snapped round. Mrs Smith was standing with her arms crossed in the door of the library. Her husband tensed as she dipped her head in frosty acknowledgement of the professor. Her expression was unreadable 'Are you ready for church, Jonathan?' she asked.

Mr Smith placed his hands on the arms of his chair and manoeuvred his great bulk into a vertical position. 'Aye, I'm coming, love.' He glanced at a watch on his wrist. 'Plenty of time.'

How long Mrs Smith had been standing in the doorway was impossible to judge. If she had overheard anything her husband had said, she was not showing it. The man himself moved past me towards the door. Professor Singh rose to his feet too, though whether out of politeness or with the intention of joining the happy couple I was not immediately sure.

Lady Fanny Leon had arrived in the entrance hall with her housekeeper and a couple of maids. She was dressed in black – wholly appropriate given the circumstances – and to look at her you would not have known this was anything other than an ordinary Sunday. She possessed that wonderful unflappability that is the hallmark of a true aristocrat, something the Mrs Smith's of this world could only ever aspire to.

'Will you be joining us, Sir Hilary?' Lady Fanny enquired as I popped my head out of the side hall. Her voice had a commanding depth, a powerful combination of age and breeding.

'I'm feeling a little tired,' I apologised. 'I think I might just sit and read the morning papers.' I have never been a great church goer and the last thing I needed was some pompous vicar droning on about charity and virtue.

Mrs Smith gave a disdainful snort. She glanced pointedly at the whisky glass in my hand. 'I don't think that will help,' she said.

I made a point of draining the glass. 'We all worship in our own way, Mrs Smith. Don't let me keep you.' Bloody woman. It wasn't as if her husband was any kind of saint, selling off her jewellery like that, without even telling her. To hell with both of them, I thought. I had better things to worry about.

The party moved along the hallway and out through the vestibule. Some of the valets and ladies maids had joined the household staff. I nodded politely to Lady Fanny as she passed me by. St Mary's Church was a ten minute walk away, on the southern side of the estate. I had a pleasant view of the steeple from my bedroom window.

Professor Singh watched quietly as the doors swung shut behind them.

'Not going to church, professor?' I asked. What kind of religion did he subscribe to? I wondered. Some heathen mumbo jumbo, no doubt.

'I am not a member of the Christian faith.'

'What *are* you then?' We moved back into the library. 'Muslim, Hindu. Buddhist?' Not that I really cared. An awkward fatalism had descended upon me. I picked up the newspaper Mr Smith had discarded and sat myself down in the leather armchair. It was warm and surprisingly comfortable.

The professor returned to his seat. 'I do not believe it is necessary to adopt the primitive belief systems of our ancestors,' he said. The fellow was incapable of giving a straight answer. 'A child may be born to parents of one particular religion, but that is not a good enough reason for adopting that same religion oneself. We must each, I believe, come to our own conclusions about the nature of the reality in which we find ourselves.'

'Right.' I frowned. 'So not a Muslim, then?' Honestly, you ask a simple question and you get a lecture in response. 'So what about killing people, then?' I asked, facetiously. 'Where do you stand on taking another man's life?'

Professor Singh clasped his hands together. I had a feeling I was going to regret asking that. 'I do not believe in absolute morality,' he affirmed enthusiastically. 'Nevertheless, for society to function, we must impose certain codes of behaviour. Human life may not be sacred in the religious sense, but it is necessary for us to act as if it were. Otherwise, it would be impossible for society to function effectively.'

I shook my head. I didn't understand a word. 'Too deep for me, I'm afraid.'

There was no stopping the professor, however. 'A civilised society cannot allow the random taking of life, since violent death – except in war time – undermines the very security that is the chief benefit of any society. Yet violence cannot be eradicated from human nature, so each community must develop mechanisms to deal with it. Our own community is a case in point; and our somewhat confused response to these recent unfortunate events has been fascinating to observe.'

'Well, quite.' I ruffled my newspaper and took a quick look at the headlines. Wall Street again. I yawned. Lord, I was feeling tired. Professor Singh had picked up a book and was starting to read it. I couldn't make out the title. I yawned again. These chairs really were *very* comfortable. It would be so easy just to close my eyes and drift away.

Anthony Sinclair was smacking me across the head with a croquet mallet. There was a loud thwack as the large hammer struck me from behind. Blood began to dribble into my eyes. 'Good show!' the Colonel exclaimed, amidst a smattering of polite applause from the combined forces of the Metropolitan Police Force. 'Nothing more than you deserve, Sir Hilary,' Sinclair snarled, standing over me and grabbing hold of my shoulder. 'Sir Hilary,' he repeated. 'Sir Hilary!'

There really *was* a hand on my shoulder. My body tensed and my eyes flipped open. I started to cough. 'Wake up, Sir Hilary.' A strange figure was looming over me. One of the valets. I struggled to focus. It couldn't be Hargreaves. This fellow had hair. 'Sorry to wake you, sir,' he apologised, as I roused myself from a deep slumber and started to take stock of my surroundings.

I was still in the library. That damned chair. I had closed my eyes for half a second and fallen asleep. How did I do it? Two murders in less than ten hours and I was struggling to keep my eyes open. I was worse than Professor Singh. I coughed and collected my bearings. The Sunday Times fell from my lap.

'Must have nodded off there,' I mumbled. The professor was no longer in the chair opposite me. He had left his book on the table top and must have departed while I was away with the fairies. Perhaps he had gone in to see the Colonel. It was probably his turn by now.

I focused my attention on the valet. 'Jenkins, isn't it?' Anthony Sinclair's man, the one I had seen at the cottage tending the dead body of his master. Poor devil, I thought. Someone else whose weekend had been less than ideal.

'That's right, sir,' Samuel Jenkins confirmed sadly. He spoke with a mild Welsh lilt, which wasn't altogether objectionable. Someone had obviously beaten out the worst excesses of his native dialect before giving him a job. And quite right too. There's nothing worse than a valet with a thick regional accent. 'Doctor Lefranc asked me to come and find you. He needs to have a word. It sounded urgent, sir.'

'Doesn't it always,' I muttered, struggling to my feet. 'I suppose I'd better go and see what he wants. What time is it?'

'Ten past eleven, Sir Hilary.'

'Lord.' I had been asleep for almost an hour. No wonder I felt exhausted. A short sleep is worse than no sleep at all. 'Where is Doctor Lefranc?'

'He asked to meet you in the kitchens, sir.'

I grunted. The far side of the house. That was typical. I bent over and poured myself a glass of whisky from a decanter on the table, purely for medicinal purposes. I gulped it down in one and, having cleared the cobwebs, I gestured for Jenkins to lead the way.

As I headed for the door, I caught sight of the book Professor Singh had been reading, resting on the table next to his armchair. *Crime And Punishment.* Very appropriate.

The morning room was directly opposite the library, on the other side of a short hallway. The door was open but there was no one inside. I could see straight through to the windows and out onto the lawn. 'What's happened to the Colonel?' I asked. Surely the interviews hadn't concluded already. I couldn't have been asleep *that* long.

Jenkins shrugged. 'I don't know, Sir Hilary. I haven't

171

seen him.'

We made our way along the entrance hall to the main stairs and then through a side door to the back hall.

Jenkins was quite a young fellow, perhaps twenty-five or twenty six. Probably hadn't seen much of life yet. He was good looking and fair haired, far too attractive to make a decent servant, though perhaps I did him a disservice. I wondered idly what he had thought of his late master. It can't have been much fun, dressing an oaf like Sinclair every day. But perhaps the journalist had been more forgiving of servants than he had been of the women in his life.

'I am sorry about your master,' I said, as we passed down a back corridor towards the kitchens. Jenkins would be looking for a new job soon, I realised. And Anthony Sinclair would not be able to provide a reference. 'It must have been a shock, finding him lying there this morning.'

'I'd never seen a dead body before,' the servant admitted. He was too young to have fought in the war, of course. 'And when it's your own master...'

'Dashed awkward,' I agreed. 'Still, you're young, Jenkins. You'll get over it. And you'll find another position easily enough.'

'I hope so, sir. But it's Mrs Sinclair I feel sorry for. The mistress was devoted to him. She'll be devastated when she hears the news.'

That was a point. I hadn't really thought about the man's family. For all I knew, there might be a whole host of little Sinclairs running around, waiting for their daddy to come home. I scowled. The last thing I needed was more guilt piling up. I felt bad enough about the whole affair already.

'The Colonel and Lady Fanny say we have to keep quiet, about how he died. They're going to say he was taken ill.'

'Probably for the best,' I agreed. There would need to be some kind of cover story, if the Colonel really was intent on covering everything up. I wondered what fantasy he would concoct for dear old Dottie. 'And you're happy to lie about it?'

'Not exactly happy, sir. But it's probably kinder in the

long run. And if it's a matter of National Security...'

'Well, quite.'

We had arrived in the main kitchen but the place was deserted. Most of the servants had accompanied Lady Fanny to church. Only Mr Townsend, my man Hargreaves and Samuel Jenkins had remained behind. It was rather lax of Lady Fanny to allow the chamber maids to go to church before all the bed sheets had been changed but, in the circumstances, the women probably needed a little divine reassurance.

The kitchen was a large, practical workspace, with a tiled floor, innumerable cupboards and several long surfaces running along the exterior walls. Ovens and wash basins shared space with a sizeable central table. Sharp kitchen implements could be seen hanging from one wall. It was an orderly, well run place, by the looks of it, but it was eerie to see it so empty. Ordinarily, a kitchen is the heart of a great house, the engine that drives the beast along, if you'll forgive the mixed metaphor.

'I thought you said Doctor Lefranc would be here?' I turned to Jenkins, unable to hide the irritation in my voice. The death of a master was no excuse for sloppiness. He would have to buck his ideas up if he wanted to find a new position.

'This is where he asked to meet you, sir.' Jenkins insisted. 'I spoke to him not five minutes ago.'

A voice piped up from a far doorway. 'Over here, Sir Hilary.' I recognised the over-enunciated French vowels.

'Doctor Lefranc?' The voice was coming from the butler's private office, just across the way. I moved over to join him.

The door to the office was open. It was the first time I had been inside, though I had stuck my head through the door earlier on when Hargreaves and I had been looking for the house keys. This time, the keys were hanging in place, on the hook above the bureau.

Lefranc was squatting down in the middle of the room, his back to the entrance. A small stream of light filtered in from a window at the far end. A pair of legs was sticking out from behind a chair on the floor where Doctor Lefranc was

173

crouching.

I came forward, a sudden chill descending upon my already strained nerves.

Lefranc looked back at me, his face suffused with sadness. 'I am very sorry, Monsieur.'

I leaned forward to get a better look at the owner of the legs.

It was my man, Hargreaves. He was lying dead on the floor, with a piece of thick gold-coloured rope wrapped several times around his neck. His familiar middle-aged face was frozen in an expression of undiluted terror.

Chapter Twenty

There are some things a woman should never have to see. Thomas Hargreaves had been my valet for over twenty years. To see him lying there, the faded remnants of his hair surrounding that familiar balding pate and with a grotesque, flamboyantly coloured rope wrapped around his neck, it was almost too much to bear. Anger boiled up inside me. 'Who did this?' I demanded. 'Who did this?' My body was shaking with rage. The pointlessness of it all infuriated me. Hargreaves had never harmed anybody. He had been the perfect manservant. I could scarcely believe I would never see that eager, nervous expression again. In killing Hargreaves, it felt like somebody had hacked away a piece of my soul.

Doctor Lefranc rose to his feet. 'Perhaps you should come through to the kitchens and sit down, Monsieur. You have had a big shock.'

I brushed Lefranc's arm from my shoulder. 'I don't need to sit down,' I snapped. 'I need to find some answers.'

I looked around the study. There was a bureau on the far side. The top of it was unlocked and Harry's revolver was lying there, exposed to the elements. The gun had a shiny silver barrel and a carved white handle. It was smaller than I remembered, almost like a toy. The Colonel had said it would be here, but it was supposed to be under lock and key.

Why didn't the murderer just shoot him, I wondered, if the revolver had been lying there when Hargreaves had entered the room? The silencer had been detached from the barrel of the Newton – a thick metal tube lay next to it on the desk top – but it would have been the work of a moment to screw it back into place.

Lefranc crouched down again and began to remove the rope from around Hargreaves' throat. It was an elaborate gold bell pull, hardly an ideal murder weapon.

I shuddered at the sight of the gash cutting across the valet's neck. It didn't need a doctor to determine the cause of death. This was no silent, quick demise, like the revolver had brought to Dorothy Kilbride. Thomas Hargreaves had suffered every moment of it.

'When did it happen?' I asked.

'Recently. Within the last fifteen or twenty minutes. The body, it is still warm.' Lefranc cradled Hargreaves' head in his hands and peered closely at the face. The eyes were staring vacantly. He closed the lids with his fingertips and gently laid the head back on the floor. 'I found him like this, just a few moments ago.' He looked back at me. 'Mr Townsend has gone to inform the Colonel.'

I wondered briefly where Sir Vincent had got to. Where had everybody got to, come to that? I hadn't seen Professor Singh since I had woken up in the library and as for Harry...

'Why would anyone do it?' I asked. 'Why would anyone want to kill my valet?'

The doctor shrugged. 'It is difficult to say. It may be he discovered some evidence that was incriminating. It is possible he deduced the identity of at least one of the murderers.'

I nodded. Typical Hargreaves. Always noticing every little detail. My hand went instinctively to the cut on my lip. He had certainly worked out the identity of the first murderer. Perhaps he had also deduced the identity of the second.

'Someone must have seen something,' I muttered, clenching my fists tightly. 'Killing somebody in the middle of the night is one thing, but strangling someone in broad daylight, in the middle of the servants' quarters...anyone might have seen it.'

'Our murderer is becoming careless,' Doctor Lefranc agreed.

'Or desperate.' And now he had made one mistake too many. This murder would not go unpunished. Even if I had to reveal my own guilt in the process, I would make damned sure the villain was caught and hanged.

Lefranc had completed his examination of the body. He shifted the legs and laid out the corpse respectfully on its back. Then he rose to his feet and disappeared for a moment to find an appropriate shroud. In the short time he was gone, I moved across to the bureau and surreptitiously slipped Harry's revolver into my jacket pocket. No one was going to bump *me* off like that, I resolved.

By the time the doctor returned, I had resumed my original position by the door.

Lefranc laid out the sheet across the floor and Hargreaves disappeared underneath the white cotton. A simple shroud for a simple man. I stared down at him sadly. Good servants are difficult to find and you never really appreciate them until they are gone.

The doctor rose to his feet. 'Did Mr Hargreaves have any relatives?' he asked, clearing his throat.

I struggled to remember. 'An aunt, I think, in Eastbourne. She's senile, though. I don't think they were close.' I stared down once more at the small body, visible now only in outline beneath the cotton sheet. He looked just like Sinclair had, over at the cottage, only with smaller shoes sticking out the end. I shuddered. Hargreaves had always been there for me but he would never be there again. 'I need a drink,' I said, stepping away from the silent shroud.

Doctor Lefranc accompanied me back to the kitchen.

Samuel Jenkins had been hovering on the edges of our conversation, not wanting to intrude. The mention of drink gave him a useful cue. 'I'll put the kettle on, sir.'

'Not that kind of drink!' I growled. 'I need a whisky.'

Jenkins looked to Doctor Lefranc, who nodded quietly. 'I believe there is a bottle of malt whisky in the butler's office,' he said. 'In the circumstances, I do not believe he will object.'

The valet went to get it.

I sat myself down on a wooden chair opposite the kitchen table. The sturdy work surface was clean and well polished. The caterers had tidied up after themselves even if the housemaids hadn't.

Doctor Lefranc took a seat opposite me. He was a strange looking man, short and plump, with thick curly hair and a rather bland face. A small moustache added a little character but it was in the eyes, as always, that the warmth of the man was most evident. He was a decent fellow, I thought. Probably the closest approximation to a gentlemen the French nation had ever produced.

'This has gone on long enough,' I told him bluntly. I pulled out my cigarette case and offered it across to Lefranc. He shook his head, but I grabbed a cigarette myself and lit it with nervous, trembling fingers.

'I agree, Monsieur,' he said. 'The time has come for answers.' The doctor's expression was commendably serious. 'And I believe I may be in a position to provide them. That is what I wanted to see you about.' Lefranc had sent Jenkins to fetch me before the body of my valet had been discovered.

I took a puff of the cigarette and exhaled gently. The Frenchman's moustache was beginning to twitch slightly. It always seemed to do that when he was about to broach a difficult subject. 'What do you mean?'

'I believe I now know who murdered Dorothy Kilbride,' he announced, with understandable solemnity. 'And the same individual of course was also responsible for the death of your valet.'

I blanched. 'Who was it?' I would damn well throttle the bastard.

The doctor's moustache twitched again. 'I am sorry Monsieur. It was your friend Harry Latimer.'

I laughed. For a brief moment, I had really thought the Frenchman had solved the puzzle. But this was no solution. Lefranc's imagination was running away with him. He had always disliked my American friend. 'Harry had nothing to do with this,' I insisted.

'I believe you are incorrect, Monsieur. It was Mr Latimer, after all, who brought the revolver to Bletchley Park this weekend. None of the other guests felt the need to arm themselves.'

'Yes, but he's an American. You know what they're like. They always carry guns. It makes them feel safe.' I had been through all this with the Colonel. 'Harry has dealings with a lot of shady characters. You know that as well as anyone. French communists. All sorts of disreputable Continental types. Sometimes he needs a little insurance.'

Lefranc acknowledged the truth of that. 'But one does

not need a silencer for self defence.'

Jenkins had returned with the bottle of malt and two crystal tumblers. The doctor waved his glass away but the valet filled the other and I gulped down the whisky in one. The liquid burnt at my throat with a reassuring intensity. Jenkins quickly refilled the glass.

'He also arrived with a considerable sum of French Francs in his holdall. Somewhere in the region of twenty thousand pounds, I believe.'

'Yes, but...'

'A sum of money, as I understand it, completely unconnected to his work in southern France.'

'Well, yes...' Harry had certainly been rather coy about the origin of that cash, but then he always was secretive when it came to business connections. When your work is often on the wrong side of the law it doesn't pay to advertise. I had simply assumed the money was counterfeit and Harry had done nothing to disabuse me of the notion.

'You knew about the money?' Lefranc asked.

'I...yes, I saw inside the holdall. How did you...?'

'Mr Townsend discovered it. He and some of the other valets conducted a search of the guest rooms this morning.'

'Yes, of course.'

Jenkins, who was hovering by the window, still holding the bottle of whisky, confirmed this with a nod. 'I searched *your* room, Sir Hilary,' he confessed, looking slightly shame-faced.

I put down my tumbler and took another puff from the cigarette. So he was the one who'd left my door unlocked. 'All right, so Harry had a large pile of cash in his bag. But that doesn't mean...'

'I believe, Monsieur, that Mr Latimer was brought here deliberately to kill Dorothy Kilbride. I believe that someone paid him that money as an advance for the murder.'

'No!' I insisted, vehemently. 'That can't be true. Harry's not an assassin. He would only ever kill in self defence.'

'But perhaps he would also kill to protect his own interests. I am sorry, Monsieur, but the evidence is very strong.'

179

I wasn't having that. 'The Colonel said the revolver was found under a pillow in Professor Singh's bedroom.'

'That is correct. In the room next door to Mr Latimer's own bedroom. And Mr Latimer would naturally wish to divert suspicion.'

I was aghast. 'You honestly think somebody paid Harry to kill Dorothy Kilbride? And then...and then he killed my valet to keep him quiet?'

'It would appear so, Monsieur.'

'But who...I mean, who on earth would do that? Who would pay him to...?'

Lefranc's moustache was twitching even more heavily now. He raised a hand to his lip to steady it. 'It pains me to say this, Monsieur, but I believe the murder was commissioned by none other than Sir Vincent Kelly himself.'

My mouth fell open. The suggestion was preposterous.

'You don't know what you're talking about,' I laughed. Sir Vincent Kelly was the most honourable man I knew. Trust some damned Frog to get the wrong end of the stick. 'Do you have even the slightest evidence...?' Jenkins had placed an ashtray on the table in front of me and I tapped out the end of the cigarette.

'The bank notes, Monsieur. The Security Service keeps a supply of foreign currency for certain important operations. The serial numbers are carefully recorded. And I am reliably informed that the currency in Mr Latimer's holdall originated from the reserves of MI5 itself.'

There was a shocked silence. Harry had said the Colonel knew nothing about the French Francs. But if it was MI5 money...

I gestured Jenkins forward and grabbed the bottle of whisky from his hands. Then I poured myself a double.

'You're seriously suggesting the Colonel arranged for the murder of his own secretary?'

'It is an explanation that fits the facts, Monsieur.'

'But what motive would he have?'

'The head of the Security Service, he must occasionally bend the rules. He must make compromises to achieve a particular aim. Sometimes, a line may be crossed.'

'And if Dottie found out and thought he had gone too far?'

'She might feel it her duty to inform their superiors. The Security Service, as I understand it, is not very popular with the new administration. The government are deeply suspicious of MI5 and perhaps with good reason. The secret service has many informers working in the trade union movement and it is the unions who finance the Labour Party. The Colonel cannot afford any controversy, Monsieur, no matter how slight. He must tread carefully if the organisation is to survive.'

I sat back in my chair. 'No, I don't believe it. If the Colonel wanted to kill his own secretary, why would he bring us all here? Why the anniversary weekend? You can't seriously be suggesting he organised all this with the intention of bumping off his secretary. That's absurd. No one would go to those lengths.'

Lefranc shrugged. 'Perhaps the anniversary was already arranged. Bletchley Park merely provided a convenient setting.'

I shook my head vehemently. 'That's utter nonsense. Other people might have got hold of that money. We're all veterans. Everyone here has worked for the service at one time or another.'

The doctor inclined his head. 'That is true, Monsieur. But the Colonel saved Harry Latimer from a long prison sentence. He rescued your friend from the French police. Why would he do that, if he did not want a favour in return?'

I took a final drag of my cigarette and stubbed it out in the ashtray. For the life of me, I couldn't think of a decent response.

The Colonel's valet chose that moment to crash into the kitchen, his expression as grim as ever. 'I've searched the house,' he informed us, arriving at the foot of the table. 'I can't find the Colonel or Mr Latimer.'

'They have left the building?' Lefranc asked, with some surprise.

'It looks that way, sir,' Townsend admitted. 'The Colonel wasn't in the morning room. I spoke to Miss Jones and

Miss Young in the billiard hall, but they hadn't seen him either.'

The Frenchman raised an eyebrow. 'So they do not yet know about the murder of Mr Hargreaves?'

'I'm afraid not, Doctor Lefranc. A dreadful business,' the valet added, glancing at me.

'Did you check upstairs?' I asked.

'I did have a brief look, Sir Hilary, but there's no sign of them anywhere.'

Lefranc shook his head, perplexed. 'It is strange that they would leave the house just now.'

'Doctor Lefranc here thinks the Colonel was responsible for Mr Hargreaves' death,' I said. 'Can you believe that?'

Townsend did a double take. It was the first time I had ever seen him looked surprised. '*The Colonel,* sir?'

I nodded. 'The doctor thinks Harry was a hired assassin brought here by your master. What do you say to that?'

The valet took a moment to consider this. 'I don't believe the Colonel would ever condone any form of murder, Sir Hilary. With respect, Doctor Lefranc, I've been his valet for some years now. He is one of the most upright and honourable men it has ever been my pleasure to serve.'

I nodded vehemently. 'Just what I was trying to tell him. It's ridiculous. The Colonel commissioning Harry Latimer to assassinate his own secretary. It's absurd.'

Townsend nodded in agreement.

'Alas, we can never be one hundred per cent certain,' Lefranc admitted. 'It is possible that someone else paid your friend to kill Miss Kilbride. But that Mr Latimer murdered her I do not think is in any doubt.'

Townsend was inclined to agree. 'I have to say, Sir Hilary, speaking as a former police man, that does seem the most likely explanation. It's the silencer that clinches it, sir. He obviously came to Bletchley Park expecting trouble.'

I bit my lip. There was nothing I could say to that. It made sense, damn it, even if I couldn't really bring myself to believe it.

A small voice spoke up from behind us. Samuel Jenkins

had been following the conversation closely. 'What about Mr Sinclair?' he enquired nervously. 'Who killed my master?'

Doctor Lefranc smiled sadly. 'Ah, that is a much easier question to answer, alas.' He looked me straight in the eye. 'Mr Sinclair was killed by Sir Hilary Manningham-Butler.'

Chapter Twenty-One

There are times in life when bare-faced denial is the only option. A choice between confessing to a particular action or denying it outright can often be no choice at all, if the consequences of that action are sufficiently severe. Jenkins was staring at me in horror but I was hardly about to confess the truth to him in front of Townsend and Doctor Lefranc. Admitting privately that I was a murderer to my man Hargreaves was one thing, but I couldn't afford the whole world to find out. Not if it meant I ended up in prison, or worse still, on the end of a hangman's noose. Unfortunately, I had not been given the time to prepare a convincing riposte. 'That's... preposterous!' I exclaimed, with a palpable lack of conviction. 'I wouldn't...I didn't have....'

Doctor Lefranc lifted a hand to forestall my protestations of innocence. 'Please do not lie to us, Monsieur. You are not very good at it and I'm afraid there is no doubt of your guilt.'

I stared at him in disbelief. Over his shoulder, I could see Townsend nodding gravely. In ordinary circumstances, I pride myself I am quite an effective liar, but these were not ordinary circumstances.

'You were the only person who *could* be responsible for Mr Sinclair's death, Sir Hilary,' the valet explained, apologetically. 'Everyone else was accounted for at the time the incident took place. Miss Jones was seen upstairs on the landing by Miss Young and most of the other guests were in the ballroom.'

'What about Harry?' I asked. He had not returned to the dance until some minutes later.

'He had the opportunity,' Doctor Lefranc conceded, 'but he would not have had time to move the body. Miss Jones spoke with him in the library shortly after her argument with Mr Sinclair. Mr Latimer returned to the ballroom almost immediately after that. But alas, it is not these details that are conclusive, Monsieur. It is the nature of the crime itself.'

That sounded ominous. 'What do you mean?'

Lefranc's moustache twitched gently. 'Professor Singh was correct in deducing that the murder of Anthony Sinclair was not a premeditated act. It was a violent altercation resulting, I believe, from a simple argument. I do not think it likely that Harry Latimer would kill a man in anger. Nor would he hide the body in such an unprofessional manner. The murderer must have panicked. He did his best to cover things up, but in such a poor and ill-thought out way, that of the possible suspects, only you could have been responsible. I am sorry, Monsieur.'

'And I did see you, sir, shortly afterwards,' Townsend added, unhelpfully. 'Coming out of the servants quarters. I thought at the time you looked rather distressed. It was only later that I connected the two events.'

I sighed, reaching for the bottle of whisky. 'And the Colonel?' I asked, pouring out a final measure.

'I believe he is coming to the same conclusion,' the valet confirmed.

The calmness of the two men explaining all this to me was rather galling. It was all so matter-of-fact. Any denials now would sound completely absurd. I gulped down the whisky and stared back at them, my lips pursed tightly together.

'Did you do it?' Jenkins asked softly. 'Did you kill my master?'

What could I say? It was clear that I had been suspected for some time and now they knew the truth. I nodded quietly. There was no point pretending any more. 'It was an accident,' I explained, in half-hearted mitigation. 'I didn't…you were right. I lost my temper. There was a fight. I didn't mean to kill him.'

Jenkins was starting to tremble. He had probably never been in the same room as a murderer before. He didn't know how to react. Townsend found him a chair and he sat down at the far end of the table, shuddering gently but doing his best to keep himself under control.

'I thought he had seduced Felicity Mandeville Jones,' I said, unable to stop myself gabbling. 'I assumed he had beaten her up. But it was a misunderstanding. I thought I was defending her honour, but it turns out that's what he was doing with Harry. God, what a mess.' I buried my head in my hands. Three murders now. And it was all my fault. If I hadn't come to Bletchley Park, hadn't brought that damn gun in Harry's holdall, then none of this would have happened.

'What…what will happen now?' Jenkins asked Doctor Lefranc.

'We must find Mr Latimer,' he said. 'And discover the truth about Dorothy Kilbride.'

'You really think Harry killed her?' I asked, looking up.

'I really do, Monsieur. I am sorry.'

I pushed back the chair and rose to my feet, wobbling slightly as I struggled to reorientate myself. The alcohol was beginning to have an effect. It was making me reckless. 'I'm going to find him,' I announced brashly. 'I brought him here. He's my responsibility.'

Townsend eyed me warily. 'I don't think we can let you leave, Sir Hilary.'

'You killed my master,' Jenkins added, unnecessarily.

'I have to,' I insisted, my hands clasping the back of the chair as I moved it to one side. 'I have to find out the truth.'

Doctor Lefranc was apologetic. 'Mr Townsend and Mr Jenkins can conduct a search of the grounds, Monsieur. It is better for you to remain here, where we can keep an eye on you.'

That was no good. I needed to talk to Harry myself. But nobody here was going to let me wander off on my own. I couldn't really blame them for that. There was already one murderer running free and they couldn't allow another one to slip through their fingers. But neither could I afford to be constrained. I moved back slowly and reached into my jacket pocket. Townsend started to move towards me, his broad, stocky frame an intimidating sight, but the man stopped when he saw the revolver in my hand.

'There is no need for this, Monsieur,' Doctor Lefranc reassured me, rising to his feet.

'I just want to talk to him,' I said. 'They can't have gone far.'

Townsend and Jenkins raised their hands. My own hands were shaking. I had never held a gun on anyone before. But I needed time to find Harry and the Colonel and there was no other way of getting it. 'All right,' I said. 'The three of you. Over into the butler's office.'

The men did as they were instructed, moving swiftly across the corridor into the room where poor Hargreaves was lying dead. I don't know what I would have done if they had refused to go. I certainly wasn't about to shoot anybody.

Luckily, nobody felt inclined to call my bluff.

I examined the room quickly from the doorway. There was a window at the far end but it was fixed shut and had a metal frame. Townsend could easily break the glass, but there would not be the room for any of them to clamber through. I could lock the door and be fairly sure the three men would not be able to get out, though there was nothing to stop them screaming for help. It didn't matter. With luck, I would only need a few minutes to locate the Colonel.

'I'm sorry about this,' I mumbled, awkwardly. 'I'll send someone to let you out in a little while.' Then they could do what they liked. 'The keys, if you please.' This last was directed at Townsend.

The valet reached into his pocket and threw a bundle of keys across to me. I caught them awkwardly with my left hand but made sure the Newton remained steady in my right.

'Both sets.'

Lefranc took the second bunch of keys from the hook above the bureau and handed them over. The three men stood well back from the door as I made to close it up and imprison them. Jenkins had not taken his eyes from me all the while.

'What are you going to do?' he asked me, breathlessly.

'I'm going to find out the truth,' I said. 'And if Harry did kill Dottie…if he did strangle my man Hargreaves.' My hand gripped firmly on the handle of the revolver. 'Then I'm going to kill him.'

Lettie Young was sitting by the large bay window on the far

side of the billiard room. Felicity Mandeville Jones was to her left, her short blonde hair framing a now sombre face. The midday sun was glittering through the window, bathing the two women in a harsh autumnal glow. They had given up practising billiards and were now engaged in what looked like a rather animated conversation. They had put the murders out of their mind for a few moments, in order to discuss a far more important topic: men.

'You're never going to marry him,' Lettie was saying. 'He ain't the type. And you're dad won't let you anyway. So just enjoy it while it lasts, that's what I say. Better to regret what you *have* done than what you haven't.'

Felicity Mandeville Jones grinned. 'I never expected it to happen like this,' she gushed. 'It really was the most wonderful thing. Not like I imagined at all. It didn't feel the least bit sordid. If only all this other business...' She cut herself off as I rushed unexpectedly into the room.

Lettie swung her head around and the two women rose to their feet at once. Lettie knew immediately that something was up.

'Where's Harry?' I demanded, before she had a chance to speak. 'Have you seen him?' I grabbed hold of the billiard table to steady myself. All that whisky had gone straight to my head. The revolver was out of sight in my jacket pocket. I had bundled it away before leaving the kitchens. The Colonel's man had told me where I could find the two girls.

It was Felicity Mandeville Jones who answered my question. 'Not recently, darling. Not since he went in to see the Colonel. That must have been... what?' She glanced at a nearby clock. 'Over an hour ago.' Her face was a picture of concern. 'Is everything all right, Sir Hilary? You do look frightfully worried.'

Lettie stepped towards me. She could see I was a bit tipsy. I was gripping rather too tightly on the edge of the billiard table. 'What is it? What's happened?' she asked.

There was no easy way of answering. 'There's been another murder. My man Hargreaves...he's dead.'

Felicity let out a sob. Her hand went to her mouth.

'Bloody hell!' Lettie stepped towards me and placed a hand on my shoulder. 'You poor bugger.' She knew what Hargreaves had meant to me, probably better than I knew it myself. She was a bright girl, for all her lack of education. I stiffened, though, when she moved forward and took me in her arms. I have never much liked hugging. It is a vulgar foreign custom better suited to hot-blooded continental types. But the gesture was well meant, so I accepted it gracefully. In truth, I wasn't quite sure who was comforting who. Lettie held onto me for some moments. Rather tightly, I have to say.

Felicity Mandeville Jones had fallen back onto the window seat and was starting to shudder. The Colonel was right, she really was very young. Lettie broke off her embrace and redirected her maternal instincts to her younger friend. Miss Jones had taken out a handkerchief and was dabbing away the tears. Lettie pulled up a chair in front of her, leaned forward and quietly embraced the young woman.

'I'm terribly sorry, Sir Hilary,' Felicity said, sniffing loudly. 'What must you think of me, blubbing away.'

'That's quite all right, my dear.'

Lettie looked up at me. 'How did he die? Your valet, I mean.'

I couldn't think of a polite way to answer. 'Strangulation,' I said. That yielded another sob from Miss Jones. 'Doctor Lefranc thinks Harry Latimer may have been responsible for his death.'

Felicity's head jerked up in astonishment. 'That's absurd!' she exclaimed, wiping away the tears from her reddened eyes. 'Harry wouldn't kill anybody. He's the kindest man I've ever…'

Lettie squeezed the girl's shoulder tightly. 'What do *you* think?' she asked me. 'You must know him better than anyone.'

I shrugged. 'I honestly don't know. The evidence is… look, Miss Jones, I'm sorry to be indelicate, but…' There was no easy way of putting this. 'You spent the night with Harry, didn't you?'

Lettie shot me a warning glance.

'I don't have a choice, Lettie. I need to know the truth.'

Felicity Mandeville Jones was not about to deny it. She held her head up proudly. 'Yes, I was with him last night.'

'Did he leave the room, at any point?'

The girl frowned. 'No. We were together all night. Until about half past six, I think. He never left my side. He couldn't possibly have killed Miss Kilbride.'

'But did you fall asleep at all during that time?' Had Harry slipped one of those sleeping pills into her glass? Or at least a small chunk of one?

Felicity considered for a moment. 'I don't know. Perhaps for half an hour or so. I don't remember.'

That was not good enough. 'Did you or didn't you?'

'I...yes, I did,' Miss Jones admitted. 'Briefly.'

That clinched it. 'So Harry could have left the room at the time of the murder.'

Felicity sighed. 'I don't know. I suppose he could have done. But...'

'Right,' I said. That was all I needed to know. The man had the means, the motive and the opportunity. I clenched my fists together.

Lettie looked up at me warily. 'You're not going to do anything stupid, are you?'

'That remains to be seen.' I picked up a billiard ball from the table and spun it angrily across the green. 'I'm going to talk to Harry and find out the truth.'

Lettie rose to her feet. 'Do you want me to come with you?' Her face was a picture of concern.

I shook my head. 'I need to do this myself, Lettie.'

'I understand.' She stepped forward, rested her hands on my shoulders and gave me a gentle kiss on the lips. I confess, I blushed. I was more used to being kissed by men than women. 'Be careful, lover boy. Don't do anything I wouldn't.' She squeezed my hand gently.

'I won't.' I tried to give her a reassuring smile.

'And don't jump to conclusions neither.' She released her grip. 'You know what the Colonel says: innocent until proven guilty.'

I felt my body tense. '*I'm* guilty,' I blurted out suddenly,

190

unable to stop myself. I didn't want to lie any more, not to people I cared about. Lefranc already knew the truth. Better Lettie should hear it from me. 'I killed Anthony Sinclair.'

She flinched, as if I had slapped her.

'I killed him. And I think Harry killed my valet.'

Lettie shrank back from me. It was painful to see the change in her, but there was nothing I could do about that.

'Now I have to find out the truth.'

Chapter Twenty-Two

Professor Singh was returning from a walk around the lake. The academic raised a hand in friendly greeting as I skidded out onto the carriage turnabout. His benign smile spoke of a man completely unaffected by the events of the last few hours. It was infuriating. Bloody academics. They live in a world of their own. I didn't want to talk to him just now, but Harry was not in the house and it was possible the professor might have bumped into him somewhere in the grounds.

'I hope you are refreshed from your sleep, Sir Hilary,' Professor Singh droned. The last time he had seen me I had been dozing off in one of those leather armchairs in the library. 'It is most important to ensure that our bodies are sufficiently rested.'

'Er...yes. Look, you haven't seen the Colonel, have you?'

The professor had been walking back along the path opposite the croquet lawn. He stopped now in front of me, his cheeks a little flushed. 'I believe he was intending to visit the stable yard.' At last, a simple answer. 'It was most unexpected. The interviews had not yet concluded, but after Sir Vincent had finished speaking to Mr Latimer, the two gentlemen left the house together. They did not give a reason. But as it appeared I would not be required for questioning, I thought I would take a turn around the lake.' He smiled. 'I find that contemplation of the natural world, even artificially sculpted as it is here, can often provide a calming influence, enabling people to transcend even the most troubling of events.'

My mouth opened and closed. There really was no answer to that. 'Good for you,' I mumbled, anxious now to get away. 'The stable yard, you say?'

Professor Singh inclined his head. 'There is a small cottage there belonging to the head groom. I believe Sir Vincent wished to make use of the telephone.'

The telephone? 'Why didn't he use the one in the hall?'

'It is not the place for a private conversation.' The

professor regarded me curiously. 'You are looking, if I may say so, a little flustered, Sir Hilary.'

'That's an understatement.' I pulled a set of house keys from my inside pocket. 'You might want to head down to the kitchens,' I told him, handing the bundle across. 'Doctor Lefranc was anxious to have a word.'

This time, it was Professor Singh who looked flustered. 'I will go there at once. But I wonder...?'

I was moving away at this point. 'I'll speak to you later,' I said, turning my back and starting to run before the professor started babbling again. At least I had managed to extract some useful information this time. The stables. And if the Colonel was looking for a telephone then he would probably be in that end cottage. And Harry would be with him. But who on earth was Sir Vincent trying to call? And why the need for secrecy?

I made my way quickly along the northern path heading away from the house. The entrance to the maze was up ahead, the large circular hedges bisected by a narrow footpath. I needed to cut left before that but, as I did so, I had a brief moment of what I believe the Frogs call "déjà vu". I stumbled into the stable yard and saw a figure emerging from the cottage on the far side. This time, it was not Samuel Jenkins, but Harry Latimer, strolling nonchalantly towards the archway. He caught sight of me and immediately changed track.

I had come to a halt outside the apple and plum store and Harry hurried across to meet me. He smiled his usual lazy smile. 'I was just coming to find you,' he said, before I had managed to utter more than a grunt of surprise. 'Listen, old man, you've got to get out of here.' He glanced back at the cottage. 'The Colonel knows you killed Anthony Sinclair.' I blinked. 'It's all my fault.' Harry lifted his hands up in an admission of guilt. 'I let the cat out the bag.'

'What the blazes are you talking about?'

'Anthony Sinclair. The Colonel knows exactly what happened. It's my fault, old man. I was chatting to Felicity this morning and she told me Sinclair had been on the phone last night, talking to his office. She figured that might have something to do with his death. I blabbed it to the Colonel during our little interview and he wanted to check it out.'

'So you came over to the stables?'

'He didn't want to be overheard. You know what it's like in that house, people coming and going all the time. But there's another phone line running from the cottage.' Harry jerked his thumb back towards the small house. The little black door, I could see, was wide open. 'The Colonel's still in there, making a few more calls. He spoke to some guy at the Daily Mail. The man said Sinclair called yesterday, asking questions about you.'

I grimaced. The telephone call had been bound to get out at some point. Not that it mattered now. My secret was already in the public domain. It was Harry I was more concerned with.

'So what did he have on you?' the American asked, with his usual impertinence. He seemed to be taking the news of my killing Anthony Sinclair with a surprising lack of concern. 'Don't tell me. He caught you with some guy, didn't he?' His eyes were twinkling now. 'You old devil. He was going to expose you as a sodomite.'

'Harry!'

'Hey, look. It doesn't bother me. Live and let live, I say. Mind you, I'd have gone for blackmail rather than exposure, but that's journalists for you. So who was the lucky guy?'

'I...'

'It's okay, old man. You don't have to tell me.' Harry was grinning again but the damn fellow would not stop talking. He was worse than Professor Singh. 'So what happened with Sinclair? I guess it was an accident, right? A fight that got out of hand. Look, I'm not blaming you. I've been in a few punch ups myself...'

This was too much. 'Harry, for God's sake, will you shut up for just one second?'

Harry blinked in surprise. 'Okay. Sure.'

I took a deep breath. 'Thomas Hargreaves has just been murdered.' My hand slipped down to rest gently on the outside of my jacket pocket.

'Jesus.' Harry took out a cigarette. 'I'm sorry to hear that old man.' He struck a match and cupped his hand around the flame as he lit the cigarette. 'How did it happen?'

'He was strangled, in the kitchens. Not half an hour ago.'

Harry rubbed his chin thoughtfully. 'That's too bad.' He took a drag of his cigarette. 'I know what the guy meant to you. Jeez, he's been with you since...well, forever.'

I snorted. 'Your sympathy I can do without.'

'Hey, look, I'm just trying to help.' He glanced back at the cottage once again. 'But you really do need to get the hell out of here. Whatever's happened. If you want to stay out of jail. I'm telling you. The Colonel knows all about Sinclair.'

'I don't care about Anthony Sinclair. I only care about justice, Harry. About the murder of Dorothy Kilbride. And my valet.' My fingers slid into the jacket pocket and wrapped themselves around the handle of the .32 calibre Newton.

Harry's eyes darted down to my waist. He was frowning now, unsure what was going on. The man had been around the block long enough to know just what I was carrying down there. He took another puff of his cigarette and tapped the ash off the end onto the gravel. 'Sure, I understand,' he admitted warily. 'Look, this has been difficult for all of us.'

I opted for the direct approach. 'Did you kill Hargreaves?'

'What?'

'It's a simple question.'

Harry was offended. 'Look, old man, I know you're upset, but that's just crazy. I've never killed anyone. Leastways, only in self defence. And anyway ...'

'Was that what it was? Self defence?'

'Hey, slow down.' Harry dropped the cigarette and stubbed it out. He had barely taken half a dozen drags. 'What is this about? You think I killed Dorothy Kilbride?'

'I don't know Harry. You tell me.' I nodded down to my pocket. 'Think very carefully before you answer.'

'Look, old man. we've been friends a long time. I've always been straight with you, haven't I?'

I laughed. If there was one thing Harry had never been, it was straight. 'So where did you get the French Francs?'

'The what?'

'The Francs. In your holdall? Where did you get them from?'

Harry was confused. 'What's that got to do with anything?'

'Did someone pay you to come here, to kill Dorothy? Is that what it was? Some kind of hit?'

'Oh, sure, yeah. I'm a hired assassin. What are you talking about, old man?'

I pulled the revolver out of my pocket. Harry's eyes didn't move from my face. 'I think you killed Dottie. I think you were *paid* to kill her, in cold blood. Twenty thousand pounds, in French Francs, to blow her brains out. Then Hargreaves found out and you killed him too.'

'That's crazy. Look, you've had a shock, old man. You're not thinking straight.' Harry stepped towards me, but halted immediately as I levelled the Newton.

'Oh I am, Harry. I'm thinking very clearly indeed.'

Harry kept his hands where I could see them. Sweat was beginning to form on his brow. 'Look, the money, it was an advance, okay? The deal in France? I was the middle man, like I told you. The Francs were a pay-off for securing the armaments. Strictly cash, strictly in advance. Only way to do business. Brought it back here after the first trip and tucked it safely away in London.'

That sounded worryingly plausible.

'So why did you ask me to bring it up to Bletchley Park?'

'I told you. It was another bit of business.' I waited for him to go on. He knew he had no choice. If he wanted to convince me he was innocent, I needed to hear the whole story. And even then, I doubted I would believe him. 'Look,' he said, 'I owed quite a bit of dough to some shady characters up in Manchester. Long story. I'd had a little problem with cash flow. You know how it is. They helped out, gave me a loan to tide me over, but with a rate of interest that would have crippled the

Bank of England. They were expecting it back by the end of the month. And these are not the kind of guys you keep waiting. I figured since I'd be coming here anyway, I might as well arrange to meet up with a couple of their goons on Saturday morning and pay them off.'

That was nonsense. The revolver had dipped slightly in my hand, but I steadied it now. 'You went for a drive with Felicity Mandeville Jones on Saturday morning. In my bloody car, I might add.'

'Sure, I took Felicity along. We had a wager, remember? Didn't want to lose momentum. I figured I could kill two birds with one stone.' He smirked briefly, hoping to rekindle a bit of camaraderie, but I kept my expression neutral. 'We had a nice drive and a pub lunch. But I told her I had an errand to run and we drove in to Aylesbury first. I figured she wouldn't mind staying in the car for ten minutes while I went and conducted a little business.'

'Handing the cash over to some hoodlum?'

'That's about the size of it, old man.'

My eyes flicked down to the revolver in my hand. 'So where does the Newton come in?'

Harry sighed. In happier circumstances, I might have been quite pleased to see him looking so uncomfortable. But I wasn't about to relieve the pressure just yet.

'Look, I figured I needed some insurance, okay? I stowed the gun with the cash when I first got paid. These are pretty nasty people. And they were expecting nice simple English pound notes not a heap of French Francs. I thought there might be a little trouble, so I made sure I had some insurance.' He gestured to the revolver. 'I arranged to meet up in a very public place, right in the centre of town. But even there, they might have got a little tricky.'

'Why did you need a silencer?'

'Like I said, old man, it was a public place. So I took that large overcoat from the vestibule. You know, the one with the pockets. I slipped the Newton inside, and kept a hand on the trigger. If I had to defend myself, I didn't want to make a public spectacle of it. I'd only just avoided a French jail. I sure as hell didn't want to end up in one over here. A silencer would keep things nice and tidy. But it was just a precaution. And luckily for me they accepted the dough. I took along a copy of the Times, to show them the exchange rate. Made sure they got a good deal. I'm no fool. Then I went back to the car and Felicity and I went off for lunch. And I started laying it on real thick with her, so I could win that fifteen guineas from you.'

'And that's it?' I said. 'That's why you had me bring the cash up here from London?'

'That's it. I couldn't get there myself, because of your crazy English weather. The boat nearly capsized on the way back from France. I ended up on the south coast, but in the middle of nowhere. I had to make all the arrangements by payphone. I'd left the holdall with an associate of mine. Small guy. Looks like a baked potato. I was going to meet up with him at Waterloo but I had to send you instead.'

That at least was true. 'What about the dirty pictures?'

Harry laughed. 'Little souvenir, from my first trip. Gave them as a gift, to my creditors, just to oil the wheels. You can't get those kind of photos in England.'

I bit my lip. It all sounded horribly plausible. But Harry had a genius for thinking on his feet. He could convince his own mother that she was his father if his life depended on it. And his life just now depended on convincing me that he was telling the truth. There was one thing that didn't add up, however.

'So let me get this straight: you're saying you handed over all the Francs to these contacts of yours in Aylesbury yesterday morning?'

'I told you, old man. The photos, the Francs. And the revolver must have been stolen from my holdall sometime yesterday evening. You saw me looking for it this morning, remember?'

I nodded. He'd pulled the bag out from under the bed and checked the side pocket. 'But if the money was gone then the bag would have been empty,' I said. 'And it looked just as full this morning as it did when we first arrived.'

'Oh, I stuffed a couple of blankets in there, just to bulk

198

it out,' he said. His eyes were darting over my shoulder. 'Didn't want to be seen leaving with less luggage than I...'

Before I knew what was happening, a hand had grabbed my arm from behind. Two men were grappling with me. It was Jenkins and Townsend. Professor Singh must have released them both, rather more quickly than I had anticipated. I felt the revolver smack against my thigh. That was Townsend's doing. I lost my grip and it clattered noisily to the ground.

Samuel Jenkins rushed forward to grab the weapon. Harry had backed away. Townsend pinned me down, yanking my arm painfully behind my back. His grip was incredible. My wrist felt like it was trapped in an industrial mangle.

'I wasn't really going to shoot him,' I protested, as Harry stepped backwards from the fray.

The Colonel's valet disagreed. 'It didn't look like that to me, Sir Hilary.'

Jenkins was standing inert with the gleaming Newton . 32 in his hand. The younger valet had clearly never handled a weapon before. His arms were trembling. I knew just how he felt.

Townsend pushed me down onto my knees, which scraped painfully against the gravel. He took the revolver from Jenkins with his free hand and then released my arm.

'Right. Back to the house, everyone. You too, Mr Latimer, sir.' After everything Doctor Lefranc had said, Harry was considered just as much of a suspect as I was. The two valets were taking Lefranc's pet theory very seriously. But my American friend had already begun to sow the seeds of doubt in my mind.

'The Colonel's over in the cottage,' Harry said, gesturing back across the courtyard. 'I figure you might want to have a word with him before you do anything hasty. He doesn't know about Hargreaves yet.'

Townsend considered this for a moment. He reached into his pocket and produced a set of handcuffs. He really was an old policeman. 'Jenkins, put these on Mr Latimer.'

'Hey, now hang on, old man....'

The valet pulled me to my feet. 'Take him over to the

cottage,' he said. 'Tell the Colonel about Mr Hargreaves. I'll take Sir Hilary back to the house.'

Harry had his hands stretched out in front of him and Jenkins moved forward to slot the metal cuffs into place.

'Behind his back,' the older valet suggested helpfully.

'Sorry, yes.'

Harry slipped his arms into position. 'Hey, not too tight,' he complained as the younger man fastened the manacles into place. He winked at me as the two of them made off towards the cottage.

Townsend pushed me in the opposite direction.

I was barely concentrating on my footing. There was something not quite right here. Ever since Harry had mentioned that empty holdall, a nagging suspicion had begun to form in the back of my mind. If Harry had genuinely disposed of all that cash on Saturday morning, as he had claimed, then there would have been no money left in the holdall for Townsend to find during his search that morning. And even if Harry was lying and still had the money, I had warned him about the search in advance, so he would have had ample opportunity to hide it.

Yet somehow, the Colonel's valet had known all about the money. And the only way he *could* have known was if he had searched Harry's bag at the start of the weekend, before Harry had driven to Aylesbury on Saturday morning. And if Townsend *had* searched the holdall at that point, he would have seen Harry's .32 calibre revolver, long before the murder of Dorothy Kilbride. An innocent man would have reported that to his master. But Townsend had said nothing.

I stumbled slightly as the valet push me forward and I turned myself towards him. It was obvious now. It was not Harry who had acted as an assassin. 'It was you,' I said, in disbelief. 'You killed Dorothy Kilbride. And you tried to frame Harry for the murder.'

Edward Townsend smiled coldly. 'Well, Sir Hilary,' he said, levelling the revolver. 'It seems you're not as stupid as I thought you were.'

Chapter Twenty-Three

Townsend gestured me along a line of trees towards the circular hedge. A path ran through a gap into the bushes. It was nicely secluded, out of sight of the house or the cottage. 'You can't fire that,' I said, as I moved into the opening of the maze. 'I left the silencer in the butler's office. If you pull that trigger, people will come running.'

Townsend was unperturbed. 'There was a struggle. You tried to wrest the gun from my hand. It went off and you were accidentally killed.' He smiled tightly. 'You're the murderer, Sir Hilary. You've already confessed to it. No one will question my account of your death.'

He was right, at that. He could kill me now and get away scot-free. The devil. He had seemed so calm and collected. But beneath that smooth façade lurked something altogether more sinister.

'I want you to know,' Townsend said, stepping into the circular enclosure, 'I take no pleasure in this.'

I tripped backwards. A curved hedge served as the opening to an otherwise traditional rectangular maze; Sir Herbert Leon's grand folly. A saucer shaped bush in the centre of the circle erupted into a sharp point, rather like an arrowhead.

'Unfortunately,' said Townsend, with some regret, 'I have come too far to stop now.' At his direction, I stepped further back. There was a small gap in the bushes behind me. This was the entrance to the maze proper.

'So why did you do it?' I asked, playing for time. 'Why did you kill Dorothy Kilbride? What did she ever do to you?'

The man frowned. 'You wouldn't understand.'

'Let me guess.' I considered for a moment. It had to be something simple. Dorothy Kilbride had been the head of payroll at MI5. It must be something to do with money. But Townsend was not a government employee, so it had to be more personal than that. 'She caught you stealing,' I guessed. 'From Sir Vincent?'

The valet flinched. I had hit the mark, first time. 'It wasn't stealing,' he insisted. There was a look of wounded pride on his rock-like face. 'It was just a few shillings, added on to the accounts. Nothing much. For my retirement. You wouldn't understand, Sir Hilary. You've never had to work for a living.'

I didn't respond to that. One lesson I have learned in life: if you keep your mouth shut, the other person will always fill in the gaps. And I needed Townsend to keep talking. If I was going to die, I wanted to know the truth before he pulled that trigger. Luckily, the fellow seemed happy to confide in me. I was the only person he *could* talk to, after all.

'When they threw me out of the police force,' he said, 'I was left with nothing at all. No character, no pension.' He spoke in a harsh monotone. 'It was the worst time of my life. I wasn't a criminal. We were striking for better wages. And then I was out on the street. It was awful. Nobody cared. But the Colonel took pity on me and I was young enough to get back on my feet. But what happens the next time?' His eyes flared suddenly. 'I don't have any family. What happens when I get old, when I can't look after myself?'

'The Colonel would have provided for you.'

'I'm sure he means to. But he's older than I am. He could keel over tomorrow and I'd be out on my ear. Left with nothing. I just…I couldn't go through that again. All I wanted was to put a bit of money aside, a little security for my old age. Was that too much to ask?' Townsend was almost pleading with me now. It was rather unsettling to watch. 'It was only the odd pound, Sir Hilary. Everybody does it. And it's not as if the Colonel couldn't afford it. But that…that woman.' His face screwed up at the thought of Dorothy Kilbride. 'She wouldn't listen. She couldn't understand. Stealing was stealing, she said. Everything was black and white to her. It wasn't hurting Sir Vincent, but she was adamant: I had to tell him the truth, confess everything and throw myself on the Colonel's mercy. I couldn't bear to do that. I couldn't bear the shame. I'd be out on my ear. No references, no job, just like before.' His teeth ground together angrily. 'But if *I* didn't tell him, *she* would.

Miss Kilbride made that very clear to me.'

'So you decided to kill her.'

'I didn't want to. It wasn't even a serious idea. She gave me a few days to come clean and I had this notion of creeping into her room and smothering her with a pillow. But it was a fantasy, a daydream. I knew it was never really going to happen.' Townsend took a deep breath. 'Then you arrived with Mr Latimer.' His lip curled up and he regarded me with something approaching distaste. 'The Colonel asked me to keep an eye on the pair of you. Particularly Mr Latimer. We were all aware of just what a dubious character he was. And I knew there was something odd about that holdall he was carrying with him. He wouldn't let me take it upstairs with the rest of the luggage. So when he was in with the Colonel I searched his room and had a look inside. When I saw the Newton everything slotted into place.' He looked down at the small revolver, almost as if he was seeing it for the first time. 'I could creep into Miss Kilbride's bedroom one night while everyone was sleeping and all my problems would be over. It would be very quick. She wouldn't know anything about it. And Mr Latimer would get the blame. He's a criminal anyway. He would be the obvious suspect.'

'And that's what you did? You crept into her bedroom?'

'I'm not proud of it, Sir Hilary. But what choice did I have? I'd have been ruined.'

'But how did you even know she'd be in there?' How did he know about the mix up over the rooms?

'I overheard Miss Young and Miss Jones talking in the corridor. I'd crept up there a few minutes beforehand to retrieve the revolver from Mr Latimer's bedroom. When I came out, I heard the young ladies laughing about it over by the stairs. It just made things easier. I waited for them to disappear and then crept back down to the servants quarters.'

'Why didn't you kill Dorothy then? Why wait until four in the morning? Or whatever time it was?'

'Because everyone was in the ballroom at that point and they would have had watertight alibis. But once all the guests were in bed, anyone could be to blame. So I kept the revolver with me and, when I came downstairs, the first person I bumped into was you, Sir Hilary, in the servants' quarters. And you seemed even more nervous than I was.'

'You knew I'd killed Sinclair?'

Townsend shook his head. 'I didn't know he was dead at that point. It was only afterwards that I made the connection. And it made everything so much easier. I was going to blame Mr Latimer. Now I could blame you too. I could make out you'd put him up to it.'

'And what about Hargreaves? What about my poor valet?'

A look of regret passed across the man's granite face. 'He was a decent enough fellow. I didn't want to kill him. But he discovered the truth. I'd locked the revolver away in the butler's office, after I'd shot Miss Kilbride. Then this morning I grabbed it from there and hid it under Professor Singh's pillow.'

'Why on Earth would you do that?'

'Well, I couldn't plant it in Mr Latimer's room, could I? He was supposed to be a professional assassin. It was much more plausible that he would try to pin the murder on someone else. And Professor Singh's bedroom was next door.'

'So what about my valet?'

'Mr Hargreaves saw me coming out of the office, as I was about to begin the search. I'm not sure if he saw the gun, but he must have put two and two together, at least later on, after the Colonel had told everybody about Miss Kilbride.'

Typical Hargreaves, noticing everything.

'I saw him in the office later. He'd unlocked the bureau with the keys from the hook and was examining the revolver. I didn't have time to think. I took the bell pull and…well, I did it as quickly as I could. Luckily, there was no one else around. They had all gone off to church. And it added to my story. You hired Mr Latimer to kill Dorothy Kilbride. Mr Hargreaves found out about it and you killed him too.'

'What motive would I have had? For killing Dottie, I mean?'

'Blackmail. She knew you were a sodomite, Sir Hilary,

204

and threatened to expose you. That was what I was going to say, at any rate.'

I nodded 'All very neat.'

Townsend disagreed. 'I hadn't expected Mr Latimer to spend the night with Felicity Mandeville Jones. That could have ruined the whole story. But then I discovered the sleeping pills on the bedside table during our search and I made a point of mentioning them to the Colonel.'

'What about Doctor Lefranc? He was trying to pin the blame on Sir Vincent. That can't have been your intention.'

'It wasn't. I was just as surprised as you were. It was my own fault, Sir Hilary, saying the French Francs were MI5 issue. I thought that would connect Mr Latimer with Dorothy Kilbride. It didn't occur to me that Doctor Lefranc would suspect the Colonel.'

'The best laid plans...' I said, looking down at my feet. 'And now here we are.'

'Here we are,' Townsend agreed.

'Well, I'm glad you've had the opportunity to unburden your conscience.' Sarcasm was dripping from my voice.

'It's a relief to be able to talk about it,' the valet admitted, gazing at me sadly. 'But I think we've talked enough now.' He raised the revolver and aimed it squarely at my forehead. 'This is nothing personal, Sir Hilary. I really have no choice.'

I took a deep breath. And Townsend pulled the trigger.

Chapter Twenty-Four

It clicked quietly but no shot rang out. I don't know who was more startled, Townsend or I. The valet blinked first, his hand flicking around to examine the weapon. I stepped backwards almost without thinking and disappeared from view between the two hedges leading in to the rectangular maze. Townsend hesitated before following me. I could hear another dull click. He was examining the revolver, to see if every chamber was as empty as the first.

I hadn't thought to check the damned thing when I had picked up Harry's gun from the bureau in the butler's office. Thank heavens for my lack of common sense. I have never been much of a one for details. That was Hargreaves' department. I had simply assumed the revolver was loaded. Now I wasn't sure whether it had been emptied out altogether or whether there was some ammunition left in there. The Newton .32 has six chambers and only two bullets had been used to kill Dorothy Kilbride.

The easiest thing to do would have been to run, to lose myself in the maze, and then to shout out, in the hope that someone might find me before Townsend drew close. Even if the gun was not loaded, I stood little chance against the valet in a straight fight. He would probably throttle me before anyone managed to come to my rescue.

My only chance was to seize the element of surprise. My miraculous reprieve had robbed me of all fear and for the first time in what felt like several years, I was able to think rationally. Instead of running the length of the maze and rounding the far corner, to end up gods knows where, I would use Townsend's confidence against him. I would crouch here, next to the entrance, and wait for him to step into the maze.

The valet had finished checking the revolver, though with what result I could not be certain. He stepped forward through the gap in the hedges, turning quickly to the left, in my direction.

I had only a fraction of a second to act.

I launched myself at him from the crouching position, knocking the man sideways and attempting to overbalance him. He staggered backwards at the unexpected onslaught, but his frame was too solid to come crashing down even with my best attempt at a rugby tackle. I managed to grab hold of his wrists, though, which were still clasping the now obviously loaded revolver. For a moment, there was stalemate, but quickly Townsend dragged the barrel back towards my face. This time it was primed and ready to fire. I had only one option. I brought a knee up to his groin and whacked him as hard as I could. The valet pulled the trigger but the pain in his nether regions caused him to shift his arm momentarily and the shot thudded into the ground. The slight recoil unbalanced him – the grass was rather slippery beneath us – and for a brief instant I managed to twist his hand away from me. A second shot fired, Townsend squeezing the trigger again, and this time there was a look of puzzlement on his face. His hands slackened and he stood for a moment, gazing down in surprise at the red stain on his otherwise pristine shirt. His mouth formed a silent 'oh' and he dropped to his knees. I pulled the Newton away from him.

There were voices shouting from nearby and figures were running along the pathway into the circular hedges just as Townsend crashed to the floor. Mr Smith was leading the cavalry. I dropped the revolver to my side, but the fat northerner saw it in my hand and immediately jumped to the wrong conclusion.

'You murdering bastard!'

I didn't have the energy to raise a voice in protest.

Mr Smith charged straight at me. I felt a heavy thud and within seconds I found myself pinned down on the grass, underneath what felt like several tons of blubber. Mr Smith pulled the weapon away from my hands. For a brief, horrible moment I knew what it was like to be Mrs Smith, struggling under that great bulk, and then somehow he flipped me over onto my front and pulled my hands expertly behind my back.

I had thought Edward Townsend was the policeman, but it seemed John Smith knew a thing or two as well.

I didn't bother to struggle. It was all over now.

207

Townsend was dead and the unpleasantness at Bletchley Park had come to a rather abrupt conclusion.

'We're not going to take the word of a murderer, are we?' John Smith demanded, his eyes flashing with barely contained anger. 'He's killed at least two people. He probably killed all four of them.'

'I do not believe so, Monsieur,' said Doctor Lefranc. 'I think Sir Hilary is telling the truth.'

A court of enquiry had been convened in the dining hall of Bletchley Park mansion. They were all there. Mr and Mrs Smith, Doctor Lefranc, Professor Singh, Lettie Young, Felicity Mandeville Jones, Harry Latimer. The Colonel himself. Even Lady Fanny Leon. And all of them were staring at me with differing levels of contempt.

Three MI5 officers had arrived from London just after midday, trundling up the tree-lined pathway in their muted green Austin 12 just as I was struggling with Edward Townsend in the maze. That had been about an hour ago. John Smith had been coming back from church with his wife at around the same time and had seen the large green van pulling up at the far end of the carriage turnabout. He went across to see who was inside and wasn't far from the maze entrance when he heard the first shot. The bluff northerner sprinted over with surprising speed, considering his enormous bulk, and the officers from London had followed in quick order.

Within minutes, most of the household seemed to have arrived at the crime scene. The Colonel, coming from the cottage with Harry and Samuel Jenkins, had quickly taken charge. Harry Latimer was still in handcuffs and could only look on in bemusement as Mr Smith held me down on the grass.

'It was Townsend!' I exclaimed breathlessly, unable to see the valet's body now with the side of my head pushed down into the muddy ground. 'He murdered Dorothy. He killed my valet. And he tried to shoot me.'

The MI5 men quickly took over from Mr Smith. I was

escorted back along the pathway to the main house. One of the officers remained behind at the maze, to examine the body of Edward Townsend and to be brought up to date by the Colonel.

Lady Fanny Leon was standing at the front of the mansion, fresh from church and as stern looking in her way as the griffins either side of her. The remaining valets and ladies' maids were lined up outside the porch, almost as if they were greeting a returning lord, but their expressions revealed somewhat darker feelings. Harry and I were being manhandled back into the house and there was only one conclusion they could draw from that.

We were responsible for everything that had happened.

Lettie was one of the group. Her pretty, painted face was a mosaic of sadness and disappointment. For the first time, I felt ashamed.

Harry winked at Felicity Mandeville Jones as he passed her by. He at least was in good humour. But then, he was in the clear; or would be once I had told everyone the truth about Townsend. My situation was rather more precarious. 'You'll be all right, old man,' Harry reassured me. He was determined to look on the bright side. 'It was self defence, wasn't it?'

I scoffed. 'It wasn't even that. Townsend pulled the trigger. His death had nothing to do with me.'

'There you are then. Home and dry.' Harry wriggled his back awkwardly as the two of us were deposited in the library. 'Hey, is someone going to find the key and get me out of these things?' His hands were still cuffed behind his back and he was finding it devilishly uncomfortable.

The two officers ignored Harry but exchanged a few brief words with each other. One of them then departed, leaving the other man standing silently in the doorway, to keep watch.

'No sense of humour, some people,' Harry muttered in my ear.

The guard wore a black suit and had closely cropped hair. He did not speak to us at all. Not that we would have had anything to say to one another. We were not about to exchange addresses, after all.

It was some minutes before the Colonel arrived. He

spoke briefly to the chap at the door, handing him a set of keys he had recovered from the body of his valet. Harry was released from his bondage and escorted across the hall to the dining room.

The Colonel remained behind. He regarded me sadly as he stepped into the room. 'All a bit of a mess, isn't it?'

'I'll say.'

There were a couple of leather armchairs opposite the fireplace. The Colonel gestured to a chair and we sat ourselves down. With a wall of books behind us, we looked for all the world like two colleagues in a gentleman's club sharing a glass of whisky. Actually, there was still a drop of the golden nectar left in a decanter on the table but my head was starting to throb and, just for once, I didn't feel like a drink. I had probably had enough this morning.

'So what happened, Butler?' The Colonel leaned across eagerly. 'The truth, mind.'

I explained, as best I could. I told him what Townsend had told me and about the struggle for the gun. The Colonel listened without interruption and when I had finished he let out a long sigh. 'You do believe me?' I asked, anxiously.

He nodded. 'I know you didn't murder Dorothy Kilbride. And I don't think Latimer did either. It fits the facts, Butler. Sadly, it fits the facts.'

'You know Doctor Lefranc suspected you were behind it all?'

The Colonel laughed. 'With good reason, so I hear. Ha ha! But no, Townsend was the chap. He was the rotten apple.' The Colonel sat back in his chair. 'Should have seen it, Butler. I should have damn well seen it.' He stared into the empty grate, looking suddenly very old. 'I've shown poor judgement in this affair. I should have realised something was up with Townsend.' He frowned. 'He had been acting a bit odd these last few days. I thought he was just worried about his sister. She was taken ill, you know.'

'I remember you saying.'

The Colonel shook his head. 'I wonder if he's even *got* a sister. Not the chap I thought he was, Butler. Not the chap at all.'

We sat in silence for a moment.

'What will happen now? To me, I mean.'

The Colonel adjusted his monocle. 'That remains to be seen. Hollis and MacLean are sorting out the bodies. But the guests are waiting for some kind of explanation and I think we're going to have to give it to them.' He grunted. 'Whether they believe it or not is another matter. But we need to convince them you're telling the truth. If we're going to keep a lid on this, Butler, we'll need everyone on board. No exceptions.'

'You think that's possible?' I said. 'To hush everything up?'

'We can but try.'

I nodded, pulling myself up. 'Let's get it over with, then.'

The dining room was almost full. Lady Fanny Leon sat imperiously at the head of the table, the female equivalent of a high court judge. Actually, her silver hair was not dissimilar to a barrister's wig. The guests were seated as they had been at breakfast, though the table now was almost bare and the servants had been banished to the back hall. The staff would be given their own explanations in due course. Samuel Jenkins was the only representative of the lower orders. We needed somebody to serve the tea, after all, and the young Welshman already knew a lot more about the day's events than most of the guests.

The room fell silent as the Colonel escorted me into position. I seated myself next to Professor Singh, but Sir Vincent remained standing and began to address the company. If this was a court of enquiry, then the Colonel was definitely one of the barristers, though whether he was acting for the prosecution or the defence I couldn't yet tell. It was obvious, however, which side the jury was on.

Mrs Smith sat with pursed lips directly opposite me, her disapproval evident without a word being spoken. The vicar of St Mary's had chosen this particular Sunday to deliver a sermon on the subject of the Ten Commandments, and there was an evangelical gleam in the woman's cold, pretty eyes.

211

Goodness knows how many Commandments I had broken in the last twenty-four hours.

John Smith was seated next to his wife, his attention flicking between me and his insufferable home counties bride. The two had clearly had words about the diamonds, but it looked as if the Yorkshire man had been forgiven. I doubted Mary Smith would feel quite as charitable towards me.

A public confession of guilt is the purest form of agony it is possible to inflict upon a man. Or a woman, come to that. I don't like making speeches at the best of times, but the audience here was far from friendly. Few of the guests wanted to meet my eye. Even Lettie Young was gazing into her lap, biting her lip sadly as I recounted the circumstances of my fateful encounter with Anthony Sinclair.

John Smith wanted clarification of the nature of the argument between us. Harry was altogether too forthcoming. 'So you're a bloody pervert as well as a murderer,' Mr Smith concluded.

Doctor Lefranc could have spoken up at this point and revealed the whole truth. He knew far more about me than anyone else and he must have guessed the rest of it by now. A woman masquerading as a man had killed another man to protect her secret. Everything else had come out, why not reveal that too? The doctor held his tongue, however – though I was past caring – and did not contradict the official story. Being a sodomite was accusation enough, a terrible crime by the standards of the day, though I haven't the foggiest idea why. More fuel for Mrs Smith's disapproval. I swear the damn woman took pleasure in being offended.

Doctor Lefranc corroborated some parts of my story and freely admitted drawing the wrong conclusions about Harry Latimer. 'I am very sorry, Monsieur,' he said, addressing the American directly. 'It appears I have misjudged you.'

Harry shrugged. 'It happens, old man, it happens.'

He had also been mistaken about the Colonel, of course, and here the doctor was profuse in his apologies. Luckily, Sir Vincent was not a man to bear a grudge.

'Don't give it another thought, old chap.'

I too had got the wrong end of the stick, if not about the Colonel then at least about Harry. How many years had I known him? Ten? Fifteen? Yet I had happily believed him to be a murderer. I had even pulled a gun on him. Lord, what had I been thinking?

When at last my account drew to a close – repeating once again everything Townsend had told me about the murder of Dorothy Kilbride – Mr Smith immediately poured scorn on the whole story. 'I'm not going to take the word of a sodomite and a self-confessed murderer,' he exclaimed.

'It wasn't murder!' Lettie Young spoke up suddenly. 'Don't you bleedin' well listen? It was an accident. An argument that got out of hand!' The young woman met my eyes at last, the whisper of a smile on her ruby red lips. She had accepted what I said and was coming to my defence. 'You stupid pillock,' she added, for good measure.

'Don't you speak like that to my husband!' Mrs Smith snarled.

'I'll speak how I bleedin' well like, you toffee nosed cow.'

'Jonathan. You're not going to let this music hall trollop speak to me like that?' Mrs Smith rose to her feet.

'Ladies, please!' the Colonel implored.

A throat was cleared at the far end of the table. All eyes turned abruptly to Lady Fanny Leon. The authority of the woman was absolute. It might as well have been the Queen Mother sitting there. 'You are all guests in my house. I would ask you to behave with the appropriate respect.'

That silenced even Mary Smith. Lady Fanny was a woman of few words, but when she spoke everybody listened. Mrs Smith returned to her seat and her husband placed a reassuring hand on her arm.

'We have heard Sir Hilary's account of events,' Lady Fanny continued. 'Sir Vincent, do you have anything to add?'

The Colonel nodded. 'Thank you, Lady Fanny. Just one thing. I believe Butler has told us the truth. My man Townsend was responsible for the murder of Dorothy Kilbride. He was also responsible for the death of Butler's valet.'

Doctor Lefranc was in full agreement.

'As for Townsend's demise, that was his own damned fault.' The Colonel had little sympathy. 'As far as I'm concerned, Butler here can only be blamed for the death of Anthony Sinclair.'

'Make's no difference,' said Mr Smith. 'Even if it's just one person, he's still a murderer.'

'That may well be true. But there are bigger issues at stake.'

Harry Latimer knew just what the Colonel was driving at. 'It was *your* valet who murdered *your* secretary.'

'Quite right,' the man admitted. 'Which doesn't reflect very well on me. As head of the Security Service, I should have known what was going on. Rather poor judgement on my part. No two ways about it.'

That was something Mrs Smith could agree with 'An honourable man would resign,' she suggested acidly.

'You're quite right my dear. And in ordinary circumstances, that is exactly what I would do. I'd be more than happy to retire and pass on the reins. But now isn't the time for a change in leadership. If I stepped down, especially if there was some kind of scandal, the current administration would use it as an excuse to wind up the Security Service altogether. They'd transfer everything over to Special Branch or merge it all under one roof with the SIS.'

'That would not be wise,' Doctor Lefranc thought.

Professor Singh nodded his agreement.

'No, it wouldn't,' the Colonel said. 'I happen to believe MI5 serves a vital role in the smooth running of this country. We keep people safe in their beds. But to be brutally frank, ladies, gentlemen: if I go, the institution goes with me. That's not idle boasting. It's my own damned fault – taking on too much, becoming indivisible with the whole show. Britain needs MI5. But if this gets out, the Security Service is finished. We'll be a laughing stock. And before we know it, the wolves will pounce.'

'So it is necessary for everything to be kept secret.'

'That's about the size of it, Lefranc. No one can ever

know what happened here this weekend. Not one word can be allowed to get out. And everyone here has to agree to keep that secret.'

Felicity Mandeville Jones was frowning. 'It will be frightfully difficult, Sir Vincent. Four people have been killed.'

'I realise that, my dear. But we're professionals here. We've all signed the Official Secrets Act. If anyone can keep this quiet, we can.'

'What about the servants?' the girl asked.

Lady Fanny had no concerns there. 'I will see to that, Miss Jones. No one in my employ will breathe a word of this to anyone.'

That I could well believe. Nobody in their right mind would risk provoking the wrath of Lady Fanny Leon.

Mr Smith remained sceptical. 'How are you going to cover up the death of Anthony Sinclair? He was on the phone to his office. They know he was here. And I was on the phone to my Mr Butterworth just this morning'

'I did ask everyone not to use the telephone,' the Colonel said testily. 'We'll transfer Sinclair back to London this afternoon. He came here for the weekend at the invitation of Lady Fanny, but was taken ill and died on the way back to London.'

'There'll have to be an inquest though,' said Mr Smith.

'I have a couple of tame coroners in London who will rubber stamp anything that needs rubber stamping, if they believe it is a matter of national security.'

'What about Miss Kilbride? And your valet?' I asked.

'I'll say Townsend has gone to visit his sister in Ireland. He can stay there to nurse her. Dottie...well, she can die somewhere else in a few days time. Don't worry, gentlemen, ladies. I'll make sure she gets a decent send off. It's the least she deserves. And we'll have a proper turn out from the office. But there'll be no connection with Bletchley Park.'

'Did Dorothy have any relatives?' Felicity Mandeville Jones enquired.

'A mother in Stoke, I believe. I'll break the news as sensitively as I can. As for your man Hargreaves. Butler, do you

215

have any special requests?'

I shook my head. 'Not really. Just a proper Christian burial. I'll meet the expenses, of course. I suppose you ought to inform his aunt. Not that she'll remember who he is. She's in a nursing home now.'

The valet, Samuel Jenkins, was standing over by the window. He had turned away from us for a moment to look out across the lawn. 'They're moving Mr Sinclair from the cottage,' he observed, by way of explanation. Two officers, Hollis and MacLean, were carrying the stretcher across the gravel. The body was loaded carefully into the back of the Austin 12.

'We're going to take *all* the bodies up to London,' the Colonel said. 'Get them cleaned up. We'll put the word out about Sinclair later this afternoon. After we've informed his wife, of course. Don't want her hearing it from anyone else, do we Jenkins?'

'No, sir. Thank you, sir.'

'You've got it all worked out,' Mr Smith observed, sounding less than impressed. 'There's just one thing you haven't mentioned, Colonel.' He nodded his head towards me. 'What are we going to do about *him*?' His eyes mirrored the righteous fury of his priggish little wife. Perhaps they weren't such a bad match after all.

'He can't be allowed to get away with murder,' Mrs Smith asserted bluntly.

It was left to Professor Singh to inject a quiet note of subversion. 'Let him who is without sin...' he whispered.

Mr Smith glared at the academic. 'Hey, I'm no bloody saint, I know that. I lied to my wife and tried to cover things up. But she's forgiven me.'

Mary Smith smiled tightly. 'I take my marriage vows very seriously.' She clasped her husband's hand on top of the table. 'I took an oath before God. For richer, for poorer. In sickness and in health.'

'But neither of us caved anybody's head in with an iron poker. And I don't reckon murder should ever go unpunished. Leastways, not in a civilised society.'

'Hey, it wasn't exactly murder,' said Harry, leaping to my defence. 'Just a little fight that got out of hand.'

'I don't call hitting someone over the head with an iron poker "a little fight".'

'But it was not a premeditated act, Monsieur.' Doctor Lefranc was rather better versed in the law than Mr Smith. 'That means it is manslaughter rather than murder.'

'Aye, well, you can put what label you like on it, it's still murder in my book. And he has to pay the price.'

'You can't just decide he's guilty,' Lettie Young declared forcefully. 'We ain't bleedin' savages. There has to be a trial. Even I know that. Judge and jury.'

John Smith shook his head. 'We don't need a trial, love. He's already admitted his guilt. All we need to do is pass sentence.'

The Colonel cleared his throat. 'There are some practical considerations here. We can't exactly throw him in jail.'

Mr Smith met his gaze. 'We don't need a *jail*, Colonel.'

'Now hang on just one bleedin' minute…' It was all too obvious what Mr Smith was suggesting. Lettie Young was horrified.

I wasn't too happy about it either. My God, I thought, swallowing hard. They want to string me up.

The clock out in the lounge hall began to chime the quarter hour. The Colonel raised a hand for silence. 'A few more opinions might be in order, Smith, before we rush in to anything. What do you think, Miss Jones?'

Felicity Mandeville Jones considered carefully before answering. 'It was an awful thing to do,' she said at last. 'Anthony was a bit of an ogre, but he didn't deserve to die like that.' There were a few nods of agreement.

'Miss Young?'

'Hilary ain't a bad bloke,' Lettie said. 'We all make mistakes.' She gave me a reassuring smile. 'I think we should let him go.'

Harry agreed with her. 'I guess that goes for me too.'

'You would bloody well say that,' Mr Smith muttered.

The Colonel raised a hand to forestall any arguments. 'Professor Singh? What do you think?'

The professor cleared his throat. There was a collective groan around the table as the academic leaned forward to speak. 'The purpose of a judicial system, it seems to me, is to protect society from an individual whose behaviour poses a threat to the well being of others within that community. If possible, it seeks to reform the individual, and in certain circumstances it seeks to punish them, as a deterrent for others who may be considering a similar course of action. It seems unlikely to me that the circumstances of this particular crime will ever arise again. Sir Hilary poses no threat to society and, since he acknowledges his guilt and has expressed regret for his actions, he is not in need of reform. Some form of public retribution might be appropriate in ordinary circumstances, but since any action we take will not be witnessed beyond these four walls, it cannot conceivably act as a deterrent to others. I believe therefore that there would be no benefit in punishing Sir Hilary any further for his crimes. His own guilt will serve to punish him and, I hope, will serve to guide his future actions.' The professor sat back in his chair with some satisfaction.

As always, when he finished speaking, there was a moment of confused silence, though Doctor Lefranc was already nodding his head vigorously. He at least seemed to understand what the fellow was going on about. Another one on my side, it appeared.

'Mrs Smith?' the Colonel asked, anxious to move on.

Her opinion barely needed stating. 'An eye for an eye, Sir Vincent. Nothing less will do.'

'Mr Smith?'

'The wife and I are of the same mind.'

'Very well.' The Colonel looked to the head of the table. 'Lady Fanny? You have the casting vote.'

The great matriarch took a moment to consider the matter. 'I do appreciate the need for secrecy, Sir Vincent. But a crime has been committed and justice must be served.'

The Colonel nodded. 'Very well. That settles it. I'm sorry, Butler, but there has to be a reckoning. Menzies, will you escort him back to the library?' The MI5 officer stepped forward from the doorway. 'We need a few moments in private to determine the appropriate sentence.'

'Now, hang on a minute...' I said, rising to my feet.

'I'm sorry, Butler,' the Colonel told me firmly. 'We won't keep you long. But this has to be done properly.'

'If you'll come this way, sir,' the officer prompted.

I looked around the table one last time. Few of the guests would meet my eye. Lettie was struggling to maintain her composure. Harry gave me a sad smile. But it was obvious now what was going to happen.

The library was as quiet as a funeral parlour. Menzies stood impassively in the doorway, a virtual automaton in a dark suit, though like the Mona Lisa his eyes followed me whenever I moved around.

The book Professor Singh had been reading lay abandoned on a table near the fireplace. I picked it up. *Crime and Punishment* indeed. I flung the damn thing onto the fire. The hearth was unlit, but that was beside the point.

I moved across to the window. I could feel the eyes of the MI5 man watching me as I gazed forlornly across the lawn. The sky was cloudy now and a few spots of rain were beginning to fall. The steeple of St Mary's Church was barely visible in the middle distance. There were too many trees in the way to see it properly from this angle. It was too late for redemption in any case.

I couldn't blame Mr and Mrs Smith. If Harry had bludgeoned someone to death, would I have defended him? Probably not. I wondered if he would miss me when I was gone. I hoped so. We had had some good times together. The smooth talking rogue.

A copy of the Sunday Times was lying discarded on the floor. I had fallen asleep having barely glanced at the headlines earlier on. I grabbed hold of the paper now and sat down, flicking through the over-sized pages. Wall Street was still the main topic of conversation. The Yanks had been lucky to survive the week, they said. But I couldn't really bring myself to care.

Occasional sounds filtered into the library from the rest of the house, but whenever I looked up I was greeted with that same expressionless face. Where did the Colonel find these men? They could have been waxworks, they were so immobile. Or Beefeaters. I wondered idly if the Crown Jewels were lying unprotected in the Tower Of London this afternoon.

Half an hour went by with excruciating slowness.

And then at last, the familiar figure of the Colonel popped his head around the door and quietly entered the room. He was carrying a small briefcase. His face was every bit as sombre as that of the automaton standing to his left. He gestured Menzies away and closed the door quietly behind him.

I did my best to smile. 'What's the verdict?' I asked.

'Not good, I'm afraid.' The Colonel came across and sat opposite me. 'You have to understand, Butler, there are bigger considerations here. If it was up to me, I'd let you go. You did a terrible thing, but you're not a bad chap.' He took a deep breath. 'But others feel, understandably, that a price has to be paid.' He reached down and opened the briefcase. 'We couldn't put you in prison. The Smiths wanted to hang you from the chandeliers. But I managed to persuade them to give you another option.' He pulled Harry's revolver out of the briefcase. 'I'm very sorry, old chap.' He placed the Newton down on the table in front of me. 'But you're going to have to die.'

Chapter Twenty-Five

I pride myself I am not a coward, but imminent death is a difficult concept to grasp with equanimity. I swallowed hard and tried not to grip my hands together too tightly. 'I understand,' I said, keeping my voice as level as I could. But the blood was draining from my face. 'Better for me to do it. It wouldn't be fair to ask anyone else.'

'Smith volunteered, but I wasn't having that,' the Colonel said grimly. 'Two bullets left in there. Should do the job nicely.' He leaned in. 'But listen, Butler.' His eyes glistened mischievously. 'I'm not really expecting you to blow your own brains out.'

'I...don't understand.'

'There may be a way out of this. But it's not going to be easy.'

I didn't know what to say. 'I'm listening.'

The Colonel kept his voice low. 'I had a quick discussion with Lefranc and my man Hollis. It's obvious that the Smiths won't be satisfied unless justice is seen to be done. So justice is exactly what we're going to give them.' He gestured to the revolver on the table. 'I'm going to leave the room in a minute. When I've gone, I want you to pick up the gun, fire a shot into the air and then lie down on the floor over there. We'll leave it a few seconds, then Lefranc and I will come into the room. The doctor will examine you and confirm that you're dead. Then we'll get a stretcher, cover you over with a sheet and my men can carry you out to the van and put you in with the other bodies. Couldn't be simpler!'

I was speechless. 'You would do that, for me?'

The Colonel nodded. 'It's not an ideal solution, Butler. It won't be easy for you. You can never go back to your wife or see any of your friends. You'll have to start everything over again from scratch.'

I shrugged. 'Better than the alternative, I suppose.'

'Well, quite. My men will drive you down to London. We can put you on a train for Dover. Lefranc has kindly given up his ticket to Calais this evening. The ferry leaves at eight o'clock sharp and we can have you in France by half past nine.

I was overwhelmed. 'I don't know what to say.'

'Don't say anything. You'll need a disguise, though, and a fake passport. Don't want anyone recognising you on the train! Lefranc suggested we put you in a frock. A wig and some glasses, should do the trick.'

I almost choked. I didn't realise Doctor Lefranc had such a well developed sense of humour. 'I don't think I'd make a convincing woman,' I said, managing to keep a straight face.

The Colonel eyed me critically. 'Neither do I. But it's only for a day or two. With a bit of make up on, you'll pass well enough. Lefranc will come back with me to London later this afternoon, when we've finished up here. We'll get some proper documents sorted out then and the doctor can bring them across the Channel and meet up with you later in the week. We'll give you a whole new identity, a clean slate. Do you have any preference for a name?'

I shrugged. I couldn't think of anything, off the top of my head. 'Just something bland. Nothing ostentatious.'

'Righty-ho. How are you for cash?'

'I can probably get by for a day or two.'

'Capital! That's settled then. We'll have to announce your death, of course. Arrange the funeral etc.'

'Ah. Right.' I didn't like the sound of that.

'Has to be done, Butler. We'll need a decent cover story, too. Did you tell anyone you were coming up here this weekend?'

'I told my wife. But I just said Buckinghamshire. And I think my maid Jenny saw the invitation, but not the address.'

'Good. We'll find a hotel somewhere and say you stayed there for the weekend. Don't want you dying in Bletchley Park at the same time as Sinclair. Let's say Wolverton, shall we? I've heard that's quite pleasant. I'll get someone to drive your car over there and you can die peacefully in your sleep this evening.'

'Lord.' This really was going to happen. 'What will you tell my wife?'

The Colonel didn't blink. 'Undiagnosed heart condition. Could have happened to anyone. We'll think of something.'

'I don't think she'll be too upset, as long as there's no scandal.' I chuckled briefly, imagining her reaction. 'She'll probably make quite a merry widow.' Society, for some reason, had a greater tolerance of widows than it did of married women. 'Do you really think you'll be able to keep all of this quiet?'

'No choice, Butler. Everyone knows the form. And I've covered up bigger secrets than this before now.' That I could believe. 'Once you're safely dead, Mr and Mrs Smith will keep mum. They've given me their word. They may not be the most charitable of people, Butler, but they know their duty. As do we all.'

I nodded. 'One question I do have, Colonel. If it's not a little impertinent.' There was one loose end I was dying to tie up.

'Go on.'

'What did Harry do for you, to get you to rescue him like that from the French police?'

The Colonel smiled apologetically. 'Need to know, I'm afraid. Can't go into details, old chap. You know how it is. But an enormous service, during the War. And no matter what he's done since then, we owed him a debt of gratitude.'

'I'm going to owe *you* a favour, after all this.'

'I may well hold you to that.' The Colonel rose to his feet. 'Well, better get on with it, eh? Try not to breathe too much when we carry you out. The Smiths will be watching.'

I stood up and shook the old devil by the hand. 'I can't believe you would do all this. For me.'

'You're family, Butler. We look after our own. And you deserve a second chance.' He moved towards the door. 'Oh, try not to damage the light fittings when you pull that trigger. Lady Fanny would never forgive me.' He was on the verge of barking out that familiar laugh, but restrained himself at the last moment. Now was not the time. He closed the door quietly behind him and I was left all alone.

I picked up the revolver from the table and cradled it in

my hand for a moment. If only I had left the damn thing back in London. It was my own greed that had got me here. I should have told Harry what to do with his fifty quid. Ah well. Life was like that. Elizabeth would not miss me. But I would miss her. And I would miss Harry too.

There was no point dwelling on the past, however. A new life beckoned. Not the light fittings, the Colonel had said.

I aimed the Newton at the top of one of the armchairs and squeezed the trigger. A bullet tore through the leather and smacked into the bookcase behind, obliterating a first edition of Boswell's *Life of Johnson*. I almost fired a second shot as a reflex action, but I managed to stop myself in time. One bullet was probably sufficient.

My life was over. I was dead at long last.

A cool breeze wafted in through the glass doors of the Café Rohan. An elderly customer shambled through the entrance and took up his regular place at a table opposite the main till. I could feel the chill on my legs as the cold air circulated across the room. The sooner I could get back into a decent pair of trousers the better. After a lifetime living as a man, I couldn't get used to wearing a skirt. My legs felt so exposed. And as for the shoes...

I gazed out across the square. The Palais Rohan stood opposite the café, an imposing Romanesque edifice competing for attention with the rather more gothic Cathédrale Saint-André across the way. I tapped my fingers irritably. I had received a telephone call the previous evening at the Hotel de Ville. Doctor Lefranc had arrived in Paris and was calling to tell me he was on his way with the new documents at long last. We'd arranged to meet up at Friday lunchtime on the Place Pey-Berland – the square I could see through the café window now – but the doctor was running late.

A surly French waiter came over and pointedly removed my empty cup. I had no choice but to order another coffee. It was foul stuff, but marginally more attractive than the tea. I like to be broad minded, but the Frogs just don't know how to brew tea properly. My French was limited to a few words and, as none of the locals could be bothered to learn English, there was no point trying to describe the correct procedure. Easier just to drink their foul coffee instead.

It had taken a couple of days to get to Bordeaux from London. That had been the easy part of the journey. The first hundred yards between the library at Bletchley Park and the back of that large green Austin 12 had been by far the hardest.

Doctor Lefranc had rushed into the library after I had fired my shot. The Colonel and a couple of his men followed him in, making sure the door was quickly locked behind them, so nobody would notice the absence of a large hole in my forehead. I laid myself decorously across the floor and kept my eyes closed, for form's sake. After a few minutes, a stretcher was brought into the room. I was loaded onto it and covered over with the ubiquitous white sheet.

Doctor Lefranc leaned in closely to me as the stretcher was being lifted. 'I will see you again, Madame,' he whispered mischievously.

The journey through the hallway to the van was the longest of my life. I had to stop myself from holding my breath, for fear that I might suddenly let it all out in one tremendous burst. Instead, I concentrated on trying to keep my stomach level. I could picture in my mind all the guests standing outside, immobile like the griffins, or perhaps like the MI5 officers, gazing solemnly at the Colonel's men as they loaded me into the back of the Austin with all the other corpses. I fancied I heard a woman crying, but perhaps that was just my vanity. None of the house guests at Bletchley Park could feel any more wretched and humiliated than I did at that moment.

Sharing a rather cramped green van with four dead bodies was a picnic in comparison, even if one of them was my own dead valet. Poor old Hargreaves, I thought. It was hardly the ending he deserved.

We made good time to London. Once there, I was smuggled into an apartment block and some clothes were provided. A photograph was taken for the passport. The Colonel's men had a good laugh when they caught sight of me in my wig and skirt. 'I don't fancy yours much,' one said to the other. There were a few mocking whistles. One of them passed me the doctored passport. I shuddered when I saw the name on the front of it: *Miss D A Kilbride*. We were in Dottie's flat. A drab, spartan set of rooms in an unfashionable district of London.

The clothes I had borrowed from the deceased were equally drab. But the point was not to draw attention to myself and that I seemed to manage with little effort.

The officers dropped me off at Waterloo Station and from there I caught a train to Dover. By eight o'clock, I was on the ferry to Calais.

That had been five days ago.

I took out my pocket watch again. The Colonel had promised me my new documents in a couple of days but so far they had not arrived. Now I was running out of money. I didn't even have enough cash to pay for the coffees, let alone my hotel bill. Doctor Lefranc was my last hope.

And there the little man was, limping slightly but hurrying across the square, his short, plump frame a welcome sight in the drab November afternoon. He caught sight of me in the window and waved a friendly hand. I was surprised he recognised me. But then, of course, he had seen me dressed as a woman once before.

The waiter plonked down another cup of coffee as Lefranc pushed through the glass doors and another gust of wind assaulted my nether regions. I will never get used to wearing a skirt.

'Sir Hilary,' Lefranc gushed, extending his hands and coming forward. 'It is good to see you. I am sorry I am late. The trains were delayed.' He gazed down at my drab feminine clothes. 'You are looking delightful, Madame.'

'Don't you start,' I growled, gesturing for him to take a seat.

'They suit you very well.' His eyes flashed in amusement. 'You have worn women's clothes before, have you not?'

'Yes, when I was pregnant. But that was just a smock.

226

You can get away with dressing like a country bumpkin when you're blown up like a weather balloon. But this…'

Lefranc frowned. 'A *"bumpkin"*?'

'Never mind.' I shifted uncomfortably in my chair. It was difficult to believe these clothes were actually *designed* for someone of my shape. They were ridiculously uncomfortable. It was the stockings that were the killer. The fastenings were so damn fiddly. And I couldn't get used to dressing myself. 'The sooner I get shot of these bloody clothes, the better. I need to find myself a new valet.'

'Or a ladies maid,' Lefranc teased.

'A valet,' I insisted. 'I'd have offered that fellow Jenkins a job, if circumstances were different.'

'I believe the Colonel is planning to take him on. Subject to the appropriate enquiries, of course. He will want to be very careful this time.' A new valet would have to be thoroughly vetted. They didn't want another murderer running loose, after all.

The waiter was standing over us. He had taken note of the new arrival and stood poised with his notepad.

I growled. 'Un café, sivousplate.'

The waiter shuffled away. 'You are learning the language.'

'Barely. How did things go at Bletchley? Did the Colonel manage to keep on top of everything?'

'I believe so. People will not talk. They know how important it is to keep everything quiet.'

'Didn't see anything about it in the papers. Not that you can get English papers out here.'

'There were a few obituaries for Mr Sinclair. One for you as well, so I understand. But nobody asked any awkward questions. I believe the press have bigger concerns this week.'

'I'll say.' The stock market in America had finally come crashing down on Tuesday 29th October and the papers were having a field day. Even I had been able to translate the horrified headline on the front page of Le Figaro. Any hopes Mr Smith had of saving his business were in tatters. But Mary Smith, I had no doubt, would stand by her husband. More fool her.

The waiter returned with the doctor's coffee. Lefranc took a sip and winced. 'Mr Sinclair was buried yesterday afternoon. Your own funeral is scheduled for ten o'clock this morning.' The doctor glanced at his wrist watch. 'It will probably be over by now.'

I frowned. I didn't like to think about that. 'Whose body will they use?' The undertakers had to put somebody in the coffin. 'Not my man Hargreaves, surely?'

Lefranc shook his head. 'No. Your valet will be buried separately. And not for some days yet, I am afraid.'

'Oh?' That was a little strange. 'Why the delay?'

'The Colonel thought it might seem odd if the two of you died at the same time. But a cover story has been prepared. Officially Mr Hargreaves is still alive.' The doctor smiled sadly. 'But he suffered a stroke after discovering your body at the hotel in Wolverton. He will thus be unable to attend your funeral. And, of course, he is not expected to recover.'

I nodded. 'What about the coffin?'

'As I understand it, Mr Townsend's body will be used, in place of your own.'

That sounded sensible. 'So how did Elizabeth take the news? About me, I mean.'

Lefranc shrugged. 'As well as can be expected, Monsieur. The Colonel says there will be a good turn out at the church. Even Miss Young will be there, paying her respects. Sir Vincent was not happy about that, but the young woman insisted.'

'That was kind of her.' I smiled. 'Lord, I wonder what Elizabeth will think, having some East End girl turning up to my funeral?' My wife was even more of a snob than I was. I grinned at the thought. Good old Lettie.

'She will not draw any undue attention. As far as the press is concerned, she is simply there as a companion of the Colonel. His niece, in fact.'

I sighed wistfully. 'I wonder if I'll ever bump into her again.'

'It is unlikely, Monsieur, but perhaps not impossible.

Monsieur. Madame.' Lefranc smiled. 'You confuse even me. I think you make a better woman than you would like to admit.'

'Nonsense.' The fellow was deranged. 'As soon as I have the new documents it's back to normal. Life as an ageing flapper is too damn complicated. You *do* have the new documents?'

'But of course.' Lefranc reached into his jacket and produced a small brown envelope. 'The Colonel has also provided a little currency to tide you over.'

'That was thoughtful of him.' Now that I was separated from Elizabeth I would have no regular income. It was a horrifying thought, but I might actually have to find a job.

I took the envelope and saw with gratitude that there was quite a hefty wad of French Francs in there. All with MI5 serial codes, no doubt. 'You've done me proud, Doctor Lefranc,' I said, flipping the currency through my fingers. 'Not just this. Everything. For keeping quiet about...well.' I gestured to my clothes. 'All of this. You could have blabbed to the Colonel. Especially when you discovered I'd killed Anthony Sinclair.'

'It was not my business, Monsieur.'

'Even so, I'm grateful.' I sat back in my chair. 'You know, now that Hargreaves is dead, you're the only person in the whole world who knows the truth.'

Lefranc's moustache twitched slightly. 'Perhaps not the only one.'

I frowned. 'What do you mean?'

'I could be wrong, Monsieur but I have the strangest feeling Sir Vincent Kelly also knows.' He raised his hands. 'Oh, I have not said a word. But I think he knows. I think he has *always* known.'

'Good lord.' The thought had never occurred to me. My father had got me the job at MI5. Perhaps he had tipped Sir Vincent the wink, all those years ago. Could that be the reason the Colonel had let me go? He had always been rather protective of the ladies.

Lefranc took another sip of coffee. 'I could be wrong, of course. It does happen occasionally.'

I returned the cash to the envelope and pulled out a few of the documents. Dottie's old passport was back at the hotel. I would have to retrieve it at some point and give it back. Or destroy it.

I grimaced as I caught sight of the name on the cover of the new passport. 'Oh, very funny.' I could just imagine the Colonel chuckling to himself as he scribbled it down. '"*Mr R J Bland*." What kind of a name is that?'

'I believe it is what you asked for, Monsieur.' Lefranc smiled, peering across at the passport in my hands. 'Where will you go next?'

'I quite fancied Spain,' I said. 'See what the Dagos are up to.' Perhaps they would know how to make a decent cup of tea.

'The Colonel asks that you leave a forwarding address. He may have a job for you, Monsieur, in the very near future.'

I put the documents down on the table. 'Oh. What kind of job?'

Lefranc took a sip of his coffee. His moustache was twitching a second time. 'That you will have to discover for yourself.'

The Red Zeppelin
by
Jack Treby

"You'll never get me up in one of those things. They're absolutely lethal!"

Seville, 1931. Six months after the loss of the British airship the R101, a German Zeppelin is coming in to land in Southern Spain.

Hilary Manningham-Butler is an MI5 operative eking out a pitiful existence on the Rock of Gibraltar. The offer of a job in the Americas provides a potential life line but there are strings attached. First she must prove her mettle to her masters in London and that means stepping on board the *Richthofen* before the airship leaves Seville.

A cache of secret documents has been stolen from Scotland Yard and the files must be recovered if British security is not to be severely compromised. Hilary must put her life on the line to discover the identity of the thief. But as the airship makes its way across the Atlantic towards Brazil it becomes clear that nobody on board is quite what they seem. And there is no guarantee that any of them will reach Rio de Janeiro alive...

www.jacktreby.com

The Pineapple Republic
by
Jack Treby

Democracy is coming to the Central American Republic of San Doloroso. But it won't be staying long...

The year is 1990. Ace reporter Daniel Parr has been injured in a freak surfing accident, just as the provisional government of San Doloroso has announced the country's first democratic elections.

The Daily Herald needs a man on the spot and in desperation they turn to Patrick Malone, a feckless junior reporter who just happens to speak a few words of Spanish.

Despatched to Central America to get the inside story, our Man in Toronja finds himself at the mercy of a corrupt and brutal administration that is determined to win the election at any cost...

The Gunpowder Treason
by
Michael Dax

"If I had thought there was the least sin in the plot, I would not have been in it for all the world..."

Robert Catesby is a man in despair. His father is dead and his wife is burning in the fires of Hell – his punishment from God for marrying a Protestant. A new king presents a new hope but the persecution of Catholics in England continues unabated and Catesby can tolerate it no longer. King James bears responsibility but the whole government must be eradicated if anything is to really change. And Catesby has a plan...

The Gunpowder Treason is a fast-paced historical thriller. Every character is based on a real person and almost every scene is derived from eye-witness accounts. This is the story of the Gunpowder Plot, as told by the people who were there...

52137466R00129

Made in the USA
Lexington, KY
09 September 2019